THE HOUSE OF MAD

L.E. REINER

The House of Mad

ISBN: 9798589801118 (paperback)

ASIN: B08RXLV5DL

Cover art by Coverdungeonrabbit

"That which you mistake for madness is but an over acuteness of the senses"

– Edgar Allen Poe

CHAPTER I

April 11ᵗʰ, 1928
Border Cities Arena,
Windsor, Ontario

I WANT TO DIE.

August DeWitt sat on the bench in *his* locker room. With his elbows on his knees and his face in his hands; his stomach twisted into knots. Too much liquor—not at all difficult for the North American heavyweight cage fighting champion to come by, even during prohibition.

As the crowd cheered his name from above, the only thought that raced through his mind was, *I want to die.*

He picked his head up, sniffling from the force of all the blood rushing to his face. They cheered his name and chanted for his victory despite him being American. But he was unbeatable. *The Unbeatable August DeWitt*, and no fan of cage fighting refuted his skill.

They all loved him.

His stomach turned, and he darted to the sink. Falling to his knees, he vomited everything he drank only minutes before.

1

After firing his manager, there was no one to tell him to take it easy on the booze. No one to caution him on the dangers of fighting inebriated, which is exactly what he wanted.

This had to be believable.

His clumsy hand twisted the water-stained faucet, and he shoveled handfuls of water into his mouth. His gaze met with his own reflection in the mirror—his brown eyes appearing black in the overhead lighting. After a few moments, he grinned and then winked. "Lookin' swell, kid!"

The crowd roared when August emerged from the locker room. Flashes of light from the photographers warmed his bare skin, and he kept his head low to avoid being blinded. He was no novice to being photographed, and keeping his head down to avoid being blinded was a common practice.

Especially since his vision was already compromised—blurred from the excessive alcohol.

As August marched through the crowd, he threw his fist in the air, and the audience roared in delight. Without hesitation, he entered the cage and threw his arms out to his side. He did not acknowledge his opponent just yet, but instead strutted around the ring. The fans loved his peacocking—showboating before the fight ever even began. Because no opponent was ever worthy enough to take down August DeWitt.

Finally, he whipped around to his opponent and outstretched his massive arm to him—pointing with a wicked grin. "You ready to lose?"

The fighter twisted his head from side to side—loosening his neck before the match. When the bell dinged, the crowd roared. With no fear or reverence, August charged toward his opponent, winding up his hook.

The fighter kept his hands up to protect his head, neck, and face. When he anticipated August's hook, he challenger turned his body to block him and instead met with the champion's jab, the force of which was so intense that he staggered back into the cage.

August grinned and thumbed his nose. When his opponent regained balance, the champion charged him again, wrapping his arms around the fighter's waist to knock him back into the cage again. He landed a few blows to his side, but a crushing sensation at the base of his skull blinded him momentarily.

The crowd groaned in unison when August staggered away from the fighter. Weakened from the blow to his head, he grimaced and ran his fingers along his scalp, smearing sticky fluid onto his fingers.

Blood.

Once more, August grinned. As he approached his opponent again, the referee stopped him. "I'm fine!"

The blow to the head dazed him, though, exacerbating his drunken state. The lights in the stadium blinded him, and he winced while shielding his eyes. The cheers and jeers echoed and faded into a high-pitched ringing. As the urge to vomit clawed at his throat, his opponent further engaged.

August stepped back, narrowly missing a jab.

He ducked his head to the left, avoiding the cross. To take advantage of two missed hits, August swung his fist into the fighter's shoulder. He missed his face, his dizziness now making him unstable on his feet. And as the crowd started to fall silent, he knew the time had come.

He couldn't keep it up anymore.

As the fighter threw his jab, August dropped his hands— taking the blow directly to his temple.

Total Knock Out.

∽◯◅

September 23rd, 1928
Port Augusta, Nova Scotia

Byron Martin, a middle-aged, well-groomed man in a business suit, removed his hat while entering the local tavern and inn on Port Augusta. The tavern was a waiting place for those coming and going—a safe place to have a drink and pass the time until their appropriate ferry arrived. The best part, Port Augusta escaped the reach of Nova Scotia's prohibition laws.

Inside was dark and gloomy, wet from the moisture that surrounded the port. The shoddy inn remained dim and cold, comparable to the outside world. An unwelcoming sort of place—one no man wished to stay very long.

"Where is he?" Byron asked the bartender.

He tipped his head to the back of the tavern. A man sat at one of the tables, alone and with an untouched bourbon in front of him. He kept his head down, and the candle on the table left the curvatures of his face in shadows. "Headed to Halifax in about an hour. It's going to take a lot of convincing."

"It's what I do best." Byron adjusted his tie and approached the table without any hesitation or apprehension. He stood over the brooding man, confident and with a warm smile. "Mr. DeWitt?" The man barely responded with an upward tilt of his head, his dark brown eyes looking somewhat black in the faint lighting. Byron smiled. "It is you, isn't it? The Unbeatable August DeWitt."

"I ain't really lookin' to give autographs."

Byron sat across from him. "While I do enjoy watching a good fight, I'm not here for an autograph."

"Oh yeah?" August grumbled and then chugged his bourbon. "Look, if you're here to give me hell about that fight, I've already heard it all before."

4

"I wouldn't dream of doing such a thing," Byron assured. "I'm sure you had your reasons for—"

"What? Throwing the fight? You can say it. Ain't no one remember it as well as I do." August scoffed. "I don't think I'll ever be able to forget. Not with people like you always here to remind me."

"I was going to say...stepped down." Byron ignored the cool glare from the fighter. Any normal, sane person would never poke the beast they assumed August DeWitt to be. A rather large man in stature and relatively dark features compared to the porcelain, blue-eyed populace that came out of Port Augusta. And if his size and assumed *ruthless* temperament weren't enough, he'd shaved the sides of his head to appear more savage to his opponents.

But Byron knew better. He'd been following August for a long time. He knew his temperament to be more comparable to a domestic house cat than a lion on the prowl. "Is there a reason you're bothering me?"

"I have a business proposition for you."

"Not interested."

"You haven't heard it yet."

August motioned for another drink, groaning in what Byron could only assume to be annoyance. "If you're askin' me to take another dive to make your fighter look good, you can save your pitch. I've been forcibly retired."

"I promise it's nothing like that." The bartender set another double shot of bourbon in front of August. He gave Byron a shrug with a sort of *I-told-you-so* expression before leaving them alone once more. "I'm looking for a bodyguard, Mr. DeWitt."

"A bodyguard, huh?" he said unenthused.

"One of three. I can assure you, you won't find another opportunity quite like this. Excitement, danger, more money than you know what to do with." August's eyebrows raised, and a glimmer of intrigue within caused Byron to smile. "Sounds like it's right up your alley."

"How much money?"

"Four hundred a week."

"You shittin' me?"

Byron smiled and pulled his briefcase onto the table. "I've never actually understood that expression, if I'm honest." He opened the briefcase and removed a wad of cash bound with a rubber band from inside.

August snatched the money. "What's this?"

"An advance. Double what you'll be making per week if you accept the job."

"You're givin' me eight hundred dollars' cash right here in front of everyone? The hell's the matter with you?"

"What's the matter? Afraid someone will mug you?"

August glanced around the room—the other patrons cowering at the sight of the retired fighter acknowledging their nosiness. "What if I don't take the job? Do I still get to keep the money?"

"Yes," Byron said, nonchalant. "Money isn't an issue for your future employer."

"Who might that be?"

"Have you ever heard of a man named Arthur Maddox?"

"That billionaire entrepreneur?"

"He's many things, Mr. DeWitt. An inventor, entrepreneur, anthropologist, famed photographer, and a brilliant scientist. But the riches of the Maddox family are nothing new. Old money, thanks in large part to them having dipped their hands into many lucrative businesses. The railroads being the most notable."

"Doesn't he own Port Augusta?" August asked.

"Yes, that's correct. The Maddox's have property in over twenty-five countries."

"So, this guy needs a bodyguard. What, too many people tryin' to off him?" August chuckled.

"He doesn't need a bodyguard. The job is to protect his daughter, Emma. And *people* are not the issue in this circumstance. Have you ever been hunting, Mr. DeWitt?"

6

A bell rang throughout the tavern, disturbing the thoughtful moment between August and Byron. "Four-fifteen to Halifax is in the port!"

"That's me." August stuffed the money into his coat pocket and chugged his bourbon, a satisfied groan escaping him as he slammed the glass back onto the table.

Byron stood and grasped August's hand. "It's been a pleasure, Mr. DeWitt, truly. I am a big fan of cage fighting. It's a shame we couldn't work something out."

"Yeah...good to meet ya."

"Have a safe journey." Byron closed his briefcase and placed his hat on his head while making his way to the exit.

"Hey, hold up a sec," August called to him. "Say I wanted to take the job...what would need to be done?"

"Well, you'd need to miss that ferry out there, for starters. Then you'd need to book a room for the night. And in the morning, you'd need to accompany me to Arthur Maddox's estate here in Port Augusta. He does prefer to meet with new employees before sending them off."

The long pause intrigued Byron. No one else had ever shown so much reluctance after being paid an advance. Even more, August had no other commitment or engagement demanding his time. Byron knew this all too well.

"All right. I'll meet with Mr. Maddox. But it don't mean I'm takin' the job. Just... thinkin' about takin' it."

"Of course." Byron backed out of the door, smirking at August all the while. "Get some rest, Mr. DeWitt. I'll meet you here at eleven tomorrow morning."

September 24th, 1928

By the time the sky turned light blue as the day came about, August resigned himself to insomnia. A heavy burden kept him tossing and turning. Guilt overcame him when his ferry left Port Augusta the previous day. And even though he had no prior engagement pulling him to Halifax, something about the new job proposition unnerved him.

He liked the promise of a new adventure, and from the way Byron spoke, the job would deliver on that promise. A bodyguard position seemed simple enough, he thought. But the inquiry about his hunting capabilities concerned him.

August had never been hunting, and he wondered if that was something he should have made clear the day before. Perhaps Byron might not have even offered the job if he knew August had never even held a rifle before. Only handguns, and even those, he did not like.

In the bar area beneath the inn, patrons already started coming and going—ordering breakfast and drinks while awaiting their ferry. Despite this, sea water dominated August's senses as he emerged from the creaking stairwell.

He contorted his face to the salty air—thick and muggy.

"Ah, Mr. DeWitt," Byron said through a crooked smile while extending his hand.

"I ain't ever been hunting before," he blurted before taking the man's hand. Byron's crooked smile faded into a smirk while withdrawing his handshake. "I just…felt I should tell you that. Never even held a rifle before. Or a shotgun."

"No matter," Byron said. "I'm sure you'll catch on quick. The weapons you use are completely up to you. We have a man who only uses knives."

August felt foolish for even losing sleep over the conversation. The two of them left the tavern and entered the chilly morning air. A gust of wind blew through, spraying them lightly with the seawater as the mariners went about their morning, prepping their boats and opening the shops along the harbor.

"Mr. DeWitt," Byron spoke, stealing August's attention away from the dismal seafarers. In front of him was an automobile. A small, sliver of happiness—at least to him—in all the gloom of the Port.

August whistled while admiring the crimson beauty—slick and polished with all black tires—none of the white trim that he usually saw. "Ever been in a car before?" Byron asked while climbing into the driver's seat.

"Course I have. Just…never one this nice." The leather squeaked beneath his weight as he slid across the smooth passenger seat. He looked out the window and made eye contact with a young, orange-haired girl standing on the sidewalk. She stared at him intently, eyes pointed and lips puckered into a hateful scowl.

"My apologies. I often forget that times aren't as bad everywhere as they are here."

Before pulling away, August glanced out the window again, but the little girl disappeared into the crowd. Still, her disapproving stare made him uneasy. August knew all too well what being on the outside looking in felt like. He would often envy the wealthy men who had nice cars, classy broads, three-piece suits. He never could afford such luxuries, and after the disgust of even a young girl, August resented himself for even pretending to be something he wasn't.

Arthur Maddox's estate was less than a mile away. When the car pulled in front of the house, August stared in awe. None of the small glimpses of high-society he managed to take in during fight nights could have ever prepared him for something as lavish and remarkable as the mansion before them.

"Come along, Mr. DeWitt. Mr. Maddox doesn't like to be kept waiting."

While following behind, August marveled at the structure. The house was newer, built with light red brick to withstand the harsh storms plaguing Port Augusta. The shutters were black, and the entryway, white with giant pillars holding up the porch's A-frame roof. They climbed the brick steps leading to the iron gates in front of the thick, oak doors, also painted black to match the shutters.

Byron unlocked the gate with a large key and led the way into the mansion. As August suspected, the interior mirrored the grandiosity of the exterior. Hardwood floors throughout the home adorned with beautiful Persian rugs, priceless artwork scattered along the painted, light blue walls, and chandeliers hanging in the main hall—it all floored him.

"Damn…I could get used to this."

"Ah yes, the house certainly does paint the picture of luxury and refinement. Would you believe if I told you this is one of the smaller homes under the Maddox name?"

August scoffed. "Yeah, I actually would."

Byron escorted August down the main hall to a room on the right just before the grand staircase. Inside was a large, oak desk centered in front of arched windows that overlooked a garden. Along the walls of the room were bookcases filled with leather-bound books, as well as a liquor cabinet and wall safe.

"Please, have a seat," Byron said while motioning to two silk chairs positioned in front of the desk. "I'll fetch Mr. Maddox. Make yourself comfortable."

"Already am," August chuckled.

A fireplace in the corner of the room warmed and comforted him with the scent of burning wood. The flames crackled, and a grandfather clock wedged in between two bookshelves ticked the seconds away.

"Ah, there he is!" a man exclaimed from the doorway, and August spun in his chair. Arthur Maddox—much younger than he assumed. If he had to guess, the billionaire looked late thirties. It came as no surprise that he was well-groomed, his dark mustache curling upward at the edges and his curly brown hair gelled into a near perfect position.

Donned in a tan suit, sans the jacket, Arthur Maddox approached August wearing a warm smile, and his green eyes twinkled in what appeared to be distinct pleasure and admiration. August stood and accepted a hearty handshake. "Mr. Maddox."

"Please, call me Arthur. Mr. Maddox was my father," he bellowed while smacking August's arm. "My, my, August. It's no wonder you've won so many fights." He clenched his bicep. "Byron, his arm is the size of your head!"

August chuckled, pleasantly surprised with his soon-to-be employer. Youthful, animated, and richer than can be. "It's a pleasure, Arthur. Thank you for having me in your home."

"But of course, my boy." He clenched his arm even tighter, a wide smile still planted across his face. "My, what a fine specimen you are. You'll do perfectly." He released him and approached the liquor cabinet. "Cigar?"

"No, thanks. I don't smoke."

"Just the brandy then." Arthur winked and poured each of the men a glass.

"Thanks." The room fell silent while the men sniffed and tasted their brandy. And when everyone seemed comfortable enough, Arthur leaned onto the edge of his desk.

11

"Do you have children, August?"

"Uh...not that I know of."

Arthur smiled warmly at him. "That's all right. Your time will come. And let me just tell you, nothing can prepare you for the moment you hold your child in your arms for the very first time. I hope you have a girl, so you know the sheer adoration and unbreakable bond a man has with his daughter."

August shrugged. "I dunno. I kinda want a boy."

Arthur's booming laughter filled the room. "Every man's dream, of course. But a girl is the sparkle in your eye. She holds the key to your heart in the palm of her little hand."

"Sounds terrifying."

"It most certainly is, but it's the best kind of terror. Emma is the greatest gift I could have asked for. And even to this day, all she has to do is crawl into my lap, look at me with those big, beautiful green eyes, and I'm putty in her hands. If she says, *'daddy, I want a pony,'* then a pony she shall have."

August huffed. "Lucky kid."

"Any child that feels the love of their father is lucky. And Emma, well... she's my little princess. So, I'm sure you can understand why I felt it necessary to meet you before offering you the job of caretaker to her."

August's gaze lifted to meet Arthur's intent stare. "Caretaker? I was told this was a bodyguard position."

"It is," Arthur assured. "But Emma..." he sighed, and his warm, exuberant smile faded into melancholy. "My sweet angel is very sick. She cannot leave the house, and some days she is completely bed-ridden. Now, I've done my research on you, August. Born and raised in Savannah, Georgia. Your parents were in an accident, which left you in charge of your brother's care. He was deaf, wasn't he?"

"Yep."

"And you brought him to Canada."

"I thought it'd be safer. Didn't like the idea of him suffering the same fate as our parents."

12

"A mugging, wasn't it?" Arthur asked.

"Something like that."

"See? You've been a caretaker before."

August sighed and chugged his brandy, wincing at the onslaught of bitterness in his mouth. "Yeah, well, if you've done your research like you say you have, you already know how that ended."

"I'm very sorry for bringing it up. But my daughter, she needs someone like you. Someone who's compassionate and who doesn't struggle to put her needs before his own."

An overwhelming sense of dread came over August. To hear that a child was sick made his heart ache for the adoring father. "Is she...contagious?"

Arthur chuckled. "Heavens, no. She suffers from a mental condition. She is on a strict regimen, of course, being looked after by the best doctor available. But seeing as how her bodyguards are almost always at her side, I do require they assume the role of caretaker once in a while. After all, no one knows her better than the Hunters."

"The Hunters?"

"Your title from this moment forward. You do care for Emma. Keep her on schedule and safe inside the house. But when you're not tending to her, you're out in the trenches hunting."

"Not literal trenches," Byron added.

August placed his glass on the table in between him and Byron. "Yeah, what exactly are we hunting?"

A cold chill shot up August's spine when he saw any bit of warmth and compassion flee from Arthur's eyes completely. "Howlers."

"Howlers?"

"Ravenous wolves hell-bent on destruction. They're responsible for the death of the last Hunter, Carlyle. And many before him."

"Arthur," Byron groaned.

Arthur held up his hands in surrender and smirked. "Full disclosure."

"Wolf is a very…loose term for these creatures."

"Quite right you are, Byron." Arthur stood and moved to the window behind his desk. He looked outward to the garden, as if losing himself in a traumatic memory from his encounter with the Howlers. "Take a wolf, paint it the blackest of blacks. Give it razor-sharp fangs, no shorter than your middle finger, and have it stand at, the very least, five feet tall on all fours. That'll give you a vague idea of what we're up against."

"What kinda wolf is that?"

Byron sighed. "Not even a wolf—"

"We believe they were derived from wolves," Arthur said. "But they appear to have…mutated, in some fashion. Perhaps something in the fog. It is…unlike any other mist I've seen before."

August nodded slowly, filtering through all the information given to him. It all seemed a bit odd, and only the immaculate surroundings made him consider the truth in Arthur Maddox's words. The wealth of the man before him was undeniable, and his willingness to pay August was all the convincing the retired fighter needed. "All right, so…we kill 'em off and take care of your daughter in the meantime. Doesn't seem too hard."

"As wonderful as it would be for the Hunters to completely eliminate the Howlers from Point DuPont, for some strange and inexplicable reason, they keep coming. Whether they breed like rabbits or they are simply indestructible, we remain unsure. But we've been hunting them for the past five years, on an island that's only about ten kilometers in size." Arthur lowered himself into his desk chair, and his animation completely abandoned him at that moment. "I wish them to be gone, August. But I get the sneaking suspicion that so long as my daughter resides on Point DuPont, they'll never stop coming."

It all seemed suspicious, August thought. But in an effort to remain polite, he kept his inquiries to himself. Questions about

14

why Arthur chose to stay away from his sick child and why he didn't move her from Point DuPont if it was such a dangerous place.

"So, what do you say?" Byron asked. "Excitement, danger...and as you can see, money certainly won't be an issue," he said while motioning around the room.

August contemplated. He remembered that his only other option was to go to Halifax and struggle through life just as he always had, he nodded. "Yeah, okay."

Arthur clapped his hands together. "Wonderful," he said through a wide grin. "You'll be greeted by Grady McCoy and Jonathan Moreau, the veteran Hunters of the household. You'll stay here tonight, and in the morning catch a ferry to Point DuPont." Arthur left the room after that.

"I apologize for Mr. Maddox's intrusion on your personal life. He's a businessman, you understand. Doesn't tiptoe around pertinent information even if it causes some discomfort."

August shook his head. "Nah, that's all right. He's doin' what he feels he has to for his daughter." August stood. "I'd question if he hadn't asked me anything about my past."

"What an excellent disposition you have. Come, I'll show you to your room for the evening."

August's room was on the fourth floor. Inside, two young maids finished changing the sheets and excused themselves with flirty giggles as they passed, and he gave a wry smile.

"I trust you'll be comfortable here."

He had everything he needed and more, a queen-sized bed, a fire burning, his own washroom, a small lounge area, and a large bay window overlooking the gravel roundabout in front of the house.

"Wow. Not sure I'm gonna want to leave come tomorrow," he said while staring down at the car in which he'd arrived.

"The Maddox House of Point DuPont surely won't disappoint, Mr. DeWitt. It is one of their oldest properties, and even though the outside maintenance has...dwindled in the past years, the

15

interior really is quite extraordinary. I assure you, you'll be quite comfortable during your time there."

August moved away from the window and sat on the edge of the bed. He bounced up and down a bit to test the firmness of the mattress, giving an approving nod afterward. "So, what now?"

"I'll need your measurements to send for some clothes for you. I expect you'll be in Point DuPont for quite some time, and there aren't a lot of shops up and running in the village anymore."

"Okay. Anything else?"

"Dinner will be served to your quarters at six. I recommend getting some rest tonight. Your ferry leaves at ten in the morning. Across the hall, you'll find a parlor with a telephone, paper, pens. It would behoove you to make contact with friends or family before leaving. Communication from the island takes some time, and there are no phones."

"Okay," he grumbled.

"Also…and I truly do loathe this portion of my job, but…after you've had your dinner, you and I will need to talk legalities."

"Legalities?"

"Yes. We'll need to update your last will and testament. It's standard for any new Hunter before heading to their post. I'm sure you can understand."

The thought made his stomach turn, but August had nothing to his name, other than eight-hundred dollars and some change. He also had no one to leave anything to if he didn't make it back from Point DuPont.

"Okay, I'll… I'll think it over," he muttered.

"I'll leave you to get settled. Our housemaid will be in shortly for your measurements. You can tell her what sort of clothing you prefer. Whatever you want, she'll get it delivered for you."

But clothes were the last thing on his mind. Just like the day before, a heavy burden befell him. He spent the last few months wanting to die—wishing some terrible accident befell him to end his *miserable* existence. But, now that it be a real possibility, he reconsidered.

He couldn't back out of the position, though. He knew that as an unemployed, shamed fighter, the proposition might be the only one he would receive in a long while. And even though he could make eight hundred dollars last a while, it just wouldn't be enough, not for the harsh conditions of the Canadian winter fast approaching.

After eating dinner alone in his room, August crossed the hall to the parlor. Inside, he found a desk, smaller than the one in Arthur Maddox's office, but just as finely designed and carved. On the desk, a stationary kit and a few pens placed neatly side by side. A globe sat beside the fireplace. He lifted the top, and just as he expected, he found a few crystal decanters and glasses.

After pouring himself a glass of scotch, he made himself comfortable behind the desk and took a sip. It warmed him from the inside out. But when his eyes fell onto the blank paper before him, that cold, unwelcoming feeling came rushing back to him.

He took another sip of scotch and placed it on a wooden coaster to his left. He grabbed a sheet of paper and one of the neatly placed, fine-tipped pens in his left hand. His hand only lingered over the page, though. He knew whom he wished to write, but deciding on what to say proved difficult for him. He decided to start off slow.

His pen lingered over the page. The words evaded him. After a few moments, a young maid entered the parlor, distracting him. Their eyes met. She smiled, and he offered a sheepish grin. He focused back on his letter to Jack while she dusted the furniture. Still, her presence broke his concentration.

The two locked eyes once more, and the upward turn of the edges of her lips gave him the sneaking suspicion that she, too, found him quite alluring.

He dropped his pen, having only written:

Jack,

I'm sorry.

17

C hapter II

September 25th, 1928
Point DuPont, Nova Scotia

Grady McCoy's riding boots stomping on the hardwood of the Maddox house often sent the servants running. They scurried for cover, or if they couldn't escape his path in time, tried to look busy. The Persian rugs silenced his march, and he sometimes managed to sneak up on one of the maids. They might even be so terrified that a gasp escaped them before turning in the opposite direction.

A strange thing to witness for an outsider, most would agree. Grady McCoy was a very handsome, youthful-looking man. Mid-twenties with golden blonde hair that glistened in the sunlight and hung in wisps along his forehead. His eyes, a fierce blue, so bright that he might even be detectable in the complete darkness of the night. His blonde goatee only became really noticeable in bright light because the color was comparable to his skin tone. Despite having a pointed nose and pursed lips, women who were unfamiliar with his temperament often swooned at the sight of him.

But the servants of Maddox House knew him all too well. The veteran Hunter dominated the household, demanded order, respect, and obedience from every person within. Not a cruel man to them, but certainly not one to be trifled with. And while stomping down one of the many corridors within the household on this particular morning, the sound of a maid coughing caused him to stop dead in his tracks.

"What's wrong?" he asked.

"Rien, monsieur."

"Why are you coughing?" He instilled so much fear in her that words failed her. Grady sighed, exasperated. "Go to the doctor straight away. If it's anything more than a bit of dust caught in your throat, I want you on quarters."

"Oui, monsieur."

A butler joined Grady at his side. "Is the room made up for the new Hunter?"

"Oui, Monsieur."

"Very good. I'll be in my room with Miss Emma if you need me."

Grady dominated Maddox House with fear, but it was a fear he felt was well placed. The only way to get so many people to do as he asked was for them to be afraid of him, and what he asked of them, he found, to be the most important work of his life.

"You seem tired this morning," Grady said while observing Emma from across the breakfast table. Breakfast time belonged to him. Even on mornings when Emma felt particularly weak, he insisted she not skip the most important meal of the day.

Emma dabbed her mouth with her napkin and placed it in her lap. "I am tired," she said. "I'd really love some coffee."

"You know you can't have coffee. Perhaps some chamomile tea to help calm your nerves?"

She smiled. "Fine."

"Marie," Grady's demonstrative voice bellowed to the servant in the corner of the room. "Chamomile tea for Miss Emma."

"Oui, Monsieur."

Emma barely touched her food, he noted. Her appetite started to wane after Carlyle's death. He reached across the table and grabbed the apple from her bowl—the knife attached to his belt sharpened to the point that cutting into the fruit seemed as easy as slicing through warm butter. While he peeled the apple and cut it up into individual slices, he continually glanced at her—her intense gaze focused on his fingers and the knife in his hand.

"You need to eat more fruit," Grady said. "And maybe I should have a talk with Jon about the two of you staying up and gossiping into the late hours of the night."

"We don't gossip."

"Then what is it the two of you do in your room so late at night? When you should be sleeping."

"He sits with me until I fall asleep."

Grady stopped cutting the apple. "If you're having trouble sleeping, you should come to me."

"I'm not having trouble sleeping."

He slid one of the apple slices into his mouth and placed the others into her bowl. "Eat," he demanded and slunk back into his chair. Before she even took a bite, though, a knock came to the bedroom door. "Come in," Grady groaned.

Emma perked up as the door opened. "Jon," Grady began at the sight of the man who always had every inch of him covered from head to toe, including his face—shielded by a white kabuki mask.

"Is it time for my bath?" Emma asked.

Grady drummed his fingers. "You haven't finished eating."

"I'm really not all that hungry, darling—" As she stood, Grady slammed his fist onto the table, causing the flatware to tremble beneath the force. "Sit down!"

Emma lowered herself back into her chair. "It's okay, Jon. I'll be there shortly."

After Jon closed the door behind him, Grady inhaled sharply through his nose. "I get one hour with you in the mornings. I'd appreciate it if you didn't try and cut that time short."

"I'm…sorry, darling. I wasn't thinking."

He averted his gaze, trying his best to hide the disappointment. Outside the window, a gray haze consumed the land. "It's particularly foggy today," he said, but Emma avoided his gaze while lifting her apple slice to her muted lips. "Are you sure you're feeling all right, sweetheart?"

"I feel fine."

"Maybe you should get some more rest."

The maid returned with her chamomile tea. "It's really not necessary, darling. I feel well-rested."

But Grady made up his mind. "I insist."

"Then I shall do as you ask."

He exhaled, the edges of his lips softening into a smile. "I only do these things because I love you."

&)&

After Grady excused her from the table, Jon returned Emma to her room. She remained distant—distracted from his company. He sensed fear from her, anxiety from the fog, no doubt. Thicker fog created harsher conditions for the Hunters. And he knew her aversion to sleep.

She always had night terrors.

Jon grabbed her white nightgown from the bureau and draped it over his forearm to use his hands to sign to her, his primary mode of communication. *Back to sleep?*

"Yes, Jon."

Is that what you want? He signed.

She shook her head. "I want to read."

Jon returned her and grabbed a corset and her favorite crimson gown instead. A smile spread across her face.

She dropped her robe and turned her back to him, grabbing one of the bedposts for stability while stepping into her corset. As Jon pulled it up, she gripped the post to steady herself. "Tighter, Jon," she said, and he pulled firmly on the straps—shifting her with every move.

After he finished securing her corset, Emma brought her hand to her abdomen and inhaled deeply. She turned to Jon, who held her crimson gown over his forearm.

Breathe okay? He signed.

"Barely."

After donning her dress, Jon retrieved her stockings from the vanity as she sat on the edge of her bed. He kneeled before her and lifted her dress above her knees. She picked up each foot as he slid the stockings up her calves to her thighs. After securing the second one, his hands lingered on her thigh.

She slid her fingertips along the smooth surface of his mask. That beautiful, warm smile she always gave him when he cared for her melted him—solidifying, on a daily basis, his unfailing loyalty and devotion to her. "My locket, Jon," she said, and he stood to retrieve the piece. "The silver one."

She held up her hair, and he fastened the clasp. When finished, his gloved thumb caressed the back of her neck. "Thank you, mon amour. You're so good to me." His hands slid down to her shoulders. "I don't know what I'd do without you. My oldest, dearest friend." Just a second later, Emma left the bedroom, leaving him alone before he even had a chance to drop his hand.

Jon entered the main hall and marched to the front door, with Grady joining him at his side. "Is Emma back in bed?" Grady asked, and Jon gave him a thumbs up. "Right. Let's get this over with."

A veil of white covered the landscape in front of the house—obscuring Jon's field of vision to only a few feet. They waited for the carriage delivering the new Hunter to arrive—a necessity when greeting someone new. Because at any moment, a Howler could come out of nowhere and attack the unknowing visitor before someone even managed to make it to the door.

"I don't like this," Grady said while standing at the edge of the porch, his rifle slung across both arms. Jon leaned against one of the pillars, flipping his hunting knife around in his hand. "If he takes any longer, we're going back inside."

Jon rolled his eyes.

Carriage wheels and horse hooves on gravel caused both of them to perk up a bit. Through the fog, two orange orbs reflecting onto the thick fog drew nearer.

Finally, the carriage came to a stop before the porch. The door swung open, and as the passenger stepped onto the gravel road, the carriage lifted significantly. Jon's eyes widened.

"You must be Mr. DeWitt," Grady said while extending his hand to him.

He gripped Grady's hand. "August."

"August. I'm Grady McCoy, this here is Jonathan Moreau—"

"You American?" August asked.

"I am. Sounds like you are too."

August smirked. "Born and raised in the American South," he said proudly while the coachman placed his bags at his feet. "What about you?"

"Detroit."

August recoiled as his gaze met with Jon's, a typical reaction when meeting someone new. Not many people were used to seeing a man dressed in all black with a white mask. "Nice giddup. What about you, partner? You American too?" Jon shook his head. "What's the matter? Cat got your tongue?"

"He's dumb."

"What's that?"

"He's dumb; he can't talk."

23

His remark wiped August's smile clean off. "Ah hell, I'm Sorry. I had no idea."

"I'm sure he'll forgive you," Grady interrupted. "Why don't we head back inside before the Howlers decide to make an appearance?"

∞CR

Grady led the way back into the mansion. Jon closed the front doors behind them and bolted them shut, and finally, August had a moment to observe, and admire, the house that would be his home from that moment forward. A home he never expected inhabiting, and one he never envisioned as being so magnificent.

While the exterior left something to be desired, the interior painted a much more valued picture. A long hallway straight ahead led to a darkened, wooded staircase. All the doors lining the corridor were closed as if guarding something within. And even though it was still day, the inside of the mansion was dark despite the intricate iron sconces on the wall emitting a warm glow.

Perhaps because of all the closed doors. And even with the large, arched windows in the main foyer exposing the outside, the fog kept the only bit of light to break through the gray sky at bay.

But despite the warmth, a cold chill came over August. He was unsettled by the home—though he couldn't quite place the reason. Perhaps all the dark wood, the faded grays, and worn reds used as a common theme throughout. Perhaps the cold chill came from the creaking hardwood beneath their boots, slightly muffled by a muted Persian rug. Or maybe the eerie faces of the wooden statues embedded in the walls. The further August walked into the mansion, the more he started feeling something wicked and otherworldly may reside therein.

The silence of the mansion disturbed him, and a door closing in the distance caused the hairs on his arms and neck to stand

24

upright. "Damn…I feel like I just walked into the past, comin' out here. The horse-drawn carriage, the candles—"

"The Maddox's have very refined tastes. And emissions from motor-vehicles are highly frowned upon out here. It is rather debilitating. The fog, I mean," Grady said while leading the way to the foyer.

"Who makes all these rules?" August asked as they stopped before the grand staircase. Along the wall of the stairwell, portraits and paintings hung of people and places unknown to him. Their eyes appeared hollow, once again sending a cold chill up August's spine.

"Mr. Maddox, of course. He owns the island. Wants it to be run a certain way. And the people living further inland seem to have no complaints."

Jon handed a scrap piece of paper to August. "Other than the Howlers," August read.

"You'll learn very quickly that there is an exact way we do things around here. Miss Maddox prefers silence, order. And all the things that remind her of the past—all the luxuries therein—"

Jon handed August another piece of paper. "Classical music, painting, reading—" Grady snatched the paper away.

"It might be best to keep in contact with someone from the outside world, so you don't get too lost in all of this. A week, it will feel like a lifetime. A year? You'll start forgetting how things work out in the real world. Two years, you might just lose your sanity completely."

"Jesus Christ," August replied through a huff. "So why even bother? Sounds like a real nightmare."

"I've been asking myself that same question since the day I arrived. Jon, would you kindly show Mr. DeWitt to his quarters? We'll meet in the parlor once you've gotten settled to further discuss your duties here on the island."

Grady disappeared down a corridor to the right. His endnote left August feeling all the more reluctant to continue.

Jon nudged him and pointed to the stairwell, and the two ascended the stairs to the second level. "Hey, Jon... I'm sorry about that crack I made outside. If I woulda known, I never woulda said anything like that." Jon shook his head and patted August's shoulder. "I just...know how it goes. My brother was deaf, and if anyone talked to him like that, it woulda been lights out."

Jon stopped. *Brother, deaf?* He signed.

August smirked. A pleasant surprise, finding that Jon had other ways to communicate. "Yeah. Born that way. Learned sign language to talk to him."

Jon tipped his head toward a darkened corridor to his right. They stopped in front of a closed door, and Jon pushed it open to let August inside. "This is my room?" he asked, and Jon nodded. "Holy cow." Inside was a king-sized, four-poster bed and a wooden fireplace with flames burning bright. Golden tiebacks held the gaudy red curtains away from the window—which was also barred. Beside it, a round table draped in a crimson table cloth and adorned with a vase of wilted roses.

Jon passed him and pulled open a set of double doors to the left. Inside, a bathroom with a claw foot tub. Jon pointed to the closet, but someone else's belongings resided inside.

Carlyle, Jon signed.

The realization that the room once belonged to the dead Hunter chilled August. After Jon left and the door creaked shut behind him, August wondered how anyone managed to sleep in such an unsettling home. He flung his bag onto his bed, but a child's laughter from the hallway startled him. His bedroom door creaked shut a bit more, yet he got the distinct impression someone might be watching him.

He crossed the room and yanked the door open.

Long, flowing ginger hair and the train of a crimson gown trailing around a corner intrigued him. "Hello?"

He turned the corner from which the figure disappeared but once again only caught a glimpse of ginger hair and the train of a

26

gown. "Miss?" A door slammed shut, and when he entered the next corridor, he saw only a set of double doors. He knocked and awaited a response, and when none came, he opened them.

Oak bookcases, filled with leather-bound books, lined the room. The fireplace cracked. In front of it, a silk chaise lounge. But still, no woman in sight.

"Miss?" he called again. When he turned a corner on the far side of the room, the ginger-haired beauty whipped around, eyes wide and an open-mouthed grin on her face. She looked rather sheepish while tucking her hands behind her back. "I'm...sorry, I... didn't mean to disturb you. You just...gave me a fright, is all."

She shook her head. "That's okay. It tends to happen in this house. The corridors are like a maze to those who are unfamiliar, and the enormity makes it difficult to really find anyone."

A smile crept across his face. This woman before him, much like their surroundings, seemed stuck in a world of the past. Her gown, a Victorian style with bustle, and her hair, long and loosely flowing behind her—a stark contrast to the short, tapered hairstyle of most women.

"What do you do around here?" he asked.

"Oh, I..." she smiled widely at him. "I just laze about and rely on other people to do everything for me. You must be the new Hunter."

"August DeWitt." He extended his hand to her, and she willingly accepted.

"Emma Maddox."

"*You're* Emma Maddox?"

"You seem disappointed."

"I was just expecting someone a little...younger."

"How rude."

August stifled a laugh. "I meant no offense, Miss. It's just that...the way Mr. Maddox spoke of you...the things he said I needed to do for you...I just assumed he was talking about a child."

"Yes. I suppose my father still sees me as a young girl, so I cannot fault you for thinking otherwise."

August started to wonder why her father and the other Hunters felt the need to baby her. A fully grown woman stood before him, one whom he already got the sense might be far more intelligent than those around her. And now, more than ever, he felt he needed a bit more clarification on her health. Because to him, she seemed sane and healthy.

But something even more suspicious required his attention. Emma kept her hands tucked behind her back. "What're you hiding back there?"

She hesitated to speak. "Oh, it's…just a book—"

"I like a good book."

"I'm not sure you'd like this book."

He held his hand out to her, and she hesitated to hand it to him. "120 Days of Sodom by the Marquis de Sade," he said, and when his eyes met with hers again, her cheeks flushed.

She snatched the book from him. "He's one of my favorites."

"Should a woman like you be reading something like this? I mean, it's just pornography, isn't it?"

"There's much more to it than that. A story of manipulation, desire, madness…the Marquis de Sade's prose is nothing short of revolutionary when compared to other writers of his time."

Even more intriguing, her willingness to defend the smut. "Well, now I'm interested. Maybe you'll let me borrow it when you're finished?"

"I'm not sure you have the stomach for such a thing. I wouldn't want to offend your delicate sensibilities."

"I'm not easily offended, Miss."

Her eyes darted over his shoulder, wiping her smile clean. "Hello, darling." August only then noticed Grady in the doorway.

"Emma. I thought we agreed on more rest?"

"Oh, I tried to rest, really, I did. But I found myself in the midst of a nightmare, you see. And without having you by my side, I thought it best to try and distract myself until you made the time for me."

He waved her over, and she sauntered to him, her hands clasping her book behind her back. Grady lifted her chin to him. "I can't be with you all the time, sweetheart," he whispered.

She nodded. "I know."

"Go to your room and wait for me so I can undress you." Before exiting the library, though, Grady took the book from her hands. "I told you, I don't want you reading this book. It's depraved." He tossed it on a nearby table and then stepped aside to allow her to pass.

"It was a pleasure to meet you, Miss Maddox."

"I assure you, the pleasure was all mine."

She left the room. After a few moments, Grady cleared his throat. "Jon is waiting for us in the parlor. Tell him I'll be just a moment."

"Sure, okay." But August lingered in the library until Grady disappeared into the hall, and his interest in learning more about Emma beckoned him to take the book Grady tossed aside.

Chapter III

August entered the parlor. An oak table lined with crystal decanters filled with various liquors and glasses on the far side of the room grabbed his attention. He passed Jon, who was sitting in one of the green velvet armchairs. "Well, Grady sure is a delight." The room stayed quiet, and only when he remembered Jon couldn't speak, did he turn to face him. "Doesn't that piss you off? Him callin' you dumb like that?"

He shook his head.

But August's thoughts remained with the charming young woman he met in the library just minutes before. "So...Emma, huh? She certainly is a looker, ain't she?" Jon did not respond. "Her and Grady a thing?" The muted man threw his head back and then twisted his chin side to side as if the question annoyed him. "Seems like they are."

Grady marched into the room. "Now that we're all here, we can begin," he said while closing the door behind him. He stood before them, above them, demanding their attention. "The fog is particularly thick today, so we won't be hunting. Which might be a good thing considering it's only your first day on the island."

"Well, that's good to know. I'd like to get a bit more...acquainted with everything before I put my life on the line."

"A reasonable request, though if the fog clears by tomorrow, we won't be able to put it off for long."

Jon began signing.

"I can't understand you, Jon," Grady snapped.

"He said the Howlers are more aggressive now. Been coming out more often."

"You know sign language? You might be more useful than I originally assumed. While I don't much care for Jon's presence, he's a formidable fighter, and being unable to communicate with him out there is maddening."

"You know he can hear you, right?"

"I'm aware. It's no surprise that Jon and I merely tolerate each other for Emma's benefit."

"Hey, what's the deal with her anyway?"

"What do you mean?"

"Well...Mr. Maddox said that she's...not really normal—"

"She's...mentally unstable."

"Okay, but...what's wrong with her?" August asked. "You're tellin' me she's sick, but...what kinda sick are we talkin' about? She talk to walls or something?"

"No one really knows what's wrong, but Mr. Maddox realized that she was a very peculiar child early on. And when she turned seventeen, he found it best to keep her inside the house, for her safety and the safety of those around her. It's because of this you'll notice that she's on a very strict schedule. A regimen, if you will, and diverting from that could have dire consequences." His eyes darted to Jon.

"So she's crazy?"

Jon shook his head.

"For lack of a better word."

31

Jon shook his head again, this time aggressively signing to August.

"If you're done romanticizing the idea of Emma, I'd like to continue."

August chuckled. "How do you know that's what he's doing?"

"Because I know Jon. Look, Emma's condition is really none of your concern. You're a Hunter under my command, and our job is to hunt down the Howlers. We kill as many as we can, keep them away from the house, and keep Emma inside. When we're not out hunting, it's our job to tend to her."

"What exactly needs to be done?"

"I'm in charge of her medication, her eating habits. I'm the liaison between her doctors and the two of you, so if something seems off about her...more so than usual, it is very prudent that you report it to me. Jon takes care of her daily schedule. Organizes dress fittings, things to help her morale, as well as overseeing her morning and nightly ablutions—"

"What, like, bathing her?"

"He supervises her. And once she starts to trust you more, it'll be your job to put her to bed and get her up in the morning."

August elbowed Jon. "Wanna trade?"

"This isn't a game, Mr. DeWitt. Emma is very unstable and requires 'round clock care. But don't let that fool you. She's highly intelligent and very manipulative." Grady turned away from them and approached the window, his hands tucked behind his back. "Her beauty alone is enough to bring a grown man to his knees. That combined with her silver tongue..." He sighed, disturbed. "If you don't have your wits about you, she'll walk all over you and destroy everything you've ever stood for. All so you'll be more inclined to do as she asks. You must establish your dominance over her, or she'll dominate you."

The room fell completely silent after that, ominously so. When August looked to Jon for affirmation, he got nothing in return but a diverted glance to the ground.

August laughed. Surely no woman could ever bring him to his knees, he thought. "Okay."

"And the most important thing for you to remember," Grady began, his eyes cold and narrowed. "Don't make her angry."

Jon nudged him. *Make her mad, not easy.*

August shrugged. "Maybe she just likes you."

"Gentlemen?" Grady said from the doorway, "If you're done chit-chatting, perhaps now would be a good time to tour the house?"

August threw his hands in the air. "Lead the way."

He soon learned navigating through the house might prove difficult with four stories of winding hallways and corridors— something he wouldn't have imagined judging by the exterior. The outside of the house did not give justice to the intricacies of the home inside, almost like an illusion, the space inside seeming much larger than the structure entirely.

On the first floor was the parlor in which they congregated, a music room with a grand piano, the kitchen, and the dining room. The second level was where August's bedroom was located. Across the hall was Grady's room. August already found the library. Emma's bedroom was not far from there, hidden away behind another set of double doors.

On the third level, doctor's quarters and a medical bay. "This is where you'll come if you're injured or sick," Grady said while entering the medical bay. "The doctor receives regular shipments of medical supplies from the mainland, so rest assured you'll be receiving the best care."

"Jesus. You guys are like a fully operational society, never having to leave the confines of the house."

"That is the general idea," Grady said. "This is Doctor Bernard. He's the lead physician here and directly oversees all of Emma's care."

"Hello," the doctor greeted with a head nod and smile.

"Good to meet ya."

"Even though we have a medical doctor on staff, all of Emma's medical concerns should be brought to me first. Doctor Bernard is the doctor to all in this house and is very busy."

"Would you like the sedatives now, Monsieur McCoy?"

"Yes, thank you for reminding me." Doctor Bernard handed Grady a pouch, who then handed it to August.

"What's all this?"

"Open it." He obliged, revealing five small syringes—each filled with a yellowish fluid. "These are the sedatives for Emma. I don't expect you'll use them any time soon. Not until you become familiar with the warning signs."

"The warning signs?"

"Of an episode. She tends to have them from time to time, but until you really start to understand her, it might be difficult for you to tell. Just keep an eye out, and I'll do my best to instruct you in the manner in which they're to be used."

August held the pouch to Grady. "Well, if it's all right with you, I'd prefer if that responsibility just stayed with you. Don't really think I have it in me to…tranquilize a woman."

"She's no ordinary woman, Mr. DeWitt. The sooner you start to realize that, the safer we'll all be."

August nudged Jon. "You agree with this?"

"Of course he doesn't. It's why he doesn't have the authority to administer the sedatives. I do ask that you reserve judgment until you witness an episode, though. And hold on to these in the meantime," Grady said while closing the pouch in August's hand. "I can't be with Emma all the time, and I need someone I can trust looking out for her when I'm not around. I'm hoping that will be you."

He had no desire to sedate Emma under any circumstance. He couldn't for the life of him imagine a situation where he'd have to. Because even if she became violent or hostile, if he could get close enough to administer a sedative, he'd be close enough to restrain her until she calmed down.

He placed the pouch in his pocket for the time being.

Grady continued with the tour of the house, but other than the servant's quarters, the armory, and a peek outside one of the parlor windows to the stables, there wasn't much left to see because most everything else was off-limits.

"What's in there?" August asked after passing a steel door on the first level.

"The basement."

"Why's it bolted shut?" August asked while approaching the door, but Grady blocked his path.

"It's off-limits. You have no reason to go down there, at least not anytime soon."

"You're freaking me out. What's down there?"

Grady smiled politely and shook his head. "Nothing that would interest you. Now, I'm sure you're tired from your travels. Rest up, wash up, do whatever you need to do to settle in. Dinner is at seven in the dining room, but only on Sundays. Every other day it's at six and served to your quarters, now if you'll excuse me."

Grady marched down the hall, leaving August at the foot of the staircase. Only when the veteran Hunter disappeared into one of the many rooms did August approach the basement again. His fingers slid across the cold, steel surface. He pressed his ear against the metal to listen, but all he heard was an electric current moving through the steel—a faint zapping that bewildered him.

ഇരു

At exactly seven o'clock, August entered the dining room. Grady sat at the head of the long, extravagant table with Jon to his right. The size and grandeur of the room captured August's attention, though. It seemed more like a ballroom, and even the massive table in the middle did little to fill the open space. The crackling from the colossal fireplace disturbed the otherwise quiet scene, and on the table, black candles in silver candelabra flickered.

August sat beside Jon. Silver plates and flatware, crystal drinking glasses, and wine goblets sat perfectly aligned in front of them. The table had a massive spread, large enough to feed a small village. Yet to August's knowledge, there were only four of them joining dinner.

Despite this, no one acknowledged the meal.

The tense silence between the Hunters unnerved him, yet before he uttered a single word, a butler entered. "The Lady Maddox," he said, and Grady and Jon stood.

As soon as Emma entered the dining room, August climbed to his feet as well. She beamed in her much more groomed state—her hair half up and curled, her emerald gown and bustle, the makeup and the jewelry she wore, all looked as if she were expected at a ball later in the evening.

"My darling, you certainly are a vision in green," Grady said as she approached.

Jon pulled her chair out for her to sit. He waved his palm in front of his face. *Beautiful.*

Emma smiled and ran her hand over the side of his mask. "Merci, tas vu ça, mon amour."

Emma's expectant eyes met with August's as he lowered himself back into his chair. "Uh...you look...real nice."

As soon as everyone sat, the servants began filling their plates and wine glasses. Without missing a moment, Emma grabbed her wine and leaned back in her chair. "So, tell us, Mr. DeWitt. What did you do before Byron tracked you down and offered you this job?"

"I was a cage fighter. And before that, I worked as a bootlegger in Savannah."

"My, my," Emma mused. "You've certainly had an exciting life so far."

"I plan to keep it as exciting, Miss. We only got one life to live."

"I couldn't agree more," she said.

36

"A cage fighter?" Grady began. "Not exactly the work of a gentleman."

August sucked his teeth. A smirk spread across his face as he snatched his wine goblet and took a sip. "I wasn't aware we needed to be gentlemen in this household."

"Oh, don't let Grady fool you. He was a hired gun before my father offered him this job."

"A mercenary, darling. It's quite the respectable career to have, despite what you've read in all your fiction novels."

"So, you're pretty good with that rifle you been totin' around?"

"I'm the best there is."

"Uh-huh." August nudged Jon. "What about you, bud? What'd you do before all this?"

I'm local, he signed.

August chuckled. "That's not very exciting."

"You can sign?" Emma asked, her emerald eyes wide as a smile crept across her face.

"Yeah, my brother was deaf."

"Was deaf? What, he suddenly started hearing again?"

Emma rolled her eyes. "Grady."

"That's all right, Miss Emma. My brother died last year. He was hit by a car while walking home from the store."

The room fell silent again. *I'm sorry for your loss*, Jon signed, and August clenched his shoulder.

"Me too," Emma said, and August nodded to her.

"Thank you."

Grady lifted his water glass to his lips, unaffected by the news. "Is that why you moved to Canada?"

"No, that…that was another accident."

Emma's eyes softened when August met her gaze again. "We certainly can relate. The fire changed Jon and me forever. Point DuPont used to be a thriving community, but after what happened, the loss of lives, the damage it did to those who survived… it's a burden we carry every day."

37

"What caused the fire?" The tension that befell the room at his inquiry intrigued and disturbed August.

Emma's eyes flitted to Jon.

"No one really knows," Grady interjected and tipped his head to Jon. "It's amazing to me how you even made it out alive."

"Well, he did. But it wasn't without…great pain and suffering. My sweet Jon was badly burned in the fire. Sustained third-degree burns over forty percent of his body." Emma rested her chin in her hand as her big green eyes settled on Jon again.

"Guess that explains the mask," August muttered.

Emma huffed. "J'aimerais que tu décolles ça."

"In English, darling."

She ignored and raised her glass to her masked friend. "You'd be a fool to underestimate him, though. Jon is a master of the blade. And quite skilled in the art of…Judo, was it?"

Jon nodded.

"You like close-range fighting too, huh?" August asked.

More intimate, Jon signed.

Grady exhaled heavily through his crooked nose while cutting into his meat. "An unnecessary risk, if you ask me. If you can take out your opponent from long range, I don't see why anyone would choose otherwise."

"I don't know, darling. I think if I were to ever end a man's life, I'd want to be close to him. I'd want to look into his eyes, feel his last breath on my face. I assume the experience would not only be very personal but highly erotic. The only experience in the world that truly allows you to be a person's first, and ultimately, their last. I imagine they'd belong to you after that."

Grady craned his neck and stared down his nose at Emma. "Cold-blooded murder doesn't really suit you, darling."

Emma grinned while lifting her wine goblet to her mouth. "Who said anything about cold-blooded?" Her emerald eyes met with August's, though he immediately diverted his gaze elsewhere and cringed. He cracked his fingers—a nervous habit. The tension in the room grew thicker than the fog outside the window.

"I think that's enough wine, sweetheart," Grady said. "At least until you've eaten something."

"I'm not really hungry, darling."

"I wasn't asking."

Eat. Please, Jon signed.

Emma slammed down her wine glass. "Oh, for heaven's sake. I won't wish to join you gentlemen for dinner if you insist on babying me every night."

"Emma," Grady warned.

Jon brought his right hand in a slicing motion down into his opposing palm—*STOP*. Through a smile, Emma became much more agreeable and took a bite of food.

"Quetchose pour toi, mon amour."

Jon brought his fingertips to his mouth, then extended them outward. *Thank you.*

"I like when you speak French. It sounds real nice. Even if I can't understand you."

When Emma took another bite of food, Grady exhaled heavily through his nose. His jaw remained clenched, and he kept his narrowed eyes directed at Emma. "You'll tire of it eventually. When you start to realize that they're most likely talking about you right in front of your face."

"I don't really care if they do. I'd be the idiot who'd still compliment her pronunciation after she called me a horse's ass."

Emma dropped her fork to her plate with a loud thunk. With her mouth full of food, she dusted her hands—as if completing such a grueling task. "It's nice to see a man show some humility around here. A humble man is an admirable one."

August scoffed, eyes wide. Never in his life had anyone *accused* him of such a quaility. Like calling a rattlesnake gentle or a lion cowardly. It just didn't fit. "I'm far from humble, Miss."

Emma snorted. "Well, then you and Grady will get along just famously."

"That's enough, darling—"

"Of course, he's not nearly as boastful as he was when he first came to the island. Always talking about being the most highly sought-after mercenary in Canada despite being an American—"

"Emma—" Grady warned.

"I guess he realized that we all started to tire of his verbal meanderings. I suspect his wife did as well—" Grady slammed his fist on the table, silencing Emma. Far from intimidated, she leaned back in her chair and took a sip of wine. "Forgive my outburst, darling. I often forget how sensitive the topic of your wife is."

August raised an eyebrow. "You got a wife?"

Emma tipped her glass to him. "And a young daughter."

"You seem very agitated this evening, sweetpea. Perhaps it may be best to call it an early night."

"Oh, I'm in a very pleasurable mood, *darling*." A power struggle happened before his eyes, one he didn't care to witness. "So, Mr. DeWitt…" she began, and he hesitated to give her his attention. "You've been given the grand tour of the house. What're your thoughts?"

"Uh… it's nice. Real big."

"Isn't that an understatement? I'm sure it must have surprised you to see the medical ward we have here as well. All for my benefit, it would seem. Surely they've told you about my condition by now."

August sighed. "I didn't get many details, Miss Emma. That's not really why I'm here."

"Why are you here?"

"To hunt the Howlers."

She took another sip of wine. Her warm, welcoming gaze became cold and narrowed. She lowered her glass back onto the table and inhaled sharply through her nose. "I've been informed that... you've been given a few of my sedatives. In case of an episode."

August looked to Grady for guidance, but his cold stare remained on Jon. "Yes, ma'am."

"I see. A man who I've only just met has been granted so much power over me, and there's nothing I can do about it."

"I wasn't plannin' on usin' 'em, Miss—"

"Oh, but you will." Her eyes glossed over. "It's only natural for a person to feel anger and annoyance at some point in their life. And from what they've told you about me, when that day comes, you'll grow frightened. You'll realize that it's so much easier just to shut me up than have to listen to all the reasons for my discontentment. Because if there's one thing man does not understand, it's his female counterpart. And given the opportunity, you'll do exactly as Grady has told you. You'll silence me. And you'll keep doing it until I no longer have the strength to fight anymore."

"You don't know anything about me."

"You see, that's where you're wrong. I know men. And I know that they'd prefer full control over uncertainties. Men fear what they do not understand. And what do you do when you're afraid, Mr. DeWitt? When you feel challenged or threatened in any way?"

"You make all these assumptions about people, but you haven't left your house in over a decade."

Emma slammed her fist onto the table. "Not by my own choosing!"

"Emma," Grady scorned.

"I didn't mean any offense, Miss Emma. I'm just asking you to give me a chance before you make up your mind about me."

"I apologize for my rudeness, Mr. DeWitt, but so long as you carry those sedatives, my trust in you will be compromised. Surely you can understand." Emma shot to her feet.

"Where are you going?" Grady asked.

41

"To get stinking drunk. And I won't be requiring the displeasure of your company, so you can all go to hell." Grady scooted his chair and darted across the room to reach her. When he grabbed her arm, she shoved him away. "Don't!" She pointed her finger at him. "Don't touch me."

Amazed by the spectacle, August only tore his eyes away from Grady and Emma when he noticed that Jon started rocking back and forth with his head lowered. "You all right?"

The flames from the candelabra flickered as if a gust of wind just blew through the dining room, and August scanned the area to try and find the source.

"Emma, it's all just a precaution—" Grady began, but then Emma gasped. Her wide eyes darted to the arched, barred window on the far side of the room.

All the color drained from her face. "They're coming."

The flames on the candelabra died out completely, and Jon groaned while rocking back and forth in his chair.

"No, they're not coming," Grady began.

"What the hell's goin' on?" August shouted.

"I can feel them. They're going to get in the house this time, I know it!" Emma rushed to the table, narrowly dodging Grady's attempt to grab her. She flattened her palms on the top. "Can you hear them howling, Mr. DeWitt?"

He hesitated—listened for any sound other than her heavy breaths. "I can't hear anything."

Grady approached Emma from behind. He brought his arms around her and stuck a needle into her neck. She whined, but as soon as he pressed the plunger, she collapsed into his arms.

August shot to his feet. "What the hell are you doing?" But Jon's desperate wails filled the room as he started smacking himself in the head. "Stop, Jon—"

"She was having an episode."

"You coulda just…I dunno, talked to her or somethin'—"

Grady lifted Emma into his arms. "You have a lot to learn, Mr. DeWitt. She cannot be reasoned with when she's like this."

Finally, Jon slammed his hands onto the table. He stood so abruptly that his chair flipped over, and he kicked it away before storming out of the dining room—leaving August in awe. "You're all stark-raving mad. All of you."

"Yes. And if you have any desire to hold on to the only bit of sanity we're awarded in this world, you'll leave Point DuPont. Now, if you don't mind, I must get Emma to bed."

Grady lifted Emma higher into his arms and carried her through the double doors, leaving August alone. He lowered himself back into his chair and stared at the scene before him. The burned-out flames from the candelabra, Jon's tipped over chair. And the untouched food.

Emma's words about the Howlers stayed with him, and he listened as best he could, but all he heard was the crackling from the fireplace. He moved to the large, arched windows and stared through the bars to the outside, but the thickness of the fog obscured his view. And still, he heard no howling.

Chapter IV

Grady put Emma to bed that night, a job usually reserved for Jon. He didn't mind and even preferred it because at least then he knew she would be going to sleep instead of staying up late with her oldest friend—something he grew restless of because, in his mind, it left her in a bitter mood the following morning.

That night was different, however. The way Emma acted at dinner wasn't something he could ignore. He wasn't content with just putting her to bed and calling it a day. His tortured mind wouldn't allow that sort of peace. So, he sat beside her bed, huddled by the fire for warmth. His bitterness stayed with him all night and through the morning when the sun started to rise. By eight, Emma's breakfast was served. And breakfast was his time.

He slammed her breakfast tray on the polished oak table in the corner of the room, causing Emma to stir. "Rise and shine, my darling. The day is upon us."

Emma's eyes fluttered open. "Where's Jon?"

He kept his back to her—facing the barred windows instead while leaning over her breakfast tray. "He's busy. Gearing up for the hunt."

Emma sat upward. "But the fog—"

"We can't put it off anymore, Emma. You know that." He turned to her. "I'm deeply troubled by the way you acted last night."

"I thought I heard the Howlers—"

"Not about that. I've noticed increased irritability in you since Carlyle's death. I can…only assume it's because you're afraid the Howlers will get to you one day. But I'm still here, Emma. I'm still alive, and I risk my life for you every day. All to keep you safe from harm, I…" overwhelmed by the notion, Grady hung his head and swallowed whole the grief rising from his chest and into his throat. "I think I'd die if anything ever happened to you, my darling."

She quivered. "Grady?"

"You treated me like dirt last night. How anyone can be so…ungrateful after everything I've done, I just…" He hung his head. A tightness grew in his chest, one he knew would send him into a fit of despondency if he didn't compose himself. "Maybe we should up your dose of the serum. You might be building an immunity, and…maybe that's why you've been more petulant lately."

"Grady, please—"

"I'll send word along to the doctor. Perhaps he can have it done before your morning dose," he said while crossing the room.

Emma flew from the bed and dropped to her knees in front of him. "Please don't, my darling. I lose myself as it is; an increased dose would only further remove me from reality."

His expression softened. Seeing her in such distress pulled any remaining bit of compassion out of him. He ran his fingers along the side of her face. "I don't know what else to do. I just want the old Emma back." He tucked a strand of her messy, ginger hair behind her ear.

"I'm still here. I still…love you."

Grady exhaled while running his thumb over her pale lips. "Prove it to me."

45

He offered his hands and pulled her to her feet. Every move she made, he scrutinized—searching for any sign of dishonesty. He did not wait for her to progress on her own. He pressed his lips onto hers and yanked her into him—taking full control of her. Claiming what he felt was rightly his. Her soft, wet lips reminded him of previous nights between them—sensual, passionate affairs from when she used to seek comfort in his arms. In his bed.

In between kisses, he panted, "I'm so in love with you." His hand twisted into her thick, ginger hair. He grabbed a handful and yanked her head back—connecting his hungry mouth with the bounding pulse in her neck. Driven mad with desire, he lifted her onto the vanity. "Spread your legs for me." As her thighs parted, the door swung open.

Emma gasped.

Jon stood in the doorway and lowered his head—averting his gaze. The sight forced a wicked grin across Grady's face. "Something the matter?"

The mute Hunter kept his eyes on the ground and pulled his pad and pencil from his coat pocket. He scribbled his words, tore the paper, and held it up for Grady to read. *It's time to leave.*

"Fine. I'll be down shortly." After Jon backed out of the room and closed the door behind him, Grady faced Emma again. "I have to go, darling." He gripped the back of her neck and pulled her lips onto his again. "Eat every last bit of your porridge," he commanded in between gentle kisses. "And try to eat some fruit too. I'll be checking with the kitchen when I return to assure you've eaten." Again, Emma nodded, and Grady took a moment to admire her before kissing her one last time.

The thick, muggy air choked August as he exited the house behind Jon. He followed him to the stables. The Hunters reinforced the small building in the same manner as the house. Barred windows and a thick, steel door, chained up and barricaded.

Jon carried the key.

Inside, the heat from the furnace combined with horse manure made it even more difficult to take a breath. "Gotta keep the beasts warm," the old caretaker grumbled while stoking the fire in the kiln.

Jon ran his gloved hand over a black horse's muzzle. "This one yours?" August asked while Jon adjusted the bridle, and he only nodded. "What's its name?"

"That one there is named Rose," the caretaker interrupted. "Brown one, that's Monsieur McCoy's. His name is Gunnar. You know how to ride a horse?"

August peered over his shoulder—eyebrows raised. "Uh, yeah. Don't know any self-respectin' southerner who don't know how. So, which one's mine?" The old man motioned to a white horse peppered with black that continually snorted and bobbed its head at him.

"That's Domino."

August smirked. "Well, all right."

Jon nudged him. *Glad you're here.*

Baffled, August chuckled. "Why's that? Don't trust Grady?" Only seconds later did Grady's riding boots on gravel trudge nearer until he appeared in the doorway of the stables.

"Saddle up, men. I'd like to make it to town before nine."

Grady and August rode side by side on the gravel road leading to the town while Jon followed behind. The fog made it difficult for August to observe the surrounding area, which caused great concern. He imagined it being rather easy to get lost in the fog if he didn't know the landscape. But the horse's hooves on the gravel, waves crashing into the cliffs in the distance, and the seagulls cawing as they flew overhead kept him grounded and oriented to the area. Over time, he managed to make out the lining of the forest.

"Don't worry. You'll learn your way to town soon enough."

August glanced over his shoulder to Jon, only detectable because of his black clothes and horse against the white fog. "You doin' all right back there?"

"Every morning before heading out to hunt, we check in with the town," Grady began, pulling August's attention away from Jon. "Mr. Maddox likes us to keep tabs on the people living there for some odd reason. More trouble than it's worth if you ask me. Our job is to keep Emma safe. Though I have to admit, the townspeople have been helpful from time to time. The Howlers mostly keep away from them. We're not entirely sure why. But every once in a while, one of them turns up."

"Well, then it's probably a good thing we go and check on them."

Grady huffed. "Why they even bother to stay is beyond me."

As they made it closer to the town, the fog started to clear enough to make out a gathering of small, derelict buildings lumped together haphazardly. Some were completely uninhabited—their foundations stained with black smoke and the windows boarded.

The livable buildings and homes were only detectable by the gas lamps giving off a faint glow at their entrances. The few people August saw outdoors hurried along from one point to another. He soon gathered that the town was not only poor but just as cautious of the fog as the Hunters.

Grady stopped in front of one of the larger buildings in sight, a two-story tavern with the upstairs balcony near collapse. And despite every other citizen hurrying out of the fog, one brave man dared sit in one of the chairs on the front porch—no doubt drunk.

The trio dismounted their horses and tied them to the post outside. "Watch the horses, will ya?" Grady grunted to the drunk man as they passed.

48

Inside, sparsely placed candles did a poor job of lighting the tavern, keeping it dim. The patrons sat at scattered tables throughout. Some drank while others ate their breakfast in peace. Despite the tavern being dark and muggy—more like a cavern—August felt a warm, tingling sensation from within. Whether from the glow of the candles, the smell of freshly baked croissants, or just being in the presence of other people, he wasn't entirely sure.

But it was the only comfort he felt since arriving.

"Yes, we're still alive!" the middle-aged bartender called to Grady in a deep, gruff voice.

"And well?" Grady asked while approaching the bar. "August, this is Telford Meyer. Owner of the rusty spoon."

Telford scoffed. "Americans with your atrocious accents. It's pronounced *Le Cellier*."

August chuckled and extended his hand to the scruffy barkeep. "Good to meet ya."

Telford's eyes narrowed, and his face contorted into an overdramatized grimace. "Not another American."

"Hello, Grady," a meek voice spoke from beside Telford, and it was only then that August noticed a young girl, face dirty with soot and hair tied up in a messy bun.

Grady tipped his head. "Hello, Darcy."

She beamed at his greeting. "Would you care for a croissant?" she asked while grabbing one from her tray and handing it to him, and he accepted. It was the most uncomfortable exchange August witnessed in a long while.

"Thank you."

"Darcy, get back to work," Telford demanded—his booming voice disturbing her trance.

"You know why we're here, Telford. Let's just get down to it," Grady said while sitting on one of the stools at the bar.

"It was a quiet night around here."

"No howling or anything of that nature? What about your animals? Have you checked on them this morning?"

"Believe me, if anything were to happen, Grady McCoy, you'd be the first to know. Now, if you don't mind, I have a business to run."

Grady forced a smile. "Not at all."

Despite Telford's obvious dislike of the Hunters, August rather enjoyed him. As if all pleasantries just completely vanished. He missed that sort of honesty. It became a rarity to find such an honest exchange after August became such a well-known fighter. It was something he looked forward to after his fall from grace— the candor.

Grady made sure to check in with the remaining senior ranking townspeople, but they all said the same thing as Telford. The Howlers hadn't made an appearance, and the news baffled Grady. They mounted their horses and left the town to be enveloped by fog once again. "It's not that I'm expecting an attack," Grady said as they rode side by side. "But after Emma's outburst last night, I suppose I was hoping that maybe she really did hear something. The alternative is a much more disturbing revelation."

"The alternative?"

"She's gone completely mad."

August looked over his shoulder to Jon, again riding solo in the back, but his mask made it impossible to gauge his reaction.

When the Hunters entered the forest of Point DuPont, all conversation ceased. Without needing any sort of explanation, August knew it was best to keep quiet.

As they rode deeper into the forest, the fog dissipated. They remained shrouded in darkness, though—the foliage being much too thick to allow any sort of light to guide their way.

It became colder as well.

Grady slowed his horse in front of a dilapidated shack and then dismounted. He slung his rifle over his shoulder. "August, come with me. Jon, keep watch."

August jumped off his horse and secured it next to Grady's. He moved to the veteran Hunter's side. They approached the shack, weapons in hand. "We always come here first," Grady said in a hushed voice. He used his rifle to push some low hanging branches aside.

"Why's that?" August whispered.

"Carlyle claimed this is where he saw a pack of them one day during the hunt. He died not far from here."

August's stomach twisted at the reminder. He slowed his pace and allowed Grady to take the first step up the splintered, creaking step leading to the shack's gaping black entrance. "We goin' in there?"

"We're just having a look." Grady's gaze met with August's. "You can wait here. I'll call if I need you."

August shrugged. "Whatever you say, boss man." And although he did his best to appear nonchalant, when Grady disappeared inside, he sighed in relief. As his eyes met with the mute Hunter's on his horse over his shoulder, he offered a head nod. A motion of solidarity.

༄༅ༀ

A stick cracked in the distance, catching Jon's attention. A gust of wind blew through the trees soon after, startling the birds within—sending them up into flight. Though bundled in layers of clothing, a cold chill shot up Jon's back. The scene unnerved him—alerting his horse to a change in his demeanor.

She neighed and kicked one of her hooves, and Jon ran his gloved hand through her mane. The shack creaked beside them. The rotted roof was caved in, and mold grew on the walls. Dead foliage lined the porch, creating a much different scene than he remembered from childhood.

He remembered a shack, yes, but a much warmer and brighter version surrounded by green grass, lush trees, and flowers. The sound of a little girl's laughter was also a distant memory, now replaced with the shack creaking in the slightest bit of wind.

51

Grady emerged after a few minutes and slung his rifle over his shoulder. "The coast is clear. We should head up the road a bit more. See if maybe they're still in the area."

The ride continued with August and Grady taking the lead once again. Jon followed behind, his head hanging low as he remembered all the times he spent in that forest as a child. That forest was his safe haven from his parents. It's where he wanted to disappear forever until he met Emma. Even after she came into his life at just ten years old, the two spent most of their time there playing make-believe.

Now infested with Howlers, years had passed since he and Emma found solace in the peace and tranquility of the forests of Point DuPont. But every time the weight of the deterioration started to crush him, he told himself, it's all for Emma. As much as he wished the two of them could leave and live the lives they always wanted, he convinced himself that he needed to endure the pain and heartbreak for her.

As she'd always done for him.

August's voice calling for him in the distance ripped Jon from his daydream. He tightened his grip on the reins and searched the area for his fellow Hunters, but he saw no one.

He slowed his horse. A flash of blackness darted in front of Rose, and she reared as a shrill neigh escaped her. Jon pulled on the reins and dug his heels into her side, but another violent kick launched him from her back, and Rose darted through the woods.

He hit the ground, the impact knocking the wind out of him. "Jon!" August called through the forest, his voice distant and echoed. But not only could Jon not respond, something much more urgent required his full attention. In front of him, towering over him, two glowing yellow eyes met with his.

Jon remained still; he knew better than to make any sudden movements while in the presence of a Howler. The beast growled and stepped closer, its hackles standing upright—similar to a dog before engaging an enemy. Jon reached for the hunting knife on his belt, but the beast snarled and launched at him.

August pulled the reins of his horse and whipped him around. He kicked his heels into the horse's sides, and he sprinted in the direction from which they came. He feared he might not find Jon. Or if he did find him, he feared only finding the mangled bits of him. Because according to everyone else, the Howlers only left mangled bits behind.

Domino darted through the woods as August clenched the reins and kicked his heels into the horse's side. "Jon!"

Even though he knew Jon had no way to respond, he hoped his voice might reassure his colleague. Or maybe, the shouting might scare off a potential attacker.

Almost as abruptly as the horse took off in a canter, it came to a skidding halt, kicking upward and neighing at the sight of one of the dark beasts growling and gnashing its teeth. On the ground behind the Howler, Jon clenched his side.

Finally, August came face to face with the animal he heard so much about. The time came to face the truth—the stories her heard, all accurate depictions of the demonic monsters lurking within the woods. And it paralyzed him with fear. He trembled. "Jesus Christ, what is that thing?"

Its yellow eyes glowed—pulsed, undulating with desire to wreak havoc and destruction. It bared its teeth—long, sharp, and dripping with saliva.

Twigs snapped as Grady crept forward with his rifle pointed right at the Howler.

"Shoot it, Grady." But he only kneeled—his rifle pointed at the intended target. Yet for some reason, he hesitated to fire. "Grady...?"

The Howler's attention turned to Jon. Instead of attacking, it backed away into the forest, and none of the Hunters moved until it disappeared from sight and sound entirely.

Grady lowered his rifle.

August jumped from his horse and raced to Jon's side. "Why didn't you shoot it?"

"I didn't want to alert any others in the area. Trust me, I would have fired if it had attacked."

"It already did," August said, and Jon leaned his head back and groaned. "We have to get him back to the house."

ℴ⁗℞

August carried Jon over his shoulder and into the parlor. He dropped him on the sofa, causing him to groan. "Shit, I'm sorry."

Grady rushed to the exit. "I'll get the doctor."

August kneeled beside the sofa. He started unbuttoning Jon's coat, but the muted Hunter pushed his hands away and shook his head. "Stop. I have to see the wound. Won't be able to do much if you don't show me." He tore Jon's coat open. "Jesus, you got a lot of layers here." Beneath his thick riding coat, Jon wore a black waistcoat and undershirt. "Not that I'm complaining. These layers probably saved your life." August ripped his clothes, exposing the burns on his body.

"It's a good bite, but…it ain't so deep. Does it hurt?" he asked, and Jon only teetered his hand. "You're pretty tough, ain't ya?"

Grady and Doctor Bernard entered the parlor.

"Okay, Jon," the Doctor said while kneeling next to the couch, and August moved away to give him more room. "I'll be asking you yes or no questions. I just want you to nod or shake your head in response, understand?"

Jon nodded.

While the doctor tended to Jon's wounds, August moved to Grady's side. "You think he's gonna be all right?" he asked in a hushed tone.

"He'll be fine."

"They're not, like, poisonous, are they? The Howlers?"

"No. But they tend to latch onto their prey. I'm amazed it even let him go, to be honest. It's strange. Almost like…the Howler was just warning him to back off. Like it didn't want to kill him, just keep him away."

"You been bit by one before?"

Grady shook his head. "But I've watched three Hunters die so far because of those damn things. I've grown accustomed to their ways. Grown numb to the grisly scene they paint when they latch onto their intended target. Animals ripped to shreds, and there are still pieces of the Hunters we haven't found." Grady's cool gaze met with August's. "He's very lucky to be alive right now."

"Why do you think they did that? Let him go?"

"Maybe because he's a cripple."

"A cripple?"

"Animals can sense that sort of thing. The wounded, the weak. Even if from another species. Maybe they choose not to prey on the weak. Maybe they know we're the bigger threat."

"Jon's not weak. And he ain't a cripple."

"To you. But those animals might feel different."

Before August thought of anything to say, the parlor door swung open, and the room turned to Emma.

"Jon?" He scrambled to cover himself. "What happened?" She gasped. "What'd they do to you—"

"August, get her out of here," Grady demanded, and he rushed to keep her away. For Jon's sake, more than anything. Because in the short time she remained in the parlor, he sensed Jon's terror and insecurity flooding out of him.

August wrapped his arms around her to push her back out of the parlor, but she fought to break free. "Jon! What happened to him? Why won't you let me see him?"

"Calm down, Miss Emma. Jon's all right—"

"Then why can't I see him?"

"Because he doesn't want you to see him like this." A tear streaked down her cheek, and her breath quivered. "Please don't cry, Miss Emma. Grady can be a real asshole when you get all…out of sorts."

"I could feel him. I knew something…something awful happened to him. He's going to be okay, August? I don't think…I couldn't bear losing him."

He didn't bother to ask for clarification. Instead, he knew he needed to calm her. So he nodded. "Yeah, he'll be fine. Just a little nip is all." But his words seemed to have no effect on her, and she ran her hand over her forehead—her frantic eyes darting to the ground. "Look, if I thought what was going on in there was life-threatening, I wouldn't keep you from seein' him. Can you at least trust that?"

"Yes, all right."

August offered his arm to her. "May I escort you to your room, Miss? Or maybe the library? I'd be glad to keep you company while the doctor finishes tending to Jon."

Emma nodded to him in approval and took his arm. "Thank you, Mr. DeWitt. Your graciousness will not soon be forgotten."

Chapter V

August escorted Emma to the library and waited with her for an update on Jon. He sat on the chaise lounge while she stood by the window, facing outward to the fog. She seemed lost in a trance, and he wracked his brain for any sort of comfort to offer.

"The fog is clearing," Emma muttered.

August thought it best to distract her. He grabbed a book on the table beside him. "The Canterbury Tales. My mom used to read this to me when I was little." Emma looked over her shoulder to him. He held the book up. "Jon told me you read to him."

"What's the matter, Mr. DeWitt? In need of a bedtime story?"

August chuckled. "Nah, I just…I think it's nice that you do that for him."

Emma returned her gaze to the outdoors. "I enjoy reading to others, that is true. And at night, I read to Jon, but it's not for his benefit. And he knows that."

"What do you mean?"

She stayed quiet for a while, lost in her own little world. "I become fearful at night. I'm afraid to go to sleep because my dreams, they haunt me. Jon sits with me until I do, but…most nights, I need a distraction. Something to deflect all the things that run through my mind. Oh, I so wish he could be the one who reads to me until I fall asleep."

"Did your dad use to read to you?"

"No. But my mother did."

"What happened to your mother?"

She sighed and turned her back on the window. She leaned on the sill and folded her arms across her chest—her narrowed eyes concentrated on the floor. "I'm not sure. One day she was there, and then the next she wasn't. We used to live in a small cabin out in the middle of the woods. It was just the two of us. She'd read me bedtime stories every night. But I can't for the life of me remember what she looked like. I remember her voice, but…not her face."

"Was this here? On the island?"

Emma shook her head with squinted eyes. "I don't think so. But I don't remember much about back then. I just remember my mother reading me bedtime stories, and…wherever we were, it was always winter. The forest around our cabin was always covered in thick snow."

"That must have been nice."

She smirked. "If you like snow."

"I get the feeling you do."

"Yes, I do. And I'm not sure why. I should be traumatized by it, but…I find comfort in it, more than anything."

"Why should you be traumatized by snow?"

She hung her head, and her frantic eyes darted along the floor beneath her feet. "I have this one memory…and for some reason, it's stronger than all the others. I was out playing in the snow one day, and…I got lost in the woods. I was only a little girl, maybe…four years old. I remember being frightened when I couldn't find my way back. I must have been gone for a long time because…I was freezing. And then the sun started to set, and…I remember crying for my mother. I had no understanding of death at the time, but I knew…I don't know how to explain it, really. I

58

knew that I would…somehow disappear forever. And then out of the forest came this…this beautiful white wolf. Bright blue eyes, fur so perfect and untouched that it seemed she was created from the snow on which she walked."

August raised an eyebrow. "Is this a true story?"

Emma smirked. "I would probably second guess it myself if it weren't so clear in my mind. I remember so well the softness of her fur and the warmth she gave me when she curled up on the ground next to me. She stayed with me all through the night, kept me warm. Kept me safe from harm."

"And then what happened?"

"I don't know," she lamented. "The only memories I have from that point on are living here on the island."

The doors to the library opened, disturbing the bizarre calmness between them. When Grady entered, they stood. "Is Jon all right?" Emma asked.

"He's fine. He's gone to bed for the evening."

"But I didn't even get to see him."

"He did not wish to see you tonight," Grady said, nonchalant. "Jon won't be going hunting with us tomorrow, August. The doctor wishes he take the day off to recuperate, which inconveniences our operation, but I cannot argue. Since it's just the two of us, we'll stick to the forest's outer region for now. But we'll talk more about that in the morning. Meet me in the parlor at six. Eat something before then, if it pleases you. I'd like to be back at the house earlier this time." Grady's eyes flitted to Emma. "Ready for bed, sweetheart?"

"Oh, why don't you let August put me to bed, darling? You've been working so hard all day trying to please me, and I want you to be well-rested before you leave in the morning." Grady's shifty eyes met with August's. Emma sauntered over to him, slinging her arm around his waist to pull him closer. "You work too hard, darling."

He slid his fingers along the side of her face, and only then did August really start to notice how much power she had over Grady.

He talked a big game, but when Emma swooned over him, Grady melted into her. "I do it to keep you safe, sweetheart."

"I know you do, my love," she whispered and turned her face into his hand to place gentle kisses on his palm. "And I adore you for it. Really, I do."

August's discomfort grew with every passing moment. The couple swooned over each other, and he wanted nothing more than to slink away from them. He'd never been a fan of public displays of affection, but Emma's insincerity was what sickened him. And How Grady didn't notice perplexed him. Too in love, he guessed—blinded by his rose-colored glasses.

"August, please put Miss Emma to bed. And make sure you give her the nightly dose."

"The nightly dose?" he asked.

"It's on her vanity in a capped syringe. She'll instruct you on how to use it." He kissed Emma's forehead. "Sweet dreams, my darling."

"Sweet dreams of you," she cooed, and August rolled his eyes.

He escorted Emma to her room, and once inside, she closed the doors behind them. It was the first time he entered a woman's room without the intention of being intimate with her. When Emma smiled at him, he did his best to appear disinterested and looked everywhere but at her.

"Wow. It's really somethin' in here."

"Mr. DeWitt?"

"Yeah?"

"I need you to undress me now."

He cleared his throat. "Sure, uh…okay."

When he came within inches of her, he froze. He'd undressed women before, plenty of times, but none of them ever wore the 19th-century garb Emma seemed so fond of. He didn't even know where to begin. "Something wrong?" she asked.

"No, I just…never had to get a lady out of such a complicated dress before. Are you sure you don't want Grady helping you?"

"I'm sure. It's not that complex. Just untie the sash in the back. Then unbutton the clasps, and it'll come right off."

His trembling hands untied the sash and then started unbuttoning the clasps along her spine. His fingers were much bigger than a typical handmaiden's, though, and he struggled to get a proper grip. His hand slipped after jerking one open, shifting Emma through the force. "Oh!" she squealed.

"Shit, I'm sorry, Miss Emma—"

"That's all right," she whispered. "Let me." She reached behind her back to undo the last few clasps. "See? It isn't so hard. You just need to relax."

August forced a laugh. "Oh, I'm relaxed."

Emma raised her hands in the air. "Your heart is pounding."

His face burned from embarrassment. How she even heard his heart thudding wildly in his chest perplexed him. He kneeled and grabbed the base of her dress. After bunching it up as best he could, he lifted it over her head. Beneath the dress, she wore even more intricate undergarments. "Holy hell."

"Never seen a corset before?"

"Not like this. I think my mom used to wear them when she was young."

"I just need you to untie it for me. I'll do the rest."

"Sure, okay." He moved into her again and grabbed the thin strands. "Do you need me to...loosen it for you?"

"If you'd be so kind." His thick fingers loosened the seam until reaching the curve of her backside, where he hesitated to continue. "Would you grab my nightgown from the bureau?"

"Yes, ma'am," he muttered, ashamed that he even dared admire her backside while in her underwear. He yanked open the bureau doors, and his eyes darted over every piece of clothing therein. "Uh—"

"It's the white, silk gown."

He snatched it from the shelves, and as he closed the door again, Emma stepped out of her corset completely, leaving her only in a pair of white thigh high stockings and short bloomers.

And then he dared admire her again.

"Jesus," he quivered. Emma's eyes met with his gaze, and it shamed him into looking away. He handed her the nightgown and kept his head down as he slunk into an armchair on the far side of the room. "Is that it?"

She pulled her nightgown over her body. "I suppose." She sat on the edge of her bed to remove her stockings. Once finished, she pulled her bloomers down and let them fall to the floor. She then grabbed a white, flowing robe from the back of her vanity chair and wrapped it around herself.

That's when he noticed the capped syringe on the vanity. He needed to give her medicine.

"So…where does this go?" he asked as she crawled into bed.

"Oh, must I take it, August? Really, I feel fine."

"What happens if you don't?"

She shook her head. "Nothing."

He contemplated while smacking the syringe into his other hand. "Why don't you want to take it?"

"It makes me feel all…foggy. Like I'm not really here. And it stays for a long while."

The pressure he felt was unparalleled by anything he experienced before, and he'd been a professional fighter. He considered what Grady might say if he found out and weighed that against the worried expression in Emma's eyes. "What should I do with it?"

She extended her hand to him. "Give it to me." He hesitated to hand it over to her. "Don't worry. This will be our little secret."

"This is only for tonight, right? I mean, you ain't gonna ask me to skip this all the time, are ya? Might just let Jon keep putting you to bed if that's the case."

"Jon doesn't give it to me either."

August nodded. "Yeah. I could have figured. You need anything else?"

Emma extended her hand to the lounge. "My water."

A pitcher of water and a crystal glass glistened on a tray beside the fire. He snatched the glass and placed it on the nightstand beside her bed. "How about now?"

Emma leaned up and took a large swig of water. She set it back on the nightstand and flopped back onto her big, fluffy pillow, a big smile on her face.

"Look at you. Snug as a bug."

"Will you stay with me?"

"What?" The two hardly knew each other, only having met the previous day. Of course, his job was to take care of her. Still, a tinge of resentment came over him for her even asking—for putting him in a situation he wanted to decline but knew he shouldn't. And after what she told him earlier about having trouble sleeping—becoming fearful at night—August relented.

He lowered himself into the armchair near her bed. "How long do you need me to stay?"

"Just until I fall asleep."

Her continued stare forced a smile across his face. "You gonna close your eyes?"

"Come closer."

He sighed and scooted the armchair closer to the bed. "This all right?" he asked, and she nodded.

She turned onto her side and creeped closer to the edge to be closer to him. She extended her hand toward him, her fingers running over the mattress between them. "I'm frightened, August."

Her words were like some kind of magic spell cast over him. The fear in her eyes, seemingly out of nowhere, weakened him. For a moment, it seemed like he looked upon a child—one terrified of the monsters under her bed. "You don't need to be scared, Miss Emma. Nothing's gonna happen to you. Not while I'm here."

He leaned forward onto the bed and placed his hand over hers. Slowly, the warmth came back to her eyes. "I dreamt of you, Mr.

DeWitt. After Carlyle died. I dreamt of a man, tall and dark, emerging from the fog. Like the white wolf."

"Oh yeah? And how'd you know it was me?"

"Because I felt you."

He hummed through a half-hearted smile. "Try and get some sleep, Miss Emma. Go ahead and close your eyes now."

Even after she closed her eyes, he never broke his gaze upon her. As much as he wanted to believe that she was comforted by him, Grady's warning about her manipulative nature dominated his thoughts.

But then there was Jon's interpretation of her—innocent, fearful. After everything she told him, he started to consider Jon's truth over Grady's.

He rested his head on the mattress beside their hands. But even when her breathing slowed, his guilt from even thinking about leaving her kept him in place. The simple act of pulling his hand from hers might wake her. The last thing he wanted to do after she found peace was to pull her back into reality.

He would stay a little while longer, he thought.

But a little while turned to hours after August drifted to sleep. The fire died down and became nothing more than a smoldering heap of ash. The clock on Emma's night table ticked along, passing through the hours of the night until four in the morning when August stirred at the sound of a child crying.

He opened his eyes. The diminshed fog allowed the moon to shine through and paint the room a dark shade of blue. He lifted his head and rubbed his eyes—disturbed by the nightmare and wanting nothing more than to reorient himself. The crying continued, though, and his eyes darted to the bedroom door.

A door that was closed before but now creaked open.

He crossed the room and swung it open. His head darted in both directions of the hall, though nothing appeared to be out of the ordinary. Perhaps just his imagination, or a dream. Only when a little girl in a white nightgown passed the hall further down did he know for certain. She headed in the direction of his bedroom.

The sight paralyzed him. "He h...hey," he called, but the child disappeared behind the corner.

He jogged to catch up to her, but when he turned the corner, he saw nothing, and a bitter chill shot up his spine, causing the hairs on his neck to stand upright. The temperature plummeted, and he panted heavy, visible breaths.

"August?" a little voice spoke from behind. He whipped around to see the young child looking up at him, pale white.

He jolted and found himself still at Emma's bedside. His hand remained on hers as she slept, and only then did he realize he had a horrible nightmare. At least, he hoped that's all it was.

The clock read five in the morning, and as tired as he felt from the discomfort of spending all night hunched over, the day was now upon him, and within the hour, he and Grady would have to set out to hunt.

Chapter VI

Jon watched over his fellow Hunters from his bedroom window as they hurried to the stables the following morning. The fog settled along the grass in the open field. The clarity of the sky painted a clearer day ahead. As Grady and August left, a carriage arrived with the flower delivery Jon was to supervise. It was no surprise to anyone that to keep Maddox House fully operational, supplies needed to be delivered monthly. Food, medicine, fabrics for new clothes. And then, of course, anything Emma wanted.

Chocolates from Italy, new paints from Paris, jewelry from Spain. The flower delivery was one that she grew most fond of because it made her feel somewhat alive in the cold and drab surroundings.

At least, that's what she told Jon.

Dozens of bouquets were delivered, of every sort of flower Emma wished and in every color. Jon stood guard while the maids brought them into the house. The last bouquet was crimson roses.

After bidding the carriage farewell, Jon bolted the door shut and then ran to catch up with the maid carrying the roses. He tipped his head to the bouquet.

"Of course, Jon."

He took one of the roses. *Thank you.*

Jon rushed to Emma's room, thrilled that her morning belonged to him instead of Grady. He knocked lightly on her door and pushed it open to see her still fast asleep. He moved to her bedside and was careful to sit on the edge. She was so peaceful and beautiful to him—the rose in his hand, hardly compared to her splendor.

He ran the rose over the tip of her nose. She stirred but didn't wake. He slid the petals over her pale lips, and when Emma opened her eyes, Jon smiled behind his mask. *Good morning.*

A wide smile spread across her face. "Jon," she cooed. She sat up in bed and took the rose from him. "C'est si beau, mon amour. Merci." She looped her arm around him and pulled him close. "Grady said you didn't wish to see me last night." He shook his head, displeased to know that Grady would tell her such things. "I was so worried about you."

He pulled her arms from around him and cradled her hands in his momentarily—inhaling a deep, sharp breath. *I'm fine,* he signed and made an X over his heart. *Are you hungry?*

Jon spent the next hour organizing Emma's breakfast—a breakfast that usually consisted of porridge or fruit. Because even though Grady made sure she ate, the veteran Hunter did not like her eating in large amounts and kept her away from certain types of food. If she grew tired of the porridge and demanded Belgian waffles, Grady left out the syrup and added strawberries instead. If she wanted a bit of dessert, he sent for a fruit salad or yogurt.

This displeased Jon to no end because he remembered Emma having a sweet tooth as a child. So for breakfast on this day, he requested the kitchen prepare a dozen crepes for her with sliced bananas and strawberries, complete with syrup, sugar, and whipped cream.

He ordered coffee with cream and sugar for her—the perfect touch to the magnificent spread on the cast-iron café table of the greenhouse. When Jon escorted Emma to breakfast, she gasped at the sight.

"Oh, look at this! Grady would be seething if he saw it," she said through a laugh. He pulled her chair out for her. "Crepes! I just simply don't deserve you."

He poured her coffee and added the exact amount of cream and sugar she preferred. As Emma devoured her breakfast, Jon sat beside her. He never ate in her presence. To do so would require the removal of his mask.

"Are you not having any?" She placed her silverware on her plate. "I'll make you a strawberry one." Before she grabbed another plate, Jon gripped her wrist. He shook his head and averted his gaze outward to the glass walls of the greenhouse—protected by an iron, pointed gate that rose nearly eight feet high to keep the Howlers away.

For the first time in months, the fog was thin enough to see the bluffs and the outstretch of the blue ocean in the distance.

"Oh, I'm going to be positively stuffed after this. I won't be able to fit into my corset."

After breakfast, Jon had the servants package up the remaining food to be delivered to town—something Emma always insisted upon when so much food was leftover.

When it was time to dress her, Emma groaned. "Not too tight today," she said as he fastened her corset, but even then, she belched. "Oh my...forgive me, Jon. Seems I really did eat too much."

He smirked behind his mask. Jon recalled her belching many times when they were children and how they used to compete for the loudest during lunchtime. Her father never minded either. It was her governess who used to strike her hand when she did such things.

Emma picked a light blue gown for the day, which was Jon's favorite. The blue made her beautiful ginger hair pop and green eyes stand out more than usual. She wore white stockings with them and her favorite silver locket.

After dressing, Emma stared at her reflection in her vanity mirror, and Jon sensed displeasure. She lowered herself into her chair, studying her reflection intently. She applied rouge to her pale cheeks and pink lip stain to her muted lips. Meanwhile, he tied up her hair.

"My youth seems to have gotten away from me. I feel as though I'm losing my vitality by the day. A woman my age should be married with children by now." Jon exhaled slowly while admiring her through the mirror. He couldn't disagree more. "Have you ever thought about that, Jon? I know it's different for men. Their vitality never really leaves, and they can continue courting up into their forties, fifties even. But have you ever thought that you're wasting your life here on the island? You, too, could be married with children right now. If you weren't so busy tending to me. I feel like I've robbed you of the life you were meant to live. You deserve better than this life."

He pointed to her in the mirror.

She smiled weakly at him, and when his fingers traced the skin on her shoulder, she reached her hand to his and held it tightly. "Do you ever think about that day, Jon? Do you ever think about what our life would be like if we made it out?"

Every day, he signed.

He released her after that and grabbed the capped syringe from her vanity. "Must I?" He shook his head, then turned to toss the syringe into the fireplace.

ᔕᐧᑕᕈ

In the village, August fought to swallow the vomit rising in his throat. The gory scene before him—strewn about the barn of one of the townspeople—made him regret eating anything for breakfast. Worse than the sight of the carnage was the smell. Despite how hard he tried, when Grady kneeled before the mess of torn sheep, August bolted to the corner of the barn and vomited.

"It happened around three. Those damned things got two of them before I got here," the owner cried.

Grady examined the mutilated sheep with narrowed eyes and pursed lips. "You're lucky it didn't kill you."

"There were three of those damned things!"

Grady crossed the barn to the entrance. "Your locks are rusted. It's no wonder they got inside."

"You're saying this is my fault? Isn't it your job to kill them?"

"Yes, it is our job. But you need to take responsibility and assure you're protecting you and yours accordingly. Replace these locks. And then consider doing the same to your house. I can only imagine the state that's in."

"And the mess?" the man asked.

"I'd recommend sawdust. Good day."

When the veteran Hunter exited the barn, August knew he needed to follow. He wiped his mouth on his coat sleeve and groaned. "Sorry about your sheep." As soon as he staggered into the chilly, morning air, he inhaled deeply—no longer plagued by the smell of rot and decay. "So that's all you do? Examine the destruction and then tell the people everything they should have done to prevent it?"

"What else can I do?"

"I dunno. Offer a bit of…compassion? Some reassurance that the problem is being dealt with?"

Grady chuckled while approaching his horse. "You have a lot to learn, Mr. DeWitt. This problem has been going on for five years. The people of Point DuPont, believe it or not, aren't stupid."

"Ugh, I feel sick."

"You're going to need a stronger stomach. You think that was bad, wait until they get their teeth on a human being."

A carriage stopped in front of Le Cellier, distracting the Hunters. "That our carriage?" August asked.

Grady groaned and ran his hands over his face. "Yes."

Two men exited, carrying large trays into the tavern. When Grady and August approached, the driver greeted them. "Monsieur McCoy, Monsieur DeWitt."

"What's going on?" Grady asked.

"Food delivery," the driver said.

"Unbelievable." He led the way into the tavern, where patrons helped themselves to platefuls of crepes, eggs, and bacon. "I'm gone for one hour, and Jon has already started to spoil her."

"McCoy!" Telford shouted from behind the bar. "We've talked about this. I lose money every time that woman sends her leftovers out here."

Grady held up his hand to the irritated proprietor.

"I think it's nice, even though the smell makes me want to hurl...again." August swallowed hard, trying his best to keep from vomiting in front of all the townspeople.

"I will talk to her," Grady assured Telford. He nudged August, and the two trudged to the exit of the tavern.

"Grady!" Darcy weaved through the patrons to reach him.

"I'm on a tight schedule, Darcy—"

"I heard about what happened to Monsieur Picard's flock. Are the Howlers invading the town now?"

Grady's eyes darted around the bar to all the patrons, now looking to the Hunters. All chatter ceased. "As of right now, they're no more a threat than they were before. Just take the necessary precautions. And talk to your father about replacing the locks on your home. I can only imagine how rusted they've become."

He tried to leave again, but Darcy grabbed his arm and beckoned his attention once more. "Grady... I'm frightened. I heard the sheep were ripped in half—"

"Shush," he whispered. "Don't be frightened, Darcy. I won't let them harm you."

August cleared his throat loudly. "Well, this has been nice. And…a little awkward, but mostly…uncomfortable. How old are you?"

Grady's firm grasp on August's coat ripped him from the tavern, and only when outside did August bother jerking away—an amused smirk on his face. "Holy shit, how old is she?"

"How should I know?" Grady spat.

"You two seem close." They climbed onto their horses, but August continually glanced to Grady, waiting for more of an explanation.

"Look, it's our job to assure the villagers that we're doing everything we can. They need to feel safe, secure," he said after climbing onto Gunnar, and August chuckled while pulling himself onto Domino.

"That ain't what you told that shepherd."

Grady scoffed and assumed the lead on the pathway leading away from the village. "Come now. You know as well as I do that women need more reassurance than men."

"First of all, that ain't no woman. That's a girl. And second, that's the dumbest shit I ever heard."

"It's the truth. It's scientifically proven that women can't handle stressful situations. Why do you think there are no women fighting in the wars?"

"Your mama didn't love you as a child, huh?"

Before even reaching the edge of the town, a blood-curdling scream put the Hunters on alert. They rode through the village, shouting for the curious and frightened villagers to clear the way.

The screams led them to a small house on the edge of the town, and already, a crowd formed outside. Grady and August's horses skidded to a halt.

Grady kicked the door in. A woman and her young son cowered before the massive wolf-like demon. With the Howler in his rifle's sights, Grady took a knee.

"Come…come here." August held his arm to the family. Before they moved, the Howler charged.

72

"No!" Grady shouted and fired—CRACK!

A familiar, high-pitched ringing echoed throughout August's ears. He winced from the pain deep within his head that drowned out all other sounds around him. Gunpowder overwhelmed the smell of molded wood.

With the Howler's attention now on the Hunters, the woman took her son through the back, evading attack.

August cocked his shotgun and fired at the beast, causing it to yelp and fall back into the wall. Blood seeped from the animal's wounds. It struggled to stand, and before the Hunters had a chance to fire again, it started to howl.

August cocked his shotgun again, but the animal darted to the back of the house, narrowly missing the buckshot that sent splintered wood shards flying through the air.

They bolted after the animal and burst through the back door. But as Grady planted his feet firmly into the ground and halted, August crashed into him.

"Mother of God."

The small family was frozen. In front of them, at the mouth of the forest, more Howlers came to aid their wounded pack member. "Ma'am…come on back now," August said while Grady raised his rifle to the pack, but the immediate threat was hard to place. "Don't be stupid, Grady. We can't kill 'em all."

"There's no fog," Grady muttered, his gaze never breaking from the pack of Howlers.

August grabbed the woman's shoulder and pulled her and her child behind him. He ushered them back into the house and stood on the steps, waiting for Grady to retreat as well. "Grady?"

The Howlers stepped forward—their yellow eyes fixated on their prey before them. A low, guttural growl escaped one of them as it stepped closer to Grady, and for a moment, August thought he might try to engage the beast. And while Grady might have the ability to kill one of them, it would only take seconds for the others to attack. "Go," Grady said quietly while backing toward the steps once more. "Run!" One of the Howlers launched, forcing Grady and August back into the house. "Go, go, go go!"

They darted through the house and out the front door again, leaping from the stairs with such quickness that they staggered as their boots met with the ground. The villagers watched in sheer terror. "Go to your homes!" Grady shouted. "Run for cover!"

The door of the house burst open in an explosion of splintered wood and black furry masses. Terrified screams erupted from the villagers. Within a matter of seconds, the town transitioned into chaos.

"The horses, get the horses!" Grady shouted, and August leaped onto Domino. Over his shoulder, Grady trailed behind on Gunnar, and the Howlers wreaked havoc on anything left behind. Doors slammed shut around them; villagers dove out of the way. Straight ahead, a man struggled to close his barn doors.

August dug his heels into Domino and whipped the reins. "Keep those doors open!"

Just when the villager started to slide the barn doors closed, August and Grady skidded through the entrance and yanked on their reins—pulling their horses to an abrupt stop. They jumped from their saddles and yanked the barn doors shut.

"Get those chains," Grady demanded while holding the door shut, and August snatched them from the barn owner.

A harsh thud on the doors shifted August's weight as he struggled to secure the door. Only when he latched the padlock did the two Hunters step away. Another harsh thud caused them to flinch and step back.

"Is it the Howlers?" the barn owner asked.

The Hunters pointed their weapons at the door, ready to eliminate any threat that broke through. From outside, the villagers' screams tormented August. "We have to do something."

"What do you suggest?" Grady snapped.

"I dunno, we have to help. It's our job to be killing those things—to help protect these people!"

"Our job is to protect Emma. If we die trying to take all of them on, no one will be able to save her when they decide to overrun the house! There's nothing we can do for them."

It was a horrifying realization. An emotion—a feeling far worse than fear overcame him. Helplessness.

ಬಃಿ

At the house, Emma spent her morning reading in the music room while Jon played the piano—a lighthearted, romantic tune to off-set the melancholic works of Edgar Allen Poe Emma read.

"You play beautifully, Jon."

He smiled behind his mask and rested his fingers on the keys momentarily. *You taught me*, he signed.

Emma smiled. "I did, didn't I?" An airy laugh escaped him, and he continued to play. Emma closed her book and set it aside. "Is that…Chopin?" Jon shook his head. "Hmm…is it Mozart?" He felt her presence draw nearer. Once more, he smiled behind his mask and shook his head.

He knew she only tested him.

She sat beside him on the bench. "I know, I know, don't tell me…" She drummed her fingers along her chin. "Is it Bach?" Jon's lips curled into a wide grin. She knew all too well it was Bach, Jon's favorite. "May I?"

He pulled his fingers from the keys.

As she started the metronome, Jon paid special attention to her fingers. She started playing. A bit heavy-handed in this particular song, he noticed. The introduction was vengeful, but then it faded into a light, romantic tune.

She played in minor.

Jon always saw the creativity in Emma and took notice when her works changed. As a child, she played uplifting music, sang about love and adventure. She used to paint with bright, pastel watercolors. Over time, her creations became darker.

Jon, although concerned for her well-being, never could bring himself to dislike anything of hers. She created from her heart; therefore, he found her creations beautiful.

"That's all I have so far. I can't think of what should come next." Her eyes met with his. "What would you recommend?"

Jon inhaled sharply. Emma's song seemed to be written about suffering—some sort of longing. A burning desire that could never be fulfilled. Of that, he knew much about.

So, he played what that sounded like to him.

That's what she wanted, and he knew it as soon as she asked for his opinion. She wanted to know what suffering meant to him—to hear *his* version. And when he finished his small addition, he looked to Emma's wide eyes.

"What a beautiful mind you have, Jon. It's absolutely perfect." She started playing again from the beginning, and as she did, Jon joined her, adding a bit more to her song until the end when she allowed him to finish up strong with his addition. When they finished, Emma clapped her hands.

"We're really quite brilliant, aren't we?"

He signed, *Again.*

She smiled. As she played, Jon closed his eyes. He envisioned a better time on the island. A time before the fire, a time when he and Emma spent every day together, daydreaming about life outside of Point DuPont.

He played beside her, losing himself in the melancholic tune. It so beautifully depicted everything he felt since the fire. The shame he felt after moving into Maddox House, relying so heavily on the kindness of others to take care of him through his recovery. And then Emma. The trauma they endured strained their relationship, and he knew it would never be the same.

He stopped playing.

Emma stopped soon after. "I suddenly don't feel well."

He slid his hand across her back. *Tired?*

She gripped the sleeve of his coat. Her eyes narrowed to the field outside of the barred window—focused on something he

76

could not see. "Something's wrong. Something's…something's very wrong!" She shot to her feet. Her eyes never left the window, yet despite how hard he tried, he could not see what she saw.

Atop the piano, the metronome's pendulum stopped oscillating. The grandfather clock in the corner of the room stopped ticking as well—the rod halted in the center. Jon stood. As Emma extended her shaking hand to the barred window, a cold chill shot up his spine.

"Stop!" she demanded.

Stricken with fear, Jon's heart pounded in his chest. After a few moments of silence, he stepped toward her.

She dropped her hand, causing him to retreat. Her green eyes met with his curious gaze. "What's wrong?" she asked, but he had no response. "Why are you looking at me like that?" The metronome's pendulum continued to sway back and forth rhythmically while the grandfather clock ticked the seconds away. "Are you all right, Jon?"

He nodded.

Chapter VII

The air in the barn became thick from the animals and heavy breaths of those seeking shelter. The Hunters kept their guns pointed at the door, even though the forceful thuds stopped. The outside quieted as well, with only the occasional shout for help in the distance.

August lowered his gun. A shoddy ladder led to the loft of the barn. "Take this." He shoved the shotgun into Grady.

"What are you doing?"

August gripped the ladder and hoisted himself up. "There's a window up there. We need some air in here. Hell, maybe the Howlers have gone now." After reaching the loft, he opened the window, and a cool breeze blew inward. He inhaled deeply—a much-needed relief from the stuffy barn. However, the state of the village discouraged him.

"What do you see?"

August climbed out of the window onto the roof. Below him, destruction befell the inhabitants of Point DuPont. Villagers worked together to put out a fire near a house. Others scrambled away with anything they could salvage from the wreckage. In the street was a turned-over wagon with a mangled horse attached, and a woman cried, "Are they gone? Have the Howlers left?"

A small child cried for his mother.

"Grady, open the door!"

The Hunters emerged from their hiding. All eyes fell on them as they walked through the streets, and for a moment, August thought they might be lynched. Grady picked up the crying child. "All of you...today was a perfect example of what it feels like to be helpless. To not be able to defend yourselves, protect what's yours against the beasts prowling in these very woods. Now is not the time to turn on each other or to blame the Hunters. We can only do so much."

"You didn't do anything but hide!"

"And what can we do? When there are two of us and six of them? But hundreds of you." An exaggeration, August noted, but he agreed. Had there been more fighters, the Howlers would not have stood a chance. "For all of those still listening or interested in protecting what's yours, meet me at the tavern! We shouldn't congregate in the streets."

Grady handed the young child to August and trudged through the mud toward the tavern—the most secure building in the village. But few followed Grady while most went on about their business, cursing the Hunters as they passed.

Only a small crowd gathered at Le Cellier. They huddled around the bar, waiting for the Hunters to address them. As Telford slid a beer to August, he plopped himself onto a stool and chugged the drink.

Grady cleared his throat. "For those of you who decided to no longer be a victim in your own town, I thank you for your cooperation." The bar remained silent. "The Hunters of Point DuPont work diligently to eliminate the threat of Howlers whenever we can. But as you saw today, we're only human. Two, even three of us will not be able to eliminate all of them."

"These Howlers never used to be a problem!"

"I can sympathize," Grady continued. "I understand your frustration. I promise you that Mr. Maddox is doing all he can to cleanse the island, but...without knowing the source of these beasts, all we can do is kill as many as possible and hope one day they'll just stop coming back. We hope to restore the island to its…former glory, but we can't do that without your help."

"So, what do you want from us?" Telford asked.

Grady glanced over his shoulder to the proprietor and considered. "We will do everything we can to keep you safe, but in moments when we're not here, you need to be able to protect yourselves."

"How do you propose we do that?"

August waited expectantly for Grady's great plan to turn the villagers of Point DuPont into fighters when all they'd ever been were herdsmen, fisherman, and merchants. "Over the next few days, whomever so chooses to make the transit to Maddox House will be armed with weapons from our armory. The Hunters," He motioned to himself and August, "will then instruct you on how to use those weapons. I do ask that you really consider who it is you want to protect you in our absence as our stock will only supply, at the most, one weapon per household."

The small crowd erupted in whispers.

"We're not fighters!"

Grady turned his nose up to them. "I recommend finding a few of you who are. In the meantime, a curfew would be wise." He pushed through the crowd to exit the tavern.

August slammed his mug on the bar. The townspeople spoke among one another, and every so often, their eyes darted to him. He tossed a few dollars on the bar and followed behind Grady. Even though the Howlers were gone, for the time being, their work was far from over.

„›Ҕ

In the dining hall, Emma sat at the head of the table with her feet kicked up on the chair beside her. She twisted her hair between her fingers while her head drooped to the side. She insisted she felt fine but remained detached since her episode in the music room.

Jon closed the book in his hands and kicked her chair, breaking her deep concentration.

"I'm fine. Just…a little tired, I guess. I need exercise. And fresh air. Being cooped up here all the time drains me more than you could possibly know."

Jon tossed the book onto the table. He crossed the room to the gramophone and sifted through records to find Tchaikovsky's Nutcracker Suite—one of Emma's favorites.

The record spun. When he placed the needle on the vinyl, it cracked, and Waltz of the Flowers began playing.

When he extended his hand to her, she sighed. "It's been so long, Jon. I don't even think I remember how." She stood and slid her frail fingers into his palm.

I lead.

She snickered. "This will be a first for you."

He yanked her body into his, and she grunted from the force. Her green eyes invaded his vision and dominated his attention, and as a smile spread across her face, he grinned behind his mask. He lifted her hand to eye level. His gloved hand slid around her waist, and he started to lead in a waltz.

Emma's stiff movements confirmed her words. Too much time passed since last she danced. Her gaze was focused, intense, as if she was filtering through all the steps in her mind repeatedly instead of losing herself in the dance—in the music.

She stepped on Jon's foot and gasped—her misstep disturbing her greatly.

Jon pulled her into him and pressed his forehead onto hers. For a moment, he broke the stance and held her. Only when her breathing calmed did he sign to her, *Calm.*

She exhaled a heavy, defeated breath and nodded. "I'm just…nervous, is all."

He couldn't think of any reason she had to be nervous when it was just the two of them. He grabbed her hands and extended his arms fully. As he spun the two of them around in circles, slower at first, then faster and faster, Emma laughed.

"What movement is this?"

He pulled her into him once more, assuming their positioning for the waltz. He danced slowly in the beginning and kept his eyes fixed on hers. When she looked to her feet, he brought his hand to her chin and tilted her head up again.

They moved in structured circles, Emma's gown sweeping across the floor as she spun, and with every passing moment, her grip on his hands loosened. "This is my favorite part," she mused as the song reached its 3rd movement, and only then did Emma finally lose herself in the music, just like when they were kids.

She tilted her head, her ginger hair swaying from their pace. She closed her eyes—a wide smile on her face as Jon guided her through the dining hall—as if lost in a fantasy.

"This is the most fun I've had in so long!" He released her, and she spun through the hall, arms out to her side, eyes closed. "Spin with me, Jon!"

He preferred to watch her—carefree and far removed from all the horrors of her life. But as the doors burst open, Emma gasped.

"Grady!"

Jon stood upright, a cold chill setting upon the room as Grady and August entered. All the warmth and joy that spread throughout the hall only moments before vanished within a matter of seconds.

"Emma, please go upstairs. Your dinner should be served shortly," Grady said demonstrably, but Emma hesitated. She looked over her shoulder to Jon, who only nodded to her.

"Please, Grady…it was all my idea; Jon didn't even want to dance—"

Grady raised his hand to her. "It's all right, darling. Off you go now. The Hunters need to discuss a few things." Emma did not argue. She pushed past August and Grady and disappeared into the hall. "The fog was particularly light today, Jon."

August scoffed. "Come on, he can't help that."

Grady's expression remained hateful, his pointed eyes focused on the masked Hunter. "Can I even trust you gave Emma her medicine this morning?" he asked, and Jon nodded. Grady's head whipped to August. "And what about you?"

"What about me?"

"You gave Emma her dose last night?"

"Yeah. 'Course I did."

Grady folded his arms across his chest and leaned his head back—his furrowed brow creating dark shadows around his icy blue gaze. "Where?"

August hesitated. "In her room?"

Grady stepped toward him. "Where on her body?" he pried.

From behind Grady's back, Jon pointed to his neck. "In her...neck?" August continued. "I mean... that's where she told me to give it to her. Was that wrong?"

Grady's head whipped to Jon so fast he thought it may be on a swivel. Still, Jon, in an attempt to appear nonchalant, tucked his hands behind his back and averted his gaze.

"My apologies, Mr. DeWitt. You've proven to be...a valuable asset. But you'll soon understand that some people around here are not to be trusted," he said while looking over his shoulder to Jon again. "Come along now. You and I will debrief in the parlor." Grady marched out of the dining room. After he left, Jon turned his back and flattened his hands on the dining room table. He exhaled a heavy breath in relief.

"You good, Jon?"

He only hung his head in response.

In the parlor, Grady handed August a glass of bourbon. He sniffed his drink—the potent smell forcing a grin. He did love a good bourbon and rarely had any trouble entertaining those who gave it to him freely.

"We'll have to set aside some weapons for the villagers. We'll give them the older ones—the ones we don't use anymore. They're simple enough to learn."

"You really think arming an angry mob of townspeople is the best idea? They hate us."

Grady leaned on the desk in the corner of the room, drink in hand. "Yes, they do hate us. They won't act on it, though. Too afraid. They're not killers, August. Did you see the looks on their faces when I suggested they protect themselves?"

"They're scared."

Grady's lips curled into a wicked grin. "They should be scared. They're now being held accountable for what happens in the village."

"Maybe if Jon were there today, things woulda been different. Maybe we woulda been able to take on those things instead of hiding."

"I highly doubt that."

"Why's that?"

Grady peered into his glass, contemplating and keeping August in mystery. He finished his drink in one go and retrieved the bottle for a refill. "August, I don't want you to think that I'm bullying Jon. My treatment of him comes from experience working with him." He approached to refill August's glass.

"What do you mean?"

"I always thought it was a mistake to let Jon stay on as a Hunter. Don't get me wrong, he's a great fighter. I mean, he has nothing to lose, and he knows that. And as much as it pains me to say, he loves Emma very much."

"Why would that pain you?"

Grady replaced the bottle on the table and stared into the fireplace—the flames casting shadows along the pointed structures of his face. "He doesn't love her like I love her. Like her father loves her. Jon would do anything for her, even if it isn't in her best interest. He only wants to make her happy. Sometimes, it's at the expense of her safety." He scoffed and twisted his glass in his hand. "He's going to get her killed."

"Nah, I don't agree with that. He wouldn't do anything to jeopardize her safety. I mean, if he really wanted to, he could take her and run away. He hasn't done that yet."

"He's not stupid, Mr. DeWitt," Grady said sharply. "Jon loves being the good guy in Emma's eyes. He's the one she runs to when she's upset because he'll always be there to comfort her. But he knows as well as I do that as soon as Emma leaves the island, he becomes irrelevant. Do you think any woman would willingly stay with a muted cripple? Jon can't survive out there in the real world. Only in here does he mean something to her. He knows that."

"Tell me something, Grady. What's a guy like you doing out here with her? Emma says you got a wife, got a little girl. Why not just go back to them?"

"Go back to them? A wife who hates me and a daughter who doesn't even know who I am?" Grady sneered and brought the glass to his lips. After polishing it off again, a satisfied groan escaped him, and he winced. "I can't go back, August." He waited patiently for Grady to continue, knowing that at any moment, the veteran Hunter might just open up about his reasons for being there. "My whole life up until this point, I've been nothing. Grew up from nothing; my parents were nothing. I learned at a very young age that life was meaningless. I hated Detroit, hated my family. As soon as I was old enough, I left. Joined an International Exhibition, doing whatever I could just to eat. I picked up my first rifle at seventeen and started working as security after that. The only time I ever felt anything was when I had that gun in my hands. But at the end of the day, I was empty. I wanted to die."

"So you came here...to die?"

"Not exactly. The exhibition life wasn't enough for me. Not enough...action to keep me going through the day. I joined a team of mercenaries operating out of Ontario, and for the first time in my life, I felt something extraordinary."

"Excitement?"

"Fear." The guilt upon Grady's face led August to believe that fear might be a shameful emotion to Grady, but the confession liberated him. "I knew on my first assignment that if I felt fear, then it meant I still had hope for something. It meant I still wanted to live for something, but for what...at that time, I wasn't entirely sure."

"Your wife?"

Grady nodded slowly and peered deep into the fire. "I truly believed I could grow to love her. But with every assignment after our marriage, I wasn't afraid I'd never see her again. Just simply afraid of dying. We had our daughter, and I thought that she would be the thing that kept me going. My motivation to stay alive."

"And?"

"I felt nothing," Grady admitted, but despite a slight grin on his face, August detected a shaking voice and glossed-over eyes. "The hole inside of me only grew larger, and I felt more disconnected from life than ever before. Truth be told, I never wanted to be a father."

"Some men ain't cut out for it."

"That's when Byron tracked me down. I took the job because...what man would turn down the money? I told my wife that I'd write every day and visit often. I told her that I'd send her every penny I made for her and our daughter. And then I met Emma...and everything changed."

"You never told your wife?"

"About Emma? Why would I tell her that I finally found my reason for living? That my own child paled in comparison to the love I felt for this woman. No, I never told her about Emma. I didn't have to."

August groaned. "What is it about her anyway? You and Jon get all goo-goo eyed over this woman who has been sheltered her entire life, knows nothing about the outside world—"

"You feel it too, don't deny it."

"No, I don't."

"You're fighting it. I commend you for doing so; keep fighting it. Because as soon as you give in to her, your life will never be the same. Nothing but *her* will matter, and everything you think, everything you do and become, it'll all be for her."

"Everything I do is for myself. Always has been."

"And look where that got you. Exactly where it got me. We're not so different, you and I."

"Yeah, well, I don't have a wife and kid back on the mainland waiting for me to come home."

"Neither do I. Not anymore. I haven't seen my family in five years." He clanked his glass onto the table between them. "She's bewitched me, August. Jon as well. Don't end up like us." He crossed the room to the exit.

"So where's your family now then? You don't even know if they're alive?"

Grady doubled back. "Last I heard from Byron, Claudia, and my daughter, Emily, were living in a grand Victorian in Calgary. I did keep well on one of my promises. They've gotten every cent I've ever made."

He left August alone after that. Despite hearing that Grady was financially providing for his family, his absence in their lives made August resent him even more. What sort of man could abandon his child, he thought? Grady's love for Emma seemed to have destroyed his life. He wondered what Jon's love for Emma had done to him.

Did Jon even love her the way Grady claimed he did? Or was it just a friendship the two had since childhood? Maybe Jon felt indebted to the Maddox's, but the mystery to Jon seemed almost as impenetrable as the mask and armor he wore every day. Armor that only a Howler could penetrate.

August climbed the stairs to the servant's quarters on the fourth floor. He wondered why Jon chose to live up there when he could be living like a king below.

He stopped in front of the door at the end of the hall and knocked gently. "Hey, Jon? It's me, August. You got a minute?" Jon moved around inside, his boots trudging across the floor. When he swung the door open, he blocked the inside with his body.

August chuckled. "You good?" Jon nodded. "Can I come in?" he asked, and Jon hesitated to step aside.

The room was small, and it reminded August of all the cheap hotels he stayed in after his fall from grace. "Why do you choose to live up here? You know there's a lot more space in the rooms downstairs."

No curtains covered the window above Jon's bed, and the clear sky allowed the full moon to illuminate the room—providing more light than the candles on his desk. Jon tapped August's shoulder. *Need something?*

"I was just… comin' to check on ya. See if you're okay." On Jon's small desk, a dirty strip of cloth haphazardly covered a large sheet of sketch paper. Beside it, a slew of charcoal pencils. "Were you working on something?" August brushed aside the bit of cloth, revealing a drawing of Emma in a long, flowing gown with her hair pinned up.

Jon snatched the paper. He examined his own work and turned his back. August sensed a protectiveness in him. Almost as if Emma herself existed in the drawing. "You're in love with her, aren't you?"

Jon hesitated. He held his hand to the side and then snapped his fingers together. *Leave.*

August retreated to his room where his dinner awaited him. He lifted the lid to see grilled and seasoned cod, asparagus, and a few small potatoes. But his appetite had not returned since the morning exertions. He was tired more than anything.

After pouring himself a glass of bourbon, August entered his bathroom and filled the clawfoot tub with water. Steam filled the room. He turned off the tap and climbed inside—the heat causing the hairs on his body to stand upright.

He took a sip of bourbon and leaned back in the tub. Pleasure enveloped him—the warm bath and bourbon providing a brief escape from the horrors and atrocities in which he bared witness to earlier that day. Atrocities that seemed worth the endurance if it meant he got to relax in a hot bath with grade A bourbon in his hand.

He closed his eyes for a moment.

But the moment turned into minutes. As August drifted to sleep, he released his tipped glass, and it fell to the rug. He slid beneath the water. All he understood in his rested state was that he was so much warmer than he'd been in so long.

He wanted to stay that way forever.

A shrill scream ripped him from his dreamlike state. August jerked upward and gasped for air. Despite the warm water surrounding him, a cold chill shot up his spine. "Emma?" He climbed out of the tub and grabbed the cotton robe from the back of the door.

He fled the bedroom and sprinted to Emma's. His heart pounded in his chest, and the lingering coldness followed him in a shroud of horror—fear of what might have sent Emma into a fit of screams. When he reached her room, he burst through the door. "Emma—"

She turned in her bed, curious and with heavy eyes. "What's wrong?" She sat up, her curiosity shifting into uneasiness. "August? What happened? You look like you've seen a ghost."

"Why'd you scream?" he asked through heavy breaths.

She shook her head. "I didn't scream."

89

"You didn't…?" August exhaled heavily and ran his hands over his face, fearing that he might be caught in an awful nightmare again. "I'm sorry, Miss Emma. I must have had…a nightmare."

She raised an eyebrow. "In the…bath?"

He hesitated. "Yeah."

"Well then, I'd say that was probably the best nightmare a person could have." She had a look of intrigue upon her face, though, one he'd never seen before. "It's funny, you know. I was just dreaming about you, and here you are."

After the things Grady said to him early that evening, her flirtatious banter no longer seemed harmless. Not only did she consume Grady's affections, but Jon's as well. And despite that, she seemed dissatisfied. "You shouldn't say things like that, Miss Emma."

"And you shouldn't barge into a lady's room in the middle of the night wearing nothing more than a bathrobe, but again, here you are."

She certainly was a force to be reckoned with, which normally he liked in a woman. But the things that attracted August to her in the first place made him retreat from her. Grady's words about her manipulative nature ripped him from the foggy mist that surrounded her, drawing the curious in for a closer look. No, he refused to be one of the many that romanticized the idea of her. Because if the other two were any indication, she'd drive him mad. "I'll be going back to my room now if that's all right with you."

"Good night, Mr. DeWitt."

"Good night, Miss Maddox."

Chapter VIII

It started to rain. A ferocious thunderstorm shielded any light coming from the sky. The pinging on the windows and roof of the mansion kept August tossing and turning. The wind howled against the old house, causing it to creak and tremble from the force. It awakened August's fear once more. The same fear he experienced when he thought he heard Emma scream. Or when he dreamt of a crying child.

The rain carried on for days, and much to Grady's dismay, hunting, once again, had to be postponed.

The Hunter's sat in the parlor together, Grady standing by the window, observing the downpour, suspicious. "It hasn't rained like this in months." Grady sighed. "By the looks of it, it's going to last a while." He turned to Jon, who was leaning in one of the corners of the room, flipping his hunting knife in his hands. "What say you, Jon? You're from the island."

Jon gripped his knife and stuck it back in his belt. He signed—hands lazy and loose.

"He said it ain't lookin' so good."

Grady groaned and turned back to the window. "At least the fog is light."

The door to the parlor burst open, and Emma entered with a big smile on her face. In her hands, she clutched a canvas. "Darling, I've finished the painting. You really must see."

"Sweetheart, we're in the middle of something right now. I'll come to see it when we're finished."

Emma scoffed. "It's here now; just take a look."

Grady grabbed the canvas and flipped it around. His pointed eyes darted all around the work, and his brow furrowed. Beside him, Emma stood, observing her work with a proud smile. "Emma…this is highly disturbing."

August and Jon rushed to their side. "You don't like it?" Emma asked.

"Why would you paint this?" Grady asked.

"Holy…" August began, but the complexity and darkness therein stole words from his mouth. She painted a woman with black, hollowed eyes and pale white skin with only the slightest tinge of purple and red to paint blood vessels along her face: her mouth, a large, blackened mass with strands of dead ivy pouring out.

Emma beamed. "I see her in my dreams sometimes."

Exquisite, Jon signed.

Emma nodded to him. "Merci beaucoup."

"Wow. Two artists in one house. Who woulda thought?"

"You paint, Mr. DeWitt?" Emma asked.

"Nah, I was talking about—" Jon elbowed his ribs, silencing him. "Er…drawing. I draw stick figures."

Emma hummed through a smirk. "Well, I suppose there's no accounting for taste."

"And how." Grady lowered the painting. "Sweet pea, you really shouldn't be painting things like this. It's…morbid, macabre. Devoid of any sort of life or happiness."

Technique, good, Jon signed.

"Well, then what do you propose I do paint, *darling*?"

Grady lifted the painting again, wincing at the woman's horrifying face. "I don't know. Landscapes, flowers?"

August chuckled. "A bowl of fruit."

"Maybe some butterflies?" Grady continued. "You like those, don't you?"

"Butterflies," Emma snapped. Her lips tightened, and she averted her pointed gaze to the ground. August felt the tension rise between the four of them. They all waited for her to react in some way. In a bad way. But Emma forced a smile. "Very well. I shall start on a landscape for you straight away, my darling." She kissed his cheek forcefully and snatched her painting.

Before leaving, though, Jon stepped forward and reached for the canvas.

"You wish to keep the painting?" Emma asked, and Jon nodded. A large smile spread across her face at Jon's request. "All right, Jon. Here you go."

Even August failed to hide a smile. "You might wanna hold on to that. Gonna go for a lotta money someday."

"You boys flatter me. But I've taken up enough of your time. If you'll excuse me, I'll head back to the music room to paint some more."

Emma exited the parlor. "You really shouldn't indulge her, Jon. Her, painting something like that, it's a warning sign. Her morale is low. She feels depressed, so we need to surround her with the brighter, more pleasant things in life. Not encourage her disturbance."

"Hey, weren't you the one who got all pissed off because she had crepes and was dancing?" August recalled.

"That's different. Sugar is bad for her, and dancing can drain her energy. Something that's in short supply already."

Jon began signing—his movements sharp and quick.

"What, Jon?"

August scoffed. "He said you're an asshole."

"Hey, I might be an asshole, but someone has to keep her from flying too close to the sun. And since neither of you is willing to

93

step up and be the bad guy—to really do what needs to be done for her—then I'll happily assume that role. Because I love her. And I want what's best for her."

Another proclamation of love for Emma, and despite August having only been in the mansion for a few days, he already started to grow bored of the topic.

Glass shattering down the hall put them on high alert. When Emma screamed, they all darted to the parlor exit.

"Emma!" Grady yelled while leading the way to the music room. They burst through the door to find a shattered vase on the floor with roses scattered among the glass and water. Nearby, Emma stood on a table. "What happened?"

"I saw a rat! The biggest one I've ever seen, just…gnawing at the train of my dress!"

"Where'd it go?" Grady asked.

She pointed to the armchairs on the far side of the room. "I think it went over there." Jon offered his arm to assist Emma off the table. "Be careful, darling. He was quite gargantuan and had monstrous teeth."

Grady peered behind the chairs. "I don't see anything."

"There it is!" Emma jumped into Jon's arms. As the rat scurried across the music room, August stepped on its tail and snatched it from the floor, careful to hold it at the very tip to avoid a bite. "Oh, don't kill it, August!"

He carried it out of the room. "I ain't gonna kill it."

"Just…take it outside and let it free!"

August trudged through the hall to the front door with the rat wriggling around in his grasp. He yanked the deadbolt and swung the door open, amplifying the thunderstorm outside. Thunder and violent winds invaded the quiet corridor. After releasing the rat onto the porch, it stopped moving, as if afraid to continue further into the outdoors.

August peered into the rainy field—squinting his eyes to fight the fog before him. He wondered if the rat sensed Howlers nearby.

Only after it scurried off into the storm, did he step back inside the house. He slammed the front doors and replaced the deadbolt.

"Oh…take me to my room, Jon. I…I feel faint."

Over August's shoulder, Jon carried Emma to the staircase.

He became resentful of Emma and her powers of manipulation over a man who, in his opinion, was no match for her. One who would do anything she asked just to please her, even if it meant slitting his own throat just so she could watch him bleed for her.

He thought of his brother, Jack, who never knew the affections of a woman. August became certain that if someone like Emma had sunken her teeth into him, he also might fall victim to her unscrupulous nature. "August," Grady spoke, ripping his attention away from the stairs, "we have a problem."

"You're tellin' me."

"I fear there might be more rats inside the mansion."

"It's an old house. It happens. Just set some traps, and that should settle it."

He moved past, but Grady grabbed his arm. "No, Mr. DeWitt. It's not getting rid of them that's the problem. It's how they're getting inside." And only then did August realize the security risk. If rats could get inside the house, it was only a matter of time before the Howlers figured out a way.

☾☙☾

Jon carried Emma into her room and placed her on the bed. When she settled in, he leaned over her. *Change clothes?*

She shook her head. "No. I only need to rest for a bit," she said while bringing her hand to the side of his mask. "Will you make sure there are no rats in here, Jon? I feel like they're…everywhere now."

He nodded and searched every nook and cranny for the little intruders. He checked behind her vanity, her lounge area, under her bureau, and finally, under the bed. But he saw no rats. He

95

picked up his head and leaned on the mattress beside her, shaking his head. *No rats.*

"Lie with me?"

He hesitated, but only for a moment. As he climbed onto the bed, she scooted closer to him. The two lie side by side, eyes locked on one another. "Thank you for what you did in the parlor." He tucked a strand of her messy hair behind her ear. "It doesn't frighten you?" He shook his head. "It's because you understand me, Jon. People fear what they don't understand, but you know me so well. All of my dreams, my fears. All my deepest, darkest secrets." Her slender fingers slid to the collar of his coat, and she smiled wryly. "Maybe not all of them."

Finally, he tore his gaze from her eyes as she unfastened the buttons of his coat one by one. She pulled it open to reveal his clothes beneath. His body tensed when she looped her arm around his waist and nuzzled her head into his chest. "You're so warm," she whispered. It's no wonder, he thought. His skin burned red hot when she touched him so intimately. Her frail body against his— clinging to him for comfort and warmth—weakened him.

"I want to be inside of you," she whispered. "I want to crawl inside your skin and have you carry me around with you everywhere you go." She squeezed him so tight that a groan escaped him. When she clasped the collar of his shirt, he peered down to her desperate gaze. "Do you want to be inside of me?"

He covered her mouth—silencing her words.

Emma's bedroom door creaked open, and Jon picked his head up. "Grady wants to see you," August said from the doorway, and Jon froze. That was never a good way to start a conversation, something everyone living in the Maddox House knew to be true. "Us," he corrected. "Together. In the same room."

"Must you leave, Jon?" Emma asked while tightening her grip on his vest to keep him in place.

He looked down at her. *Rest.*

ಐﾂ

In the parlor, Grady discussed his plans to secure the house. The presence of rats posed a difficult problem for them, and Grady felt the need to be proactive about the intrusion. But August's attention wavered. He continually glanced at Jon, who also seemed distracted.

The masked Hunter stood in the corner, arms folded across his chest. And though his face remained hidden behind his mask, his head tilted downward. And his eyes never moved from the rug beneath his boots. His temperament always seemed faded after interactions with Emma.

August's resentment started to rise from within—festering inside until the very thought of her made him shake with anger. Because now, all he saw when looking at Jon was his brother.

"Mr. DeWitt?" August tore his gaze from the Persian rug beneath his feet. Now, the Hunters' eyes were on him.

"Yeah?" he griped.

"Emma's birthday. It's two weeks from now. Not that you have any personal investment in her well-being, but we tend to throw her a celebration every year. I'd like you to organize this year."

"Me? You just said yourself that I have no personal investment in her, so why would you have me do it?"

"Consider it part of your training. God willing, you'll be taking over many of the responsibilities Jon and I have been shouldering the past few years. Get with Jon if you have questions." He didn't linger for a debate and instead marched across the room to exit—leaving the two Hunters to ruminate.

A birthday celebration for a woman he hardly knew. One he hardly knew *and* one who he suspected didn't particularly enjoy him after what transpired between the two. August regarded his and Emma's relationship as complicated, at best.

97

Plan, I will, Jon signed.

August sighed in relief. "Thanks."

As he stood, Jon reached for him to grab his attention. He stiffened his hand upright and motioned it back and forth between the two of them. *Between us.*

August tipped his head to him. "Deal."

That night, August remained detached while assisting Emma through her evening routine. He untied her gown and corset and placed her nightgown on the bed, but other than that, he left her to tend to herself. He sat in one of the armchairs, flipping through a book he snatched from her bedside.

"You seem agitated this evening, Mr. DeWitt." She sat at her vanity, removing her jewelry. Their eyes met through the mirror. "Did your nightmares keep you tossing and turning?"

"No, they didn't." For a brief moment, he lost himself in the delicate nature she did so well to parade in front of him. But he thought of Jon, no doubt hidden away in the servant's quarters obsessing over her, drawing a new picture of her while her horrifying painting watched over him.

August closed his book. "Hey, I have a question I been wantin' to ask you."

"Oh?" Emma responded, never breaking her sights away from her own reflection in the mirror.

"It's about Jon."

"What about Jon?"

"He's mute, right? So, how come he can make noises and stuff? I thought mutes couldn't do that."

His question seemed to have no effect on her. She combed through her hair—still admiring her own reflection. "There are many causes of muteness, Mr. DeWitt, despite the popular belief that it comes from lack of intelligence. But you're right; the fact that he can use his vocal cords does indicate an ability to speak. There is nothing wrong with that part of his body."

"So, what then?"

"Jon suffers from something referred to as conversion disorder."

"What usually causes…conversion—"

"A traumatic event. Usually, the symptoms go away in a few days, sometimes weeks or months, but not for Jon. I suspect he suffered something quite horrendous when he was too young to even remember. And without proper care, he just never learned to speak. It's some sort of cognitive disconnect. Something is happening in his mind that just doesn't translate to his tongue. Or, it does, but Jon lacks the ability to decipher the mechanics."

"So…he can talk; he just chooses not to."

"It's not that he chooses silence. He's become convinced that he's incapable, despite medical reassurance that he can. And he's never uttered a single word in his entire life, so proving so now would be difficult. Like…learning a new language when your mind has been taught to only understand one. To put things into perspective for you, Jon trying to speak now would be comparable to a human's attempts to communicate with a feral mutt."

August scoffed. "So you compare him to a dog."

"You misunderstand me. You're the dog." The rising tension between the two burned hotter than the flames in the fireplace. August looked away from her, eyes pointed and lips pursed. "Have I satisfied your curiosity about Jon? Perhaps you might consider asking him if he continues to plague your mind."

August inhaled sharply through his nose and stood. "All right, time for bed."

"I'm not sure why you're so frazzled this evening, Mr. DeWitt. Maybe you should fix yourself a drink when you're finished here."

"You know something, Emma, I've been trying my hardest to be a gentleman with you. What you're going through, I can only imagine. And it must be difficult for you to find reasons to get out of bed every morning. Maybe you're like this out of boredom. I'm not really sure, and frankly, after seeing the way you treat the men of the house, I don't really care—"

"The men of the house?" As she stood from her vanity, the fiery flicker in her eyes disappeared—replaced with a cold, unflinching glare. "There are no men of *this* house. This is the House of Maddox, and I am the only Maddox that resides here. You make the mistake of thinking there is anyone higher ranking than myself."

"Do I make that mistake? Because by the looks of it, you're just some helpless little girl who relies on the *men* to do everything for you."

"You live in my home free of charge. My servants serve you; your accommodations are fit for a king. Yes, you make the mistake of thinking that I am not the reason for that."

"I make no mistake, Miss Maddox. I just refuse to fall victim to the sick game you play with the *men* of this household. I see right through you. Everything you do is calculating and from a very dark place in that screwed up head of yours. I won't fall for it. Not like Grady, not like Jon—"

"You will do whatever I ask of you."

August's words jumbled at the base of his tongue, and he composed himself for a moment before stuttering an incomprehensible response. Though, all he had was, "How can you do this to him?"

Emma's eyes narrowed. "What?"

"Jon's in love with you, Emma. But something tells me you already knew that. And yet, you string him along, make him think he actually stands a chance with you. You give him hope one minute, and the next you're cuddled up with Grady while he's brushed aside, standing off in the corner somewhere. Forced to watch you love another man."

Her eyes darkened—the green of her iris' becoming lost in the shadows of the room that the rising flames exaggerated. "Careful, Mr. DeWitt. You don't know what you're talking about," she said in a low, guttural tone.

100

"Is it because he's mute? Or maybe because you can't stand the idea of his scars touching your perfect skin..." a forceful sting across his face silenced him. She'd struck him, the force being powerful enough to knock even him *'The Unbeatable August'* off-kilter.

"How dare you?"

No woman had ever struck him so hard. He'd made her angry—something Grady and Jon warned him about doing. "Emma, just calm down—"

"I will not!" she screamed. The flames of the candles and fireplace danced violently—burning brighter than before. "You know nothing about Jon and me. You know nothing more about him than the fact that he can't speak and has been burned in a fire. How dare you presume to tell me about him? How dare you ever think for one second that I don't know everything that goes through his mind every second of the day and that it doesn't destroy me? That makes you the foolish one between you and me, Mr. DeWitt."

The wind howled outside the house. The ground beneath his boots trembled ever so slightly, and the glass creaked against the wind. At any moment, the storm might shatter it completely. "Emma, hang on—"

"Get out," Emma demanded. "Get out!" The bedroom doors burst open, causing August to flinch.

"What the hell's going on?"

"Get out, get out, get out, get out!" She acted feral, screaming, pulling at her hair, and stomping her feet—lost in a fiery rage.

August started to panic. "Emma, please, you have to calm down." He grabbed her arms—her skin ablaze. He shook her, trying his best to reorient her. As much as he wanted to help her, though, Grady entered the room. A sight much more frightening than the unexplained monstrous dancing flames, the bedroom door flying open without any outside interference, was Grady loading a syringe.

"Emma, sweetpea?"

August released her and backed away—holding his hands up in retreat.

"Grady," she gasped and fell to her knees. It was only after he entered, all the madness seemed to die down. "I'm sorry, darling, I... I'm fine, really," she said through a shaky voice.

Grady ignored and kneeled beside her.

The sight sickened August. "Come on, Grady. It...it was my fault, not hers. I upset her—"

"The fault is not the issue." He stuck the syringe into her neck, and after pushing the plunger, Emma groaned and collapsed onto his shoulder. "There you go, sweetheart. It'll all be over soon."

As angry as August became with Emma before, it all faded at that moment. Now, he felt unshakeable guilt for what he did. She didn't deserve to be put down when he was the cause of her anger. "This is so...wrong."

"I warned you about making her mad. You did it anyway. What would you have me do? Let her kill you?"

"Kill me?" he said, astounded. "If anyone in this house is completely off their rocker, it's you. And what the hell was all that just now?"

Grady ignored.

Moments later, Jon appeared in the doorway. He moaned when his eyes landed on Emma—a heartbreaking sound, one that translated to August as great despondency.

"Help me get her to bed, Jon—" Jon snatched her from his arms and cradled her in his own. When Grady reached for her again, Jon shoved him away. "She needs to be put to bed—"

"Just let *him* do it."

"You've done enough this evening, Mr. DeWitt."

When August's eyes met with the cold glare of the masked Hunter, his guilt became overwhelming.

The topic of Jon proved to be a very sensitive matter to Emma. A topic that—despite her cool and calm nature—could send her into a fiery rage if not approached with the utmost respect and delicacy.

102

August hardly slept that night. He wanted to make things right with Emma, but mostly, he wanted to make things right with Jon. His meddling caused more problems than he expected, and he wanted them to know that he meant no harm—that his motivations were only to protect the brooding Hunter.

The next morning, August tried to catch both of them during her morning routine. As he extended his fist to knock on her bedroom door, a gloved hand snatched his wrist. Startled, August's eyes darted to a white kabuki mask beside him.

Jon shoved August's hand away and shook his head.

"Is she all right?"

Sleeping. Jon signed.

"She's still sleeping? It's past nine—" Jon turned on his heels and marched down the hallway. "Jon!" he called after him, and Jon stopped. "We fought about you. The way she treats you." His head only turned slightly. "You know, you...remind me of Jack. And I can't help but feel this...need to protect you from her. But now I'm starting to think I was wrong about her and you. Was I wrong?"

The masked Hunter didn't respond. Instead, he continued marching down the hall until disappearing in the shadows of the stairwell—leaving August in curiosity. And confusion.

ΣΟ∞ΟΛ

Before the day's end, August met with Grady in the parlor. He expected to be chastised for what happened with Emma the previous night. A part of him felt as though Grady might relieve him of his duties for putting Emma in so much distress.

And it was all because of him.

When he entered the parlor, however, Grady smirked and handed him a glass of bourbon. "Have a seat." August lowered himself onto the sofa—unnerved by Grady's continued stare. "How are you feeling?"

103

"Like shit." He chugged the bourbon and set the glass aside. "So, how much trouble am I in?"

Grady shook his head. "No trouble."

He raised an eyebrow. "Is that right?"

"Mr. DeWitt, last night was the first night since Carlyle's death that I wasn't deemed the bad guy in Emma's eyes. I think that calls for a toast."

August cringed when Grady raised his glass to him. "So... you're praising me for sending Emma into a fit of...rage?"

Grady finished his drink, grimacing at the taste. "I'm not praising you. But maybe you're better suited for this job than I expected." He gathered their glasses and headed to the liquor cabinet once more. "I'm sure you've noticed that Jon likes to baby Emma to no end. As much as I love her, and I do love her, she's a spoiled, entitled brat who has never been told no before." Grady poured two more glasses of bourbon. August declined.

"I'm good."

"Look, I know that was... an uncomfortable situation for you. But it was a great opportunity for you to see the sort of fits she's prone to. It was a key moment for you to witness when her sedatives should be administered."

"I think I got a pretty good indication of when to use them my first night here."

"Do you have them on you?"

"No."

"You should."

August scoffed. His narrowed eyes studied Grady—searching for any sign of insincerity in his gaze. The darkness and hard shadows along his face made it difficult to tell if he was joking. But after a period of silence, the tension started to rise, and Grady remained resolute. "She ain't some wild animal that needs to be put down whenever she gets emotional; she's a woman. Being emotional comes with the territory."

"Don't presume to tell me about women, Mr. DeWitt. While you might be quite the ladies' man where you come from, I am a married man."

"That's rich, McCoy. You, of all people, have nothing to brag about there. Where is your wife?"

Grady hesitated to respond. He set August's glass of bourbon on the table next to him and chugged his own, wincing again at the taste. "That's all for now, Mr. DeWitt. You can go." Grady's disregard for his reputation made August's blood boil. No man ever dared speak to him in such a way—not after he reached his celebrity status in the arena. In any other circumstance, August would have ended their conversation with his own thuggish methods. But seeing as how Grady was his supervisor, he bit his tongue instead. He gripped the arms of the chair and shot to his feet—towering over the veteran Hunter. An intimidation method, one that was wasted on Grady McCoy, who only sneered. "Oh, and...start carrying those sedatives on you. That's an order."

Chapter IX

August stood before Emma's bedroom door but hesitated to knock. He felt foolish standing in front of the doors, flowers from the greenhouse clenched in his hand. Never in his life had he ever groveled to a woman who wasn't his mama. But, he also knew that life on the island could be utterly miserable if on Emma's bad side. Any time his pride tried to take over and send him away, his guilt and compassion kept him grounded in place.

Finally, he knocked.

The door swung open, and Jon shielded the inside with his body. His body language alone fished August's insecurities right out of him—making him feel unwelcomed and tempting him to leave. Only when Jon saw the flowers in his hand did he allow him to enter on his own.

Another moment of hesitation came over August. Entering Emma's room after the tumultuous interaction terrified him, and he likened it to walking into a viper pit or a lion's den. When he entered the bedroom, Emma's cold glare almost sent him right back out again. "Can we talk?" Emma slid into her vanity chair and tore through her thick, ginger hair with her comb—her lips pursed into a sour expression. "I, uh…brought you these."

She peered over her shoulder to the outstretched flowers. After only a few seconds, she exchanged the comb for the bouquet. "Lilies. Did Jon tell you to bring these?"

"Nah, I wanted to bring them to you. As a peace offering." She set the flowers aside. "Emma, I don't…really even know where to begin. Me saying sorry just doesn't make up for last night. And if I woulda known what was gonna happen, I woulda kept my mouth shut. I feel…guilty as sin, and I wish there was a better word than I'm sorry."

Once again, she grabbed her comb and fought to run it through her thick hair—more focused on her own reflection than him groveling behind her. "I forgive you, Mr. DeWitt."

"Do you really forgive me, or…am I gonna pay for this later?"

"No, I really do forgive you. I believe whole-heartedly that you never intended things to go that far. And even though I'm thoroughly repulsed by your expressed opinion of me, I can't help but admire you for your protection of Jon."

"He talked to you, huh?"

"He reminds you of your brother. And I think that's very sweet. It pleases me to know that someone is looking out for him. Especially out there in the fog."

Finally, she regarded him through the vanity mirror—her big green eyes glossed over. "I'm not going to let anything happen to him, Miss Emma."

She nodded at him and wiped a tear that streaked down her cheek. "Thank you."

"So, what do you say? Friends again?"

She combed her hair again. "We were never friends, Mr. DeWitt. But this is a good start."

The downpour started again in the evening. The pinging on the rooftop progressed into a vengeful thudding by sunset. The fierce wind shifted the old house, and its foundation creaked and moaned against the force. It was the sort of weather that brought nightmares for Emma, and Grady always made sure to check with her before bed on these occasions.

He marched down the corridor to her room but was at a loss to only find Jon there. He stepped through the doorway, and Jon's gloved hand grazed the syringe on her vanity. He snatched it behind his back.

Grady slow-blinked to him. He sighed and extended his hand. "Give it here." Begrudgingly, he handed it to him. "Where is she?" The masked Hunter shrugged. "Jon," Grady groaned, but he only shook his head. "You're not helping her, you know. You think you are, but you're not."

Grady stormed back into the darkness of the corridor, slamming the bedroom door shut behind him. After having lived on the island for five years—in command of Emma's care for three—she never surprised him anymore. He knew exactly where he'd find her if not nuzzled up with Jon in her bedroom.

"A bit late to be starting a new one, sweetpea."

Emma's green eyes darted from her book. She shot upright from the chaise lounge, rigid and fearful. "Grady? I was just—"

He smiled and shook his head. "It's all right, Emma." As he sauntered over to her, she cowered beneath him. "What are you reading?" His fingertips grazed the edges of the book, but she pulled it into her chest and shielded it with her arms. He held his hand out to her, demanding to see. Despite her reluctance, she gave him the book. "Memoirs of a Woman of Pleasure…" His words trailed off at the end, and his lips pursed as he inhaled a sharp breath through his nose. "Where do you get things like this?"

Emma snatched the book. "Don't act like it's so beneath you. I distinctly remember you narrating a bit of prose from The Marquis de Sade's *'Justine,'* for me." She opened her book again, a satisfied smirk upon her face. "I remember your face going red as a tomato the first time you said the word *cunt*—"

He snatched her chin—pulling her lips inches away from his face as he bent over her. "I will not have you talking like that. Do you understand me? It is beneath you."

"Why? Because I'm not the sweet, innocent girl you fell in love with?"

He sat beside her. His fingers released her chin and slid across her cheek to the base of her skull. "You are," he assured. "Stop trying to be something that you're not. I love you just the way you are."

His lips lingered over hers. As he raised the syringe, though, her eyes widened, and her breath caught in her throat. "Grady, please."

"You must, sweetpea."

Her slender fingers grazed his wrist. "Why must I?" She tossed her book aside and climbed to her knees—rising above him on the chaise lounge but keeping her lips hovering over his. "I'll be good tonight. I promise."

"Emma—"

She crawled on top of him, lifting her dress as she placed a leg on either side of him. Despite Grady's reserved nature—his demonstrative demeanor in every aspect of their lives—he melted into her when she seduced him. And as those instances became few and far between, his resolve faltered more and more.

She pushed him back, her fingers sliding into his palm as she took control of him. When he dropped the syringe to the rug, she smiled. "I remember the first time you made love to me, right here, in this very spot," she whispered while entangling her fingers in his hair.

The memory sent shivers down his body.

She had him read to her—a graphic sex scene from one of her naughty books. The more he blushed, the more aroused she became. She squirmed and dragged her hand between her thighs. It was the first real indication she'd given him that she wanted him. "What happened to us, Emma?"

Her gentle lips brushed against his. Her tongue, sliding against him, stole the breath from his mouth. "You stopped concerning yourself with pleasure and became consumed with pain. *Darling*."

Before responding, Emma tore his shirt open—her motion so abrupt that he jolted beneath her. His furrowed brow was of no concern to her, though, and she dug her nails into the flesh of his chest—causing him to groan in pain. As she dug deeper, blood trickled down his stomach.

He sat upward, snatching her wrists away from him. With his firm grasp tightening around her, Emma snickered through a grimace. "You like it. Don't act like you don't like the pain I cause—"

His mouth enveloped hers. Consumed and addicted, he held her tightly against him despite her hitting, biting, clawing at him. She became a feral animal—one intent on causing further pain while rewarding with small amounts of pleasure.

He winced when she pulled his hair. And when her hand gripped his throat, he tensed—his cool gaze meeting with her mischievous one. "Tell me you love me," he demanded.

"No."

"Do it, or I'll stick you."

She remained firmly in place on top of him—her thighs tightening around him if he moved even a little. Her taunting smile enraged him, but as he reached for the syringe on the rug, she dug her nails into his throat. With her other hand, she unbuckled his belt.

His fingers grazed the syringe, but he didn't grab it—his attention now dedicated to her as she positioned herself on top of his erection. He threw his head back and whined. In moments like this, he never felt powerful—she only ever weakened him, and he often wondered why feeling helpless enamored him so. As she rode him, dominated him, he became lost in her once again.

Nothing in the world mattered but her. She was the center of everything.

His hands gripped her sides—his fingers digging into her as she moved faster and harder. She closed her eyes as satisfied moans bellowed from deep within her. Her cheeks flushed, and a pleasured grin spread across her face.

"Look at me," Grady demanded, but she ignored him. "Look at me, Emma." His desperation broke through his tough exterior. She truly was a master of doling out pain and pleasure in equal amounts. His heart shattered as he reached his apex. "I'm so in love with you."

Her body shook on top of him, then tensed. As her nails dug further into him, that wicked grin remained. With her eyes shut tight, she trembled and bit her lip in delicious satisfaction.

He knew she thought of someone else—imagined another man beneath her. But true to his temperament, he grabbed the back of her neck and pulled her mouth onto his—swallowing his grief, and her dislike of him, completely whole.

ഇ⊃ᖆ

The next morning, the Hunters worked diligently to sift through the weapons in the armory to select the proper arsenal for the inexperienced villagers of Point DuPont. Grady recommended keeping it simple and straightforward with shotguns and revolvers.

Once they gathered the weapons and enough ammo, August and Jon brought them to the foyer in two duffle bags. Before the hour of nine, villagers already started to arrive, but only twelve showed—mostly men and two young women.

One by one, they entered the house—their heads darting in every direction to get a look around. The first young man

111

approached, hardly acknowledging the Hunters. He dedicated his attention to the walls around him—his mouth agape.

Grady shoved a shotgun into his chest. "You know how to use one of these?" He handed him a box of shotgun shells.

"Nnn...no," he stuttered. "To be honest, I really just wanted to see inside. I've always wondered what it looked like in here. Much nicer than I expected. And warm too." The young man's eyes darted behind Grady, though, and his mouth dropped once more. "Wow."

All conversation ceased. On the stairwell, Emma regarded the crowd with a stern expression and disappeared up the stairs. An onslaught of whispers and curses erupted from the onlookers.

"Is that Emma Maddox?"

Grady only smiled at the crowd standing before him. "Next, please." He pushed the man aside, and a young woman approached. Grady handed her a pistol. "Don't worry, miss. We'll show you how to use it."

The young woman's eyes darted to the duffle bag on the floor. "I want one of those." She tipped her head to a shotgun.

Grady smirked. "Shotguns are very difficult to manage. The kickback alone sends this one to the ground," he said while tilting his head to August, eliciting a booming laugh from the retired fighter.

"Can't be much more difficult than providing for a family of seven at eighteen. My mom's dead, my dad and brothers are all drunks. I need something that can protect my sisters and me."

Before Grady even had a chance to respond, August handed the shotgun and a box of shells to the young lady, who snatched them away with a grin. "No one leaves until we've had a chance to show you how to use your weapons! These guns in inexperienced hands can do more harm than the Howlers."

Once the weapons were distributed, the Hunters took the villagers outside to teach them. Grady instructed while Jon assisted those struggling. Meanwhile, August kept overwatch on his horse in case any Howlers showed during their training session.

Grady showed them how to disassemble the weapons for cleaning, stressing the importance of their upkeep. He showed them how to do it safely, ensuring the gun was not loaded, the chamber was empty, and that never, under any circumstances, should they ever point it toward themselves or anyone else.

He then covered the basic fundamentals of how firearms work, starting with the revolvers and pistols before graduating on to shotguns and crossbows. Throughout the entire lesson, though, August remained in a world of his own, staring off toward the forest until a looming suspicion came over him. Shivers crawled up his spine, a similar sensation to a set of fingertips tickling his back.

He tipped his head to the second story, and through one of the windows, Emma looked down on him—on all of them. There she stood, the ghost of Point DuPont—her outline hazy from the light fog settling around the house. Only for a moment did he look away, curious if any of the villagers saw her too. When he looked back at the window, though, Emma left.

Sadness, as well as guilt, overcame him.

ഇൗങ്ക

August knocked on the bedroom door. "Emma?" It creaked open, and Emma sat on the edge of her bed with her back to him. Only slightly did she turn her head. "You all right?"

"I'm fine."

He chuckled. "Why you just sittin' there like a weirdo?" She turned her body—her soggy eyes meeting with his and wiping the smile from his face. "I was just teasing."

She wiped her cheek and crossed the room to rip the curtains shut—blocking out any bit of light that managed to break through the fog. "I'm not crying because of you. I know you think I'm strange."

113

Her abrupt, forceful movements made him smirk. "Yeah, but being strange is a good thing."

His words stopped her angry tirade. She stiffened—her eyes narrowing as if trying to figure him out in some way. "Don't patronize me."

August held his hands up in surrender. He realized that now might not be the time for games. As fiery as he enjoyed his women, his experiences with Emma thus far made him reconsider his usual tactics. "I'm not trying to patronize you, Miss Emma. Whatever that means." The edges of her lips tightened, and she whipped her head away from him. He detected a grin she fought well to hide. "Believe it or not, there are some people around here that don't like seeing you sad."

"People? Or just you?"

"Not just me. Jon too." She squeezed her eyes shut so tight— forcing a tear from the corner to stream down her cheek. He feared upsetting her like before. He crossed the room to her and grasped her arm to pull her into him. "Come on, now, that's no reason to cry." He yanked her into an embrace, forcing a groan out of her.

Her breath quivered. There was no hiding her tears. "I've done such…horrible things, August."

"So? Me too."

She shook her head. "No, you don't understand. I hate myself for the sins I've committed. I'm stuck in this house, in this body…hating myself…disgusted with who I am…" She quivered again and pressed her hands over her mouth to muffle her cries.

"I think you're too hard on yourself, given the circumstances." He laughed. "Hell, if you knew half the shit I've done—" she picked her head up. "I mean…*stuff.* If you knew half the *stuff* I've done, you'd probably send me away and never want to see me again."

"No. You have a good heart."

"So do you. And I know Jon thinks so too."

"You think so?"

He laughed, cocking his eyebrow at her words. "You could commit cold-blooded murder, and I don't think Jon would ever think any less of you. That man's damn near crazy about you." He regretted his words as soon as he spoke them, especially when Emma looked up at him—a twinkle in her green eyes.

"You said he was in love with me too. Is it true? Has he…told you these things?" she asked, hopeful.

It wasn't his place to speak on such things. Jon never confessed his true feelings to Emma; whether it was because of Grady's interference, or Jon's insecurity, August wasn't sure. But one thing was certain—the hope in Emma's eyes made his heart sink into his stomach, and he gained a sneaking suspicion that something bad might come of his confession. "I, uh…it's just a hunch."

"A hunch." She rested her head on his chest again, and he grimaced at the thought—the damage he may have just caused.

෨൦൚

Emma's birthday was a very special occasion in Maddox House—far more important than any other holiday, and it was because Jon made it so. After Mr. Maddox left Point DuPont, he gave Emma's oldest friend the task of boosting her morale. Orchestrating her birthday was always something he took pleasure in doing.

He entered the kitchen and handed a scrap of paper to the head cook. "Three-tier strawberry with chocolate frosting?" he asked, and Jon nodded. "We'll get it done, Jon."

On top of preparing the cake, the kitchen prepped for Emma's favorite meal for dinner—sole meuniére with pommes vapeur and roasted asparagus. Along with the three-tier strawberry cake the kitchen prepared, Jon requested they served tarte tatin after her dinner as well to appease her sweet tooth.

Something he knew Grady would object to.

The servants spent all day decorating the dining room in subtle black and gold embellishments and décor, while in the parlor, they hung a *Happy Birthday* sign and delivered every gift and

115

flower bouquet shipped from the mainland. By the evening of her party, presents and bouquets of blowers filled the parlor.

Jon stood in the doorway, admiring the arrangement when August joined his side. "Holy…I ain't ever seen so many presents in one room."

Seconds later, Grady appeared. He groaned. "I thought I made it very clear that I wanted you to plan this party, Mr. DeWitt."

August outstretched his hand to the adorned room. "I did—"

"Don't. This has Jon written all over it." Grady tipped his head closer to Jon and lowered his tone as two servants passed with more flowers. "This is why she's spoiled rotten. You give her absolutely everything she asks for."

℠℟

Emma wore a black satin gown for the evening. While Jon fastened a diamond necklace around her, he continually glanced to her reflection in the vanity. Her contempt for her own reflection saddened him, and after securing her jewelry, he slid his gloved hands to her shoulders.

Emma clenched his hand and inhaled sharply while meeting his gaze in the mirror. "Is my father coming tonight?" she asked— her green eyes wide and glossy.

Jon reached into his coat pocket and pulled an envelope from within. On the front, Arthur Maddox's handwriting addressing Emma. She snatched it from him and crumpled it in her palm. A quivering breath escaped her.

Instead of crying, she faced him on her chair. "Shall we?"

But even through dinner, Emma remained distracted— distanced from the celebration. The dining room remained silent for a long while—the only sound coming from the crackling fire in the colossal fireplace.

Grady's hand slid to Emma's on the table. Instead of reciprocating, she grabbed her wine glass and turned her head from him—as if not to notice his efforts.

Jon grinned behind his mask.

Grady's sharp inhale disturbed the silence. "You look beautiful tonight, sweetheart."

August shoveled food into his mouth—the only one of the group indulging in the birthday spread. "She looks beautiful every night."

"Yes, of course, she does," Grady snapped and lifted his wine glass to his lips. "But especially tonight."

Jon met Emma's gaze from across the table, but in a similar fashion to her dismissive nature of Grady, she averted her gaze and sipped her wine.

In the parlor, August sat beside Emma on the sofa—lounged back with a bottle of champagne in hand. Grady lurked behind them—his fingers wrapped around a glass of whiskey while Jon sat in one of the armchairs nearby. All the while, the servants unwrapped Emma's presents from her father.

They held up another gown for her approval.

August winced. "I don't like that one."

"What's wrong with it?" Emma asked.

"It's so old-fashioned."

"Old-fashioned?" She extended her glass to him. The champagne bottle clanked into the brim of the flute, and bubbles flooded over the lip onto Emma's hand.

"That's quite enough champagne," Grady began.

The dissatisfied expression on August's face remained as he crossed the room to better observe the gown—his massive frame towering over the servants.

Jon longed for his confidence. He wished to be the sort of man that could draw the attention of an entire room. Magnetic, jubilant. The way Emma's eyes lit up as August commanded their attention vexed him.

"You're an absolute sheba," August began. "You need something that really shows that off, you know? Plunging neckline, low-cut back. Lotsa sparkles." He waved his hands over the dress, splashing champagne from his bottle and forcing a giggle from Emma.

"Mr. DeWitt, that's enough."

"Don't be such a bore, Grady. August is right. I deserve something that better displays my figure."

"For what reason? I already know what you look like."

The reminder always sickened Jon. His eyes darted to Emma, whose gaze met with his as she lifted her champagne glass to her lips. She chose silence as her response. From beside the old-fashioned, gold tulle evening gown, August snickered.

"Maybe we should open the presents from us," Grady said while tipping his head to the servants. They replaced the gown and left the room. Within seconds, Grady took a knee in front of Emma and outstretched his present to her. Wrapped in green tissue paper with a gold bow, Emma set her champagne glass aside and accepted the gift.

She tore through the paper easily, revealing a wooden box set. Inside, every watercolor paint imaginable. "Oh, Grady," Emma cooed while running her fingers over them.

"I know you typically use acrylic paint, but…I wanted to give you more variety. To expand your portfolio." Jon cringed at the sight of Emma smiling at him—her hand touching his face in gratitude.

"Merci, my darling. It's wonderful."

Grady gripped her hand and kissed the backside. "Jon, do you have a present for Miss Emma?"

Of course he had a present, he thought. Never had Jon in the history of their friendship ever missed giving Emma a birthday present. He leaped from the armchair and extended his hands to them—signaling for them to wait.

He marched out of the parlor. One of the servants waited with his box in the corridor, and he thanked them by tipping his head. The box was small—16x10" but required both hands to securely carry. As Jon entered the parlor again, Emma perked up. Now, it was his turn to kneel before her.

The box shifted in his hands, and scratches from within caused Emma to gasp. She gripped Grady's sleeve—now tense while staring at the box before her.

Jon shook his head. He set the box on the ground and reached inside. Already, he sensed the presence of those in the room drawing nearer—towering over him as he rummaged around for Emma's present.

Finally, he revealed a slender white cat.

"Oh..." Emma gasped while handing her glass to Grady. "Jon, you...you got me a kitten?" He held the little animal to her. Tears swelled in her eyes as she pulled it into her chest. "What's her name?" Jon shook his head and pointed to her. "I can name her?"

August sneezed.

"Jon," Grady began, "you should have spoken to me first before you just brought a cat into the house—"

Once more, August sneezed. "Why? It's perfect!" He began with a stuffy nose. "You're the one that said rats gettin' into the house was becoming a problem."

Emma's head darted up. "Rats?"

Jon's gloved hand on her cheek pulled her back into the thoughtful moment between them. She beamed while the cat burrowed herself into the crook of her neck. When she meowed, Emma laughed. "I'll name her...Bones."

Perfect, Jon signed.

Another resounding sneeze from August tipped Grady over the edge. "Are you allergic, Mr. DeWitt?"

August groaned and wiped his nose. "Very. I'm just... I'm gonna head out." His long strides carried him out of the parlor quicker than Jon ever saw him move.

"She's so sweet, Jon. I already love her so much."

An agitated sigh from Grady was the single most satisfying sound to follow Emma's proclamation. Soon after, he too marched across the parlor—leaving the two of them alone entirely. As much as Emma loved her watercolor paint set, her new cat stole the entire evening.

C hapter X

The servants tended to the remainder of Emma's gifts. After finishing a bottle of champagne, Jon sent her to bed with Bones. Despite her birthday evening having started off on a more somber tone, the resolution satisfied him. He hadn't seen Grady since he left the parlor, and August retreated to a safer, cat-free part of the house. Because of the ex-fighter's allergic reaction, Jon thought it best to tend to Emma before bed. The last thing he wanted was another Hunter against the decision to give Emma a little companion.

Jon knocked on her door. From the vanity, Emma brightened at the sight of him.

"Hello, my love." Bones, already finding her place in Emma's bed, slowly blinked at him.

Jon closed the bedroom door and retrieved her favorite white nightgown from her bureau. As he used to do every night, he untied her gown, then her corset, and helped her undress. After slipping the nightgown over her head, he gathered everything and set it aside for cleaning. When he faced her again, though, Emma stood before him naked while untying her hair.

He froze. Of course, he'd seen her naked body many times, even just seconds before. But never had she stood before him so openly, her eyes burning into him. Confused, he contemplated the reasons for disrobing once again.

A different nightgown.

He raced to the bureau and grabbed a black one.

"It's not the nightgown, Jon." Her voice came from directly behind him—startling him. He stepped back but only crashed into the bureau. "Are you all right?" He nodded and then pointed to her. A wry smile spread across her face. "I'm lovely." Her fingers slid up his chest to the buttons of his thick coat. The same coat he always wore in her presence—in an attempt to appear larger than his traumatized frame allowed him to grown.

As she unfastened it, his eyes met with hers, looking for any sign of insincerity. The only thing he noted that seemed unusual were her bright red cheeks. Too much champagne, perhaps. "I'm sorry," she muttered. "I'm nervous."

He started to understand.

The heavy breathing and quick rise and fall of her chest distracted him from her eyes. There she stood before him, offering herself to him. Her perfect body only inches from his—the very same body he often obsessed over in the privacy of his own room.

The body he became a master of drawing.

He slid his hands to her waist and pulled her closer. He imagined so many times what being with her would be like—how he'd pleasure her if given the chance. He raised his hand to her, and cupped one of her breasts in his palm—the sensation alone sending a wave of heat through his body.

She moaned. The sound made him retreat. He snatched her robe from the bureau and wrapped it around her.

"Jon," she begged, her voice pulling him back. "Don't turn away from me." She dropped the robe and then grabbed his coat lapels to pull him closer.

For as long as Jon could remember, he loved Emma. From the moment he met her—when they were only just children—she became the most important person in his life. His appreciation of her grew into a deep love and devotion. And as a teenager, he often fantasized about the two of them running away together.

She never cared that he couldn't talk.

She was the only one.

But after the fire, Jon knew he needed to forget about a future with her. Being mute, in his mind, was bad enough. Being a burn victim, too, limited the ways in which he could care for her. And ever since his accident, Emma never saw his face.

Her lips brushed against the mouth of his mask. He gripped her shoulders and forced her back. When her curious eyes met with him, he shook his head.

"Don't you want me, Jon?"

Her words pained him. Never had the wish to speak been more powerful, but the words jumbled at the base of his tongue—getting caught in his throat. No matter how hard he tried, he couldn't talk. He never could.

She stepped closer—his mind drawing a blank when she reached him again. She gripped the sides of his mask and pressed her red lips onto the mouth—smearing her lipstick over the smooth, white surface.

Her body crashed into him as he yanked her closer. It can't be true, he thought. That someone like her might love someone like him had to be a dream. Surely, he'd awake in his bed early in the morning, drunk or hungover from champagne.

"Make me yours, Jon."

His body trembled. He wished he could say to her:

You're my entire life. My obsession. I've plummeted into the deepest, darkest crevices of my mind in search of you. I've driven myself to madness, all to be closer to you.

He forced her back into her vanity and buried his masked face in the crook of her neck, inhaling her deeply as his gloved hands ravaged her body. With almost just as much force as before, he spun her around and yanked her into him again.

So small, so delicate against him. His hand trailed up from her pelvis to her breastbone. She moaned again and craned her neck to trail her tongue over the lips of his mask. "Take your gloves off. Touch me." She slid his gloved hand between her thighs, but her words froze him. Their reflections in the mirror stopped his beating heart. The vision of her, screaming in horror at the sight of his burned body—his disfigured face forced him to release her and back away. "Jon?" She snatched her robe from the floor and covered herself.

Stay away, he signed.

The very reason he kept his distance for so many years presented itself to him. He knew he could never show her what became of him for the sheer fact that he could never recover if she rejected his scarred body.

The will to live would abandon him.

"What's wrong?" she asked, eyes red with tears.

He chastised himself. How he let himself get lost in the fantasy, he didn't know. As she reached for him, he turned away from her. And already, he blamed himself for the whirlwind of destruction that might soon follow.

"Jon!"

He refused to look at her. Ashamed and discouraged, he marched to the exit of her bedroom instead.

ഇര

The slamming of doors startled August as he ascended the stairs. Jon stormed down the hall toward him, and in the distance, Emma cried.

"Jon?" He began. "What's wrong?" Jon pushed past him and ran down the stairs, leaving August conflicted. Emma's cries beckoned him, but something deep within his core sent him after

123

the brooding Hunter. "Jon!" August called while chasing him down the stairs.

"What in God's name is going on here?" Grady barked while exiting the stairwell to the basement, and August skidded to a halt.

"I, uh…Jon and I are playing a game. *Tag*. I'm it."

Grady's eyes narrowed. "You insult my intelligence—"

The front doors burst open, interrupting the two. Thunder boomed, and the storm raged. When Jon stepped into the madness of it all, August's heart fell into his stomach. "Jon!"

"Jon, stop!" Grady yelled, and he and August darted to the front door. "Get the doors, quick." But August hesitated. "Do as you're told, August!"

"We can't just leave him out there."

"We can't keep the doors open. Howlers could be nearby."

"I'll go," August said while backing out of the doorway. "You just stay by the door and wait for us."

Grady groaned and then closed the doors. Once the deadbolt was replaced, knew he only had a matter of time to track down Jon. He wasn't entirely convinced Grady wouldn't just leave them out there to die if they took too long.

The wind howled, and the ferocity of the downpour soaked August, chilling him to the bone. The rainfall had only just started, but it flooded the earth beneath his feet. "Jon!" he shouted into the darkness. But his intended target wore all black, and even though the fog dissipated in the recent days, the heavy rainfall would not allow the moon to light his way.

August ran through the gates. The open fields surrounding the mansion remained dark, and he could hardly see three feet in front of him. Running after Jon was a bad idea, he thought. He wasn't prepared for a fight, not in the darkness of the night. Not when the Howlers' fur was blacker than the black. "Jon!" August yelled.

"August?"

He whipped around to find the same little girl he'd seen late at night in the mansion, pale skin washed out by a white nightgown, drenched by the rain. The hairs on his body stood upright, and he

124

became rigid at the sight of her. "Wha…what are you doing out here?"

She seemed despondent. Heartbreakingly so, and if it weren't for the unsettling manner in which she'd come to him, he would have been much more concerned about her disposition. But the girl didn't respond. She looked to her side and then started running away from him, further into the open field where a bolt of lightning lit the scene momentarily.

"Hey!" August called after her. "Come…come back, it's not safe!" He ran after her.

"Come on!" she yelled, and another bolt of lightning guided the way to her.

He raced after her, chased her into the forest, but she was much faster than him. The entire time he ran, he thought he ran straight for his death. Through the rain and thunder, the Howlers' wicked cries emerged.

"Slow down!" he yelled. "Please, stop!"

When he lost her, panic surged throughout his body. He emerged from the forest to find the dilapidated shack before him. He scanned the area for any sign of the little girl but saw no one.

He climbed the splintered steps to the porch and peered inside, but other than a large, empty dwelling space with a hole in the roof, he saw nothing and no one.

Only after entering, did he notice another doorway in the back of the shack. "Hello?" Inside, Jon sat on the floor—leaning back on one of the walls with his head in his arms and his mask beside him. "Jon? Have you lost your mind?"

Jon tipped his head upward, careful to keep his face in the shadows. But as August kneeled before him, for the first time ever, he saw Jon's burned face.

Immediately, he averted his gaze. The sight chilled him—the extent of his burns being much worse than anticipated. "What happened back there?"

Jon moaned and leaned his head back against the wall. It was the sort of moan someone might make when experiencing gut-

125

wrenching pain—severe turmoil rising up from the core of him. He smashed his head back into the wall, startling August.

"Stop, Jon," he demanded while leaning over him to grab his hands. "Stop...stop doing this to yourself. Why do you hit yourself when you're angry?"

Finally, Jon raised his hands. He bent his hand to its shoulder and ran his opposing index finger along the elbow. *Punish.*

"Don't do that."

Jon waved his hand to him—dismissing him.

"Nah, I'm not leavin' you out here to die." He scooted beside him and leaned back onto the wall for support. The boarded window beside them allowed a gust of cold wind to blow through the sagging wood. A potential entry site if a Howler wanted inside. The ceiling above them, caving in—another probable point of entry. And then, the front entrance, of course, which had no door. As the wind blew against the structure, the old, rotten wood creaked. If not the Howlers, the collapsing shack would do them in, he thought.

Jon lifted his hands again, and at the slightest hint of movement, August whipped his head to him. *I love her*, he signed.

"So, what happened?" Jon scoffed. He motioned to himself—to his face. "Don't give me that shit. You know there ain't a man alive that loves that woman as much as you do. She needs that kind of love. Not that fucked up shit Grady parades around and dresses up as love." Jon shook his head. "Why do you constantly try to convince yourself that you're not good enough for her?" The brooding Hunter kept his hands folded in his lap. With no hope of a response, August groaned, battling his conscience and integrity in equal measures. "Jon, I may have...done something that...may or may not make things just a little more complicated."

Jon craned his neck and tilted his head inquisitively.

"I may have let slip to Emma that...well, you know...that you're in love with her, and—" Jon stood, stealing away any inspiration August mustered to come forward with the truth.

I trusted you, Jon signed.

"Easy, pal. It's not that big of a deal. She seemed happy to hear it; you just have to follow through."

Jon's stance wavered, and he shook his head. *You ruined everything.*

August stood, throwing his hands to the side. "Well, what do you want me to do, huh? I chased you out into a thunderstorm; I followed you all the way out to this shack so you wouldn't be alone. The worst thing I've ever done to you was accidentally tell Emma how you really feel. Something you should have done a long time ago."

Jon pointed his rigid arm to the door.

August seethed. After chasing the masked Hunter through the woods in the middle of the night—during a thunderstorm—he expected a more pleasant interaction between them. Even if he did meddle in his personal affairs. "Fine. But just so we're clear, you choose to be alone. Whatever happens as a result is outta my hands." August pushed past him and stormed out of the shake into the black, stormy evening. With his memory muddled, the unfamiliar area painted a tumultuous return to the house, especially in the darkness of the night and raging storm.

An internal compass guided him to Jon. One that seemed to have abandoned him for his return. He considered waiting for the brooding Hunter instead, but his pride sent him off the porch and into the thunderstorm.

A snapping twig made him freeze. "Change your mind about comin' back?"

A pair of glowing yellow eyes gazed at him, and August gasped at the sight. The familiar pitfall in his stomach when he saw the little girl forced the hair on his neck to stand upright. It was a sickening, unshakeable terror that paralyzed him when the animal stepped toward him.

The Howler growled, its sticky saliva dripping from its mouth while its hackles stood upright in a razor-like manner. "Jo...Jon?"

It launched at him.

The force of the impact knocked August onto the soggy forest ground. He anticipated the attack. Just like he anticipated all his attacks in every fight he'd ever won. As the Howler pounced on him, August crossed his arms in front of his face and grabbed the thick black fur around the Howler's mouth.

He shouted when the Howler snapped at his face and shuddered when the warmth of the saliva dripped onto his forearm. Despite his strength, his arms shook from the brute force of the creature snapping at him. He'd never met a man stronger than him in all his life, never came across anything he couldn't put down. But the Howlers were far from anything he ever encountered before, otherworldly in their strength and magnitude.

His arms started to give, and the Howler snapped closer to his face. He groaned in annoyance—an aggression being unleashed from his impending loss. A loss that would end his life.

A warm, viscous fluid sprayed onto his face, invading his mouth and causing him to shout in terror from the bitterness. An even greater force knocked the Howler further onto him, collapsing his arms to his chest. Only then did he realize the Howler went limp.

"What the—"

It flew off of him and landed to his side with so much force that the water puddled around splashed him. Practically defeated and out of breath, August's wide eyes met with Jon's piercing gaze. He stood over him, wearing his coat and mask again. In his hand, his hunting knife that dripped with blood.

ഇരുള

It took only ten minutes to make it back to the mansion with Jon leading the way. Flashes of lightning momentarily lit the area around them while thunder boomed in the distance. It was only in those brief moments of light that August finally saw the outline of Maddox house. "We'll be lucky if Grady even bothered waiting," August shouted through the storm.

Jon smashed the iron knocker into the polished wood as hard as he could. The deadbolt shifted. When the door swung open, Grady's eyes narrowed at the sight of them—his lips pursed into a sour expression. He stepped aside to allow them entry, inhaling a sharp breath as they scurried past. He slammed the door and replaced the bolt. "I've been in hell here. Everything has gone to shit, and the two of you, for some ungodly reason, thought it would be…acceptable to run outside in the middle of a storm."

"You think you've been in hell? It's nothing compared to what we just been through."

Grady sneered—his eyes frantically scanning August's attire that was soaked with rainwater and blood. "Yes, I see that. I'm not even going to ask what that little charade was about. But Emma has been inconsolable since you both left. She thought you wouldn't return."

August scoffed. "Well, why the hell did you say anything?"

"I didn't have to. She knew."

Asleep? Jon signed.

"If you're wondering if I've sedated her, the answer is *no*. She's been rather agreeable, albeit very dejected. I recommend you get upstairs and talk to her so she knows you're alive and well." Both August and Jon turned to the stairwell. "Not you," Grady barked, and they both faced him. "I'm not exactly sure what you've done, but Emma does not wish to see you. Your extra duties will now be divided between Mr. DeWitt and me. From this moment forward, you're no longer a caretaker to her. You're only a Hunter. Do I make myself clear?" Jon nodded. "Go, Mr. DeWitt," Grady demanded. "And for God's sake, clean yourself up before you see her."

August hurried to his room. He cleaned the blood off and threw on a new pair of pants and a wool sweater. Before leaving, he snatched her birthday present from the nightstand. Nothing fancy, nothing wrapped, but something he thought might improve her mood. When he made it to Emma's bedroom, he entered without knocking.

"Oh, August," she cried and crawled to the edge of the bed. As he sat beside her, she wrapped her arms around his neck, pulling him in for a tight embrace. "I was so worried about you...about Jon—"

"Shush." He rubbed her back. "It's all right, Miss Emma. We're fine."

Her tight embrace loosened, and she pulled away from him. Her green eyes—almost glowing in the candlelight—glossed over. "The Howlers got to you."

His brow furrowed in confusion. "No, it's just raining really bad. We're fine; nothing happened."

"Promise me you won't do that again. Promise me...promise me you won't leave me behind again."

He nodded. "Yeah, I promise." Shortly after, a violent sneeze shot out of him. Bones sat at Emma's side—her little green eyes blinking slowly at him. "I just realized that I never gave your present earlier." He handed her a Vogue magazine. "It's nothing fancy. Not like a kitten or...new paints."

Her attention wavered with every turn of the page. Her eyes narrowed, and with every picture she came across, she lifted the magazine closer to her face, causing August to smile. "This woman's hair is very short."

He peeked at the page. "Yeah, that's how a lot of women wear their hair now. It's all the rage."

"Really?"

"Emma?" Grady appeared in the doorway, and Emma stashed the magazine under her blanket. "You see, darling? He's all right. Now it's time for bed."

Disturbed by Emma's insistence to hide her present from Grady, August's smile faded into a hateful scowl. He and Emma exchanged solemn glances. "Good night, Miss Emma. I'll see you in the morning."

"Good night, Mr. DeWitt," she muttered.

There had been many times since meeting Grady McCoy that August wanted to pulverize his *pretty-boy* façade. Seeing the satisfied smirk on Grady's face as he passed engrained that urge so deep inside of him that his muscles twitched and as their bodies grazed each other.

It took everything in the retired fighter's being to refrain.

"I'll be just a moment, darling," Grady said and then closed the bedroom doors. "Mr. DeWitt, a moment? Since Jon will no longer be involved in Emma's care, it'll now be our job to take over his duties."

August huffed. "Yeah, you mentioned that."

"I'll take the morning shift. You'll take the evening. Her bath time, nightly dose, putting her to bed—"

"So, should I—" Grady stepped in front of him, blocking his attempts to return to Emma.

"I'll take tonight. You should rest. But since I'm already busy running the security of this house and overseeing her care, I expect you to take over anything remaining. The things Jon did to help with her morale."

"You mean all the shit that got him in trouble?"

Grady forced a laugh. "Ordering supplies for her. New materials for new gowns, flowers, books, jewelry. I need you to make her...happy."

"Shouldn't that be your job? She is your ol' lady, ain't she?"

"I'm busy with more important tasks. Keeping her safe and healthy, for example." Grady peered over his shoulder to Emma's bedroom doors. He closed the gap between them and lowered his tone. "I'd be lying if I said I wasn't happy about Jon being brushed aside for the time being. He has a way of turning her against me, and I trust you'll do as I ask when it comes to caring for her. The right way."

"Don't worry. I'll make her happy."

Grady's eyes narrowed. "Not too happy. She needs to understand the severity of the situation she's in. The delicate nature of her life on the island. You hear me?"

"Loud and clear, compadre."

"Have a good night."

As tired as he felt, August tossed and turned all evening. His troubled thoughts stayed with the dead Howler in the woods and the mysterious little girl who continued to appear and disappear since his time in the mansion.

With no meeting time set for the morning, August assumed the Hunters wouldn't be hunting the next day. Not with the storm only building stronger outside of his window. And when the sun started to rise, he finally found enough peace to sleep for a few hours, until a knock came on his bedroom door.

"Who is it?" he shouted, but no response came. He rolled over to look at the clock on the table next to his untouched dinner tray. It was past eleven in the morning, and he hadn't slept so late in weeks. But another knock came on the door. "Just…hang on a sec," he grumbled while climbing out of his bed in his boxers.

He staggered to the door and yanked it open. *Grady.* "What do you want?"

"We have a problem. Get dressed and meet me in the parlor in an hour." After what happened the previous night, August immediately thought of Jon.

Twenty minutes later, he barreled down the steps, passing a young maid. "Hey, where is everybody?" he asked, but she only hurried along her way. "Parlevouz Francais?" August said through a smirk, and she giggled.

A somber tune coming from the music room distracted him. He followed and peered inside. Emma sat at the grand piano—a rare sight to find her on the first floor without supervision. He figured Grady must not be too far. He waited in silence as she played, admiring her as her head swayed back and forth with the music. When she stopped, he resisted the urge to clap.

Applause didn't seem fitting for the mood.

"That was really beautiful."

Emma gasped and spun on the bench. "Mr. DeWitt! I wasn't aware I had an audience."

He stood over her, and she scooted down to allow space for him on the bench. He ran his fingers along the keys and played an unsettling tune. "I always wanted to play the piano. We were too poor to learn. What was that you were playing?"

"Moonlight Sonata. I never really enjoyed the song growing up, but now…it breaks my heart and then puts it back together again. It's devastating but…comforting in that someone else has felt the pain of life. A life shrouded in guilt and disenchantment. There's so much longing and yet…so much suffering."

"Emma?"

She outstretched her bony fingers to the keys again. "How is Jon?"

"I haven't seen him." She played again, but the sound tormented August. He wanted to distract her. Or at least comfort her in some way. "Stop playing that."

"It hurts you too, doesn't it? There's so much pain behind your eyes, August. Oh, how I wish to be as strong as you and keep that pain hidden away."

"No, you don't. It's poison."

"A bit of poison seems merciful." She buried her face into the crook of her arm and coughed.

"Emma—" She moved into him, silencing him. Her soft face pressing against the side of his stubbled chin, the warmth of her, the scent of lavender upon her, it dizzied him.

"Am I ruined, August? Have I completely lost all my value as a woman? I gave myself to a married man, and now I fear no one will have me."

"You're not ruined, Emma. You're perfect."

"I don't feel perfect. I'm an old maid."

"No. No, you're not." While he held and consoled her, his mind drifted to possibilities of the two of them. A thought he hadn't entertained since his first week in the house—not after seeing how the other men fawned over her. Even in her sadness, she mesmerized him in the same way as the first time he saw her.

"I grow so afraid that I'll never find someone who loves me. That I'll never be married, never have children. I'll just spend my days wasting away in this house. Completely alone."

He paused—taken aback by her words and the ridiculousness of them. "I don't think finding someone to love you is the problem here, Emma. We just need to get you out of here. Once we kill off all the Howlers, we can get you out of here, and you'll get that…happily ever after you girls always go on and on about."

Emma pulled away from him, her green eyes wet with tears. "So naïve, Mr. DeWitt. But at least someone in this house still has hope." She wet her lips. Just that little act drew him in closer. He wanted to taste her. He wanted to know what it was like to be the man she loved, even if only for a second. "August?" she whispered against his lips.

But instead of meeting with a kiss, August wrinkled his nose and sneezed. "Shit," he cursed and buried his face into the crook of his arm.

MRRROWOW!

Bones pounced onto the piano—as if the keys were a rat. Her slow-blinking, green stare transfixed on August until a violent sneeze sent him away from the bench. "Damn cat."

Completely satisfied with herself, Bones groomed and purred as Emma scratched her chin. "She's a good cat. She keeps the monsters away."

August sniffled. "The monsters?"

"Things that go bump in the night."

"So you've seen her too?"

Emma's inquisitive gaze met with his. "Her?"

"The little girl."

"I'm afraid I don't know what you're talking about." She soothed the young cat into submission. Bones rolled onto her back and pawed at Emma's fingers. "That's a good girl," Emma cooed.

She coughed again, and August wondered if she also might be allergic.

As the urge to sneeze built in August's nose, he turned his blurry vision to the exit. He liked the idea of a cat to deal with the rats. But not at the expense of his own comfort. And it seemed that Bones already took it upon herself to be Emma's personal bodyguard.

It's for the best, August thought. As he left the music room, he grew ashamed of his attempt to kiss Emma. Broken of her brief spell, he marched down the corridor—distancing himself from the thick haze that surrounded her. And lured men in for a closer look.

Chapter XI

August entered the parlor. In the corner, Jon stood beside the window with his hands folded behind his back—his gaze fixed on the storm building outside. Moments later, Grady entered, and August stiffened— that violent twitch returning at even the sound of his voice.

"Gentleman, there is a storm coming."

August scoffed. "I think it's already here."

"No, a bad storm. Not just a bit of light rain."

"All right. So, what does that mean?"

Grady hesitated—his shifty eyes darting back and forth between the expectant Hunters. "Mr. Maddox wishes to evacuate the staff. The liability of having them here during the storm... it's too much of a burden."

"What about Emma?"

Jon turned his back to them.

"She'll stay here," Grady said. "As will we. And a select few others, but you won't have any interaction with them—"

"But if it's so dangerous, shouldn't we all be leaving?" A storm so perilous surely warranted the evacuation of his only daughter to a safer place.

"We cannot evacuate Emma. It's too dangerous."

"For who?" August snapped.

Grady's lips tightened. "I'll make the arrangements for the servants, the doctors. They need to be off the island by tonight."

"What about Emma's medicine?" August asked while following Grady to the exit of the parlor. "If the doctors are leaving, how will she get the quality of care she needs?"

"The storm should only last a few days at most. Emma has enough medication to last that long—the doctors have made certain—"

August grabbed Grady's arm and stopped him from walking any further. "Are you not concerned for her safety at all?"

"I've been here for a long while, Mr. DeWitt. We live on an island, surrounded by water. This isn't the first storm we've encountered—it isn't the first time we've had to evacuate. Emma will be fine." He left the parlor, and his dismissive behavior baffled August. Even Jon—Emma's biggest advocate—kept quiet on the matter.

"What a fucking circus. This is ridiculous. If the servants can't be here, Emma should leave too. Her safety should be her father's main priority." But Jon only marched past him. "Jon!" he bellowed, grabbing the attention of the masked Hunter. "What is going on here?"

Jon shook his head.

"Don't shake your head at me," August boomed.

Carlyle, Jon signed.

Stunned, August wracked his brain for a response. No thoughts came to him, though—Jon's signing having perplexed him into questioning the translation. He left the parlor, leaving August to dwell on the revelation about the late Hunter, one he'd been told was killed by a Howler.

Before the end of the day, the time came for the servants evacuate. In groups of four, the carriage transported them to the docks to catch a ferry to Port Augusta.

Jon supervised in the hall and kept an eye out for Howlers. The servants mostly talked about the storm, how bad it had to be if they were being evacuated, and if they should be worried about the boat ride, but Jon kept quiet. Only when a young maid started coughing did he feel the need to interact in some way.

He reached for the young maid.

"I'm fine, Jon," she murmured, and he tipped his head to her. She smiled sweetly at him. "I'm all right. Just a cough is all." Jon released her and allowed her to enter the carriage, but the progressive cough concerned him.

Grady entered Emma's bedroom to find her standing at the window. He moved by her side. Below, servants climbed into the carriage to leave.

He turned his back to them. "Everything all right, sweetheart?" he asked while leaning on her vanity.

"Why doesn't my father want me with him?"

Grady sighed. "He knows you'll be safer here. With me."

Emma scoffed and shook her head. "Trapped on an island with bloodthirsty Howlers in the wake of the worst storm Point DuPont has seen in over a decade. I'm no fool, Grady, despite what you may think. My father hates me."

He grabbed her hand, and finally, she looked at him. He sensed desperation in her, a vulnerability he hadn't seen her give him in months. "He doesn't hate you. He loves you. I love you. We both want what's best for you," he said while pulling her closer to him.

"You love me?"

Grady smiled, his eyes peering down at her. A sort of triumphant victory beamed through him as he gazed upon her. "I've loved you since the first moment I saw you." His fingers grazed her chin, and he lifted her head. His lips lingered over hers—his thoughts carrying him back to the library. Darkness overcame him when he envisioned her on top of him, riding him and calling his name. He clasped her neck—her pulse pounding against his thumb. "You are mine, Emma."

"Grady, let go—"

MRRROWOW!

Grady's shifty eyes met with Bones' pointed stare from the bed. He released Emma and turned to the cat—resentful of its presence in her bedroom. Bones hissed, and as Grady went to shoo her off the bed, she swiped at him. "The cat shouldn't be in your bed, Emma. It's not good for you."

He snatched the back of Bones' neck.

"Grady!" Emma shouted.

EEEAAAAARRRR! Bones hissed—her body stiff in Grady's grasp. As he carried her to the bedroom door, though, she swiped at his face—scratching his cheek deep enough that he groaned and dropped her. She sprinted from the room—disappearing into the darkened corridor.

Grady wiped his face, smearing a bit of blood on his cheek. "I don't want that thing in your room. You understand me?" he snapped over his shoulder.

"She has more of a right to be in here than you." He whipped around. The sight of Emma leaning on her vanity with tears streaking down her face made him recoil. "If you ever touch her like that again, I will kill you."

"Emma," Grady warned.

"Get out." She wiped her face and fell into her vanity chair—keeping her back to him. "I'm tired, Grady. I want to go to bed." He had nothing to say in response. Instead of arguing, he turned on his heels and marched out of the room—slamming the doors shut behind him.

139

All life seemed to leave the mansion when the servants evacuated. August spent the early evening hours wandering the corridors. He even wished Grady was around for a bit of company. But oddly enough, he couldn't find him anywhere. He found no one—not Jon, not even Emma in her room.

The chilling sensation that came over him from his burgeoning isolation sent him straight to his own room for a bit of comfort. Because if he were to be alone, he at least wanted to be in the place most familiar to him.

A fire burned in the fireplace—one he built earlier in the evening. A first since arriving on the island. He flopped down on the bed and stared up at the ceiling. On the nightstand, Emma's naughty little book from their first encounter sat—untouched.

It seemed the perfect night to find comfort in a good book. But there was no comfort to be found in the pages of '*120 Days of Sodom*.' Despite his intrigue when Emma defended the piece, her insistence on doing so disturbed him. He told her he wasn't easily offended, and it was true. But nothing could have prepared him for the atrocities within that book, and for the first time ever, he sided with Grady on his decision to keep it away from her.

Emma had no knowledge of the outside world. And the last thing August wanted was for her to think '*120 Days of Sodom*' might be an accurate depiction of humanity.

Or maybe in her eyes, it was.

But as the storm raged on and the sky faded into darkness, August's eyes became heavy. Lazing about all day made him lethargic, despite reading disturbing anecdotes of sexual torment for the past few hours. Before he even had the chance to hide the book away from anyone who might come calling on him, August drifted asleep with the book opened on his stomach.

The hours passed, and the fire died down, now only a smoldering pile of ash. It wasn't the crash of thunder that awoke August from his sleep, though. Not the bright bolt of lightning hitting a nearby tree, lighting up his room momentarily. Not even the sound of his bedroom door creaking open awoke him. It was the sudden drop in temperature and a crushing sensation on his chest that suffocated him.

"August?"

His eyes shot open, and he gasped for air. He panted heavy, visible breaths into the cold air. When his eyes met with the same pale-faced little girl he'd seen before, the hairs on his body stood upright. Frozen with fear, August never tore his gaze from the sadness in her eyes.

"Come on," she whispered and then ran for the door. It creaked behind her as she disappeared into the darkness.

"Wait..." he called and climbed out of bed. He yanked the door open but saw nothing in either direction. He ran his hands over his face in an attempt to gather himself. Just a dream, he told himself. But when he dropped his hands, the little girl stood before him—staring up at him. "Jesus!"

"Shush," she whispered while placing her finger over her lips. "Come on, August." She grabbed his fingers, but a tingling sensation moved through his fingertips and up his forearm, raising the hairs once more.

"Don't," he gasped and snatched his hand from her. This was no little girl, he thought. A ghost, perhaps. Or perhaps still a dream. Yes, he convinced himself he must still be dreaming, just like all the other nights. And when he saw her outside the mansion after Jon ran out into the rain, his subconscious must have hallucinated her. To him, it was the only logical explanation.

But the girl cried, her voice fading into a faint echo. "Please hurry," she begged and disappeared down the hall again.

His curiosity got the better of him, and he followed. The cold stayed with every move he made. The little girl stood at the top of the stairwell, waiting for him. As he approached, she scurried down the stairs.

As he descended into the darkness behind her, the only sensation that kept him grounded was the slick, polished wood of the banister he clung to for guidance.

The first level glowed from the sconces, and hushed voices at the bottom of the stairs slowed his pace. He peered over the banister where the girl sat on the bottom step, staring up at him. She brought her index finger over her lips.

"So, what you're saying is, the cube is no longer operational." It was Grady's voice.

"Oui, Monsieur, but it is not our fault. The rats chewed through the wires…all electricity has been compromised, and without that—"

"I get it, Monsieur Leroux. How long until it's back up?"

August crouched to better hear their conversation.

"We can have it operational again in a few weeks, but if the rats keep coming, our efforts will be wasted—" A thud startled August. He snuck further down the stairs, only stopping again when Grady's hushed yet aggressive voice began again. He spoke too quietly for August to piece together what was said. The only portion he managed to hear was *danger*.

"Oui, Monsieur."

Grady sighed. "Very well. Show me."

A clank echoed through the stairwell, and August leaned over the banister to better see the source. The metal door to the basement creaked shut behind. It echoed through the halls, making August cringe—similar to nails on a chalkboard.

The looming coldness crept up August's spine. He gasped and whipped to his side where the girl stood next to him. She raised her little finger and pointed down the stairwell. "It's down there," she whispered.

"What's down there?"

She trotted down the stairs without answering. And without any more questions, August followed.

He stood before the basement door. Grady's warning about never going down there without him banged around in his mind. Surely, he'd be caught if he went down there. Surely someone would see, but what would happen? He wasn't sure, and there was really only one way to find out. And even though the little girl seemed to have disappeared once more, her presence remained and beckoned him to approach the door. The desperation he felt, he assumed, came from her.

He grabbed the handle, and a jolt of electricity—or perhaps fear—shot through the entirety of his body. Bitter cold enveloped him, paralyzing him to a point that he could no longer breathe.

He gasped—bolting upright in bed and panting in a cold sweat. '*120 of Sodom*' was on the bed next to him. The storm raged outside his window, and the fire in his room danced vivaciously. With his heart pounding, he glanced to the clock on his bedside table. It was eight in the evening. He'd only been asleep for twenty minutes.

MRRROWOW!

August flinched when Bones pounced between his legs. Frozen momentarily from his heightened senses, a shudder shot through his body at the sight of her. She kneaded her paws into his comforter—her green eyes slow-blinking at him just like always.

His face wrinkled and contorted, and a violent sneeze shook him from his terror.

"Go on, scram!" he shouted while waving his arm at her, and she bolted from his bed and out the creaking door. A door he was certain he closed behind him.

August awoke the next morning to heavy rainfall thudding onto the rooftop. He feared the worst of the storm had yet to come. Thunder rumbled, and from his window, waves crashing into the bluffs in the distance painted a chaotic picture of the sea. Yet, for the time being, it was only a thunderstorm.

After getting dressed for the day, August wandered around the mansion, searching for comfort or camaraderie. "Is anyone alive in this house?"

He made it to the first level—stopping momentarily to regard the thick, metal basement door. But muffled thuds coming in sets of three from the dining room distracted him.

After a long pause, the thuds came in a set of three once more. "What in the...?" He crossed the hall and opened the door.

A knife whipped past his face and pierced a slab of wood, paralyzing him. Jon recoiled at the sight of him.

August held his hands up in retreat. "I'm a friendly."

Jon fiddled with the knife a bit and settled back into his stance. He propelled his last dagger right toward the target, and it penetrated the middle of the bullseye.

"This what you do when you're bored?" August asked. Jon marched to the target and pulled his knives from the slab. "Hey, I hope you're still not sore about what we talked about the other night. I wasn't trying to piss you off or anything. Just wish you'd realize that the only person who should be with Emma is you." Jon repositioned himself and threw another knife into the slab. "You ignoring me now?"

Jon huffed. *I can't talk.*

"Mind if I give it a try?" Jon held the knives to him. Spared from the embarrassment of being dismissed by the brooding Hunter, he jogged over and took them. They were lighter than he expected. He gauged the weight of one with his left hand and bundled the other two in his right. The target didn't seem too far.

144

But as soon as the knife left his hand, he knew he failed. A slip of the wrist and the knife bounced off the wooden slab and hit the ground.

August winced.

Sloppy, Jon signed.

"Really? I thought it was pretty good." He rolled his eyes and refocused. Before he had the opportunity to throw the next knife, Jon held up his hands, causing August to retreat.

Left-handed? August nodded. Jon grabbed his hand and positioned the tip of one of the knives between his index finger and thumb. Afterward, he slowly guided August's hand, turning his wrist inward, then outward at full extension.

"Yeah, all right." Jon stepped aside, and August positioned himself again. The masked eyes burned into him, making him feel even more anxious. It was a foreign concept to him, feeling insecure about his performance. For the first time in any regard, he was inferior—something he never used to feel when fighting in the arena.

August extended his arm, flicking his wrist out just as Jon instructed. When the dagger penetrated the wooden slab, he grinned. Even if he only hit the edge.

Jon slow clapped. He brought his fingers to his lips and then flicked them outward. *Better.*

"Thanks. Hey, how'd you get into all this anyway?"

He brought his index finger to the outside of his nose and twisted once. *Bored.*

August chuckled. "Yeah, I can relate to that. Give me a few more weeks of this damn rain, and I'll probably end up bein' better than you."

Jon tipped his head to the target.

With his newfound confidence, August propelled the third blade through the air, missing the target entirely. "Aw, what the…" Jon crossed the room and yanked the other knives from the slab. "What about that massive thing?" August asked, and Jon glanced at the knife on his belt. The very knife he used to kill Howlers.

He only shook his head. As he packed away his throwing knives in a small black case, August closed the gap between them. "Have you, uh…talked to Emma since…?"

Jon's rigid posture made him cautious about continuing. Before he even had a chance, a tickle in his nose forced a violent sneeze from him.

Bones weaved herself in and out from between Jon's legs—rubbing herself against him in an affectionate manner.

"She likes you—" Once more, that tickle formed, and August turned away to sneeze—this time twice.

Jon scooped up Bones and scratched her chin. With his free hand, he grabbed his knife kit and headed to the exit of the dining room. "Hey, Jon!" August yelled through a stuffy nose—stopping the muted Hunter's stride. "What's in the basement? There are people down there, aren't there? Workers that are too important to have to leave. What are they doing down there?" August asked in an accusatory tone. "What happened to Carlyle?"

He gave no response—only snuck out of the dining room with the slow-blinking cat in his arms.

Chapter XII

August's failure to gain any insight from Jon unnerved him. He wondered if Grady had been right about him all along, that even though Jon loved Emma, he might be part of the problem. He and Grady were hiding something, and although the two never saw eye to eye on anything else, they seemed to share their sentiment on one thing.

August could not be trusted.

The evening came with heavier rainfall and thunder booming loud enough that it seemed to shake the house's foundation. Every once in a while, lightning struck nearby, illimunating the darkest corners of the home. The storm had officially hit Point DuPont, and August found himself in the company of the other two Hunters.

He nestled himself deep into one of the armchairs in the parlor with a thick coat wrapped around. Continually, his eyes shifted back and forth between his colleagues—his paranoia of them growing with every passing moment.

Were they the ones who killed Carlyle?

No, that's crazy, he thought. It had to be the Howlers. Because what reason would they ever have to kill another Hunter? "It's so black out there. Even if Howlers were surrounding the house, we wouldn't even know." August sneered at Grady's back. As the fire cracked, he flinched—his eyes darting to Jon flipping his massive blade around in his hands.

"How do I look?"

The Hunter's directed their attention over August's shoulder to the parlor entrance. Grady recoiled—a horrified expression on his face. "For goodness sake, what have you done?"

Jon stood upright. His rigid stance intrigued August, who whipped around to Emma standing in the doorway—her ginger hair cut to her chin.

"Holy—" He bit his tongue. She waited for their approval, but it didn't come, and her softened expression made August cringe. Guilt burdened him. The magazine, he thought. She tried to cut it like the women in the Vogue magazine.

"Emma! Why would you do this to your beautiful hair?" Grady cried while crossing the room to reach her. He snatched her arm, and she cowered.

"You don't like it?"

"No, I don't like it. You look like a boy," he whined.

Emma's glossy eyes darted across the room. "Jon?" The masked Hunter hesitated. Without any encouragement from him, Emma sobbed. She shook away from Grady's grasp. "Oh, I've made a terrible mistake."

Of all the things August saw so far in Maddox House, the moment of Grady degrading Emma's appearance outraged him most. He slammed his whiskey glass down. "I think it looks great. We just need to straighten it out a bit." With both of his massive hands on her arms, he escorted her from the parlor.

148

Emma sat in her vanity chair, and August reshaped her short hairstyle. He moved slow—cutting only when certain, while glancing periodically at the magazine for reference.

She covered her mouth and coughed.

"It's just crooked, is all," he assured.

"Have you cut hair before?"

He snipped a piece from the side of her face. "My mama taught me how to cut her hair when I was young. She never really did anything fancy like this."

"I've never seen Grady look so disgusted before. Maybe that's a good thing," she muttered.

August scoffed. "Let's face it, though. Grady's kind of a dick." He never understood the pairing—neither one of them had anything in common. "No offense, Emma. But does your father know about you and him?"

"No. In an attempt to keep me locked away, guarded by the Hunters, and protected from the perversions of society, my father seems to have forgotten one thing from his various studies and readings throughout his time. The question is called to light by the Roman poet, Juvenal."

"Which is?"

"Who will guard the guardians?"

"I don't get it."

"His poem refers to the impossibility of enforcing moral behavior on women when the enforcers are corruptible."

Their eyes met in the mirror again. Her intense stare unnerved him, and almost just as quick, he averted his gaze back to the magazine for reference. As if her words had no effect on him whatsoever. "What about Jon? You think he's corruptible?" She said nothing in response. "What started the fire? The one that burned him and killed all those people?"

"I don't know. No one knows. Some believe it was a fallen gas lamp. Others believe it was arson."

"What do you believe?"

She shrugged and shook her head. "I'm not sure. All I know is, the fire happened, and then I wasn't allowed to leave my house anymore."

⁊⊃(⊂⧽

August marched down the corridor, his thoughts consumed with Emma's words. While turning the corner to retreat to his own room, he crashed into a solid figure. He jumped back, raising a fist to protect himself if needed.

"Jon," he huffed, "what are you doing?" The masked Hunter pointed to Emma's room. For a moment, in the dark corridor lit only by sconces, he was able to detect worry behind Jon's eyes. "She's fine. She's tired, though."

Jon hung his head.

Seconds later, the jingling of a little bell grabbed their attention. As Bones ran past, August grimaced at the sight of a rat wriggling between her teeth. "The cat!" Before she made it too close to Emma's room, both Jon and August darted to her.

⁊⊃(⊂⧽

August entered the parlor with the dead rat in his hand, holding it high for Grady to see. "Bones caught a rat."

He tossed it onto the table between them, and Grady groaned. "Please...tell me you did something, anything to help with what she did to her hair."

"You're a real asshole, you know that?"

"I'll take that as a no." He took a swig of whiskey. After a while of staring into the empty glass, he flung it into the wall, shattering it into little pieces.

150

The act threw August on high alert. "Just calm down," he bellowed. "It's just hair; it'll grow back. And I made it look…somewhat presentable."

"Once more, you and Jon fail to understand that her doing something like that is a cry for help. There is something wrong with her. No woman just rationally cuts off all her hair!"

"That's not true. Women do it all the time in the real world—"

"This isn't the real world!" Grady shouted, pleading with August. "Emma is not a normal girl, and this isn't 1920s Ontario, or Savannah, or wherever it is you're accustomed to living. Emma is sick. Any unordinary act from her is to be taken very seriously, or we risk—" Grady stiffened as Emma entered the room in her white, silk nightgown. She clenched a record in her hand. "Sweet pea?"

She said nothing while crossing the room to the gramophone. August and Grady watched in anticipation. When the record started to spin, a scratchy, jazzy tune began. "Whoo!" Emma shouted and threw her hands in the air.

"You keep jazz in the house?" August asked.

"I don't know where she got that."

She started dancing in a peculiar way—how someone who's never heard jazz before might dance. Unstructured and loose, all her classical training abandoned her as she flung her arms and spun around.

But this was not a moment of admiration for August. As much as he enjoyed seeing her have a good time, something was terribly wrong with Emma. She never looked at them, never acknowledged them, and she seemed unstable on her feet. Just as Grady mentioned before, peculiar behavior was cause for concern. And this behavior certainly was peculiar.

August groaned. "Might be a bit late for dancing, Em."

As she spun, Grady tried to grab her. She only pulled away, though, and continued twirling—laughing as she did. Her face flushed bright red, and her brow furrowed. Through her chaotic

151

dancing, she bumped the record, and as it skipped, she spun around over and over again.

Grady wrapped his arms around her. As soon as he did, Emma stiffened. "She's burning up. Get Jon," he demanded.

"Jon!" But August never left the room—too transfixed on the scene in front of him. She was fine only moments before. Grady lowered her to the ground, and she started seizing. "Jon!"

ಬಂಜ

The three Hunters stood over Emma's bed. She writhed in discomfort. Her seizure stopped, and she had no memory of her actions in the parlor. But her violent cough is what worried them. Jon sat beside her and handed her handkerchief, but she pushed his hands away.

"How long has she been like this?" Grady asked with his arms folded across his chest.

"I was with her earlier, and she seemed fine. She maybe coughed a little bit, but—"

"And you didn't think to tell anyone?"

August scoffed. "People cough. I didn't think anything of it. Maybe if the two of you would set your ego aside and actually look after her, like you're supposed to..." he boomed and directed his attention to Jon. "We woulda caught it sooner. But I can't be the only one—"

Grady raised his hand to silence him. "Very well, Mr. DeWitt. I see Emma's welfare is too big a task for you now; that was my mistake."

"You smug little bastard." Grady snatched August's suspenders and jerked him closer. "You really wanna do this with me? Don't you know who I am?" August pried Grady's fingers from his clothes. "Never forget that while you tote around a rifle like some fuckin' hotshot, I could snap your neck in a second if I wanted to. *With* my bare hands."

152

"Stop," Emma groaned. She struggled to sit up in bed with Jon's assistance. "This is no one's fault but mine. I've been feeling…weary for days now. I just didn't want to be a bother. I know the staff…needed to leave the island—" a violent coughing fit started again.

"It's tuberculosis," Grady muttered.

"No, it's not."

"So, you're a doctor now?"

"How the hell would she even come down with tuberculosis? She's been locked up since she was a teenager!"

"Enough!" Emma shouted and then winced.

Jon shot to his feet. He grabbed fistfuls of their clothes from their backsides and escorted them out of the bedroom. When in the hallway, he shut the door behind them. He signed to them, hurried in his movements.

"What's he saying?"

"He said she's right, you wurp."

Before the two could take another crack at each other, Jon stepped between them. He signed to August, *call the doctor.*

"Didn't we send the doctor back to the mainland?"

Grady smacked Jon's chest. "The phone."

"We have a phone?"

The Hunters sprinted down the darkened corridor. They stopped in front of a set of double doors. Arthur's study, of course, would house the only phone.

Grady unlocked the door, and the three Hunters entered. On Arthur Maddox's massive oak desk, a phone rested, waiting to be used for emergencies.

Grady snatched the receiver and sat at the edge of the desk, his back turned to Jon and August.

The storm roared outside, and a flash of lightning lit the room momentarily, followed by a crack of thunder that shook the house's foundation. In that brief moment of light, something in the corner of the room caught August's eye. "What was that?"

The room faded to black again.

August approached a corner—eyes fixed on the spot as he waited for another flash of lightning. "Jon," he called, and when the room lit up again, he pointed to an oil painting of a little girl. "Jon, who is that?"

Emma, he signed.

It couldn't be, he thought. It was the same little girl he'd been seeing since arriving at Maddox house—the same little girl that haunted his dreams. The little girl who led him to Jon in the woods and to the discovery of the cube. It was the childlike version of Emma.

Grady slammed the receiver down. "There's no dial tone. The storm must have knocked the line out."

ℰℭ

The night was long, and the storm raged outside. Emma's condition began to worsen with the presence of blood in her sputum. The Hunters took shifts tending to her, but without a doctor present, they weren't sure how to help other than to keep her temperature down.

"It had to have been one of the servants," Grady said while August searched the medicine cabinets in the medical bay. "Coughing up blood is a sign of tuberculosis."

August fought the urge to retaliate with some witty remark when he noticed the distress on Grady's face. "If it were tuberculosis, we'd all have it," he muttered.

"Maybe we do. Maybe it's only a matter of time before we start showing symptoms as well."

"There could be a ton of reasons why she's coughing up blood." August grabbed a bottle of quinine from one of the cupboards. "This could help with the fever. I ain't no doctor, though."

Jon appeared in the doorway, grabbing their attention. They waited for terrible news, the tension in the room rising to an unbearable level. "What, Jon?"

154

Back in Emma's room, August fed her a spoonful of quinine, causing her to gag. She knocked the spoon from his hand and rolled onto her side, coughing so hard that blood stained her lips.

August set the bottle aside and touched her forehead. "I dunno if this is gonna work."

Grady shoved him aside and sat next to Emma. He ran his hand over her face. "She's burning up. Even if the quinine does help, it'll take too long. Jon, get an ice bath ready." The mute Hunter unfolded his arms and stood upright—his posture rigid. "What is it?" Grady snapped.

No ice, Jon signed.

"We'll just have to run a cold bath. As cold as it can get."

Once the bath was filled, Grady carried Emma and placed her in the cold water. She gasped and clung to him—clawing at his neck and face. "Emma, darling, we have to break your fever."

"It's too cold!"

"It's all right," Grady consoled. Even when her body was completely in the water, Grady held her, trying his best to calm her. As much as August hated him, at that moment, he saw the love the veteran Hunter had for her. Only when Jon left the room was August's gaze on the two broken.

He followed him into the hallway. "Jon." The brooding Hunter stopped. "You can't do this. You can't run away every time shit gets hard."

I sit. Watch. She suffers, he signed.

"She needs to know you're here for her. You abandon her in times of need, and she'll never be able to trust you again." Jon's breath shook as he tipped his head to the ground. "I know it's hard for you. But this ain't about you." He grabbed Jon's shoulder and pulled him into the doorway. "See that? At the end of all this, when she gets better, she's gonna remember he stayed, and you ran off. You want her to think that?"

Jon shook his head.

August shoved him inside. "Get in there." Jon approached the tub. "Grady, a word?"

155

Finally, Grady relinquished control to Jon. "Stay with her," he demanded, and Jon nodded. "What?" Grady barked from the doorway as August stayed hidden in the shadows of the hall.

"We need medicine."

"I know."

"Proper medicine. We got a boat down at the docks. There are doctors in Port Augusta. It ain't that far."

"Are you completely insane? The worst storm we've seen in centuries is going on right outside our door, and you want to take a boat to Port Augusta?"

"If we don't, she dies."

Grady considered. "How do we even know what she needs? How can the doctors make a diagnosis without examining her?"

"We bring one back to the island."

"That would never happen. We might be insane enough to travel through a hurricane for Emma, but the rest of the world would not. As far as they're concerned, she's just another patient—one that can't be helped."

Grady tried to enter the bathroom again, but August grabbed his arm. "So that's it? We give up? Or maybe we start comin' up with solutions instead."

"Solutions. Such as?"

"We take her with us."

"She's too sick. I would never risk her safety for that. And don't give me the whole *'if we don't, she dies'* argument. Taking her onto those waters might as well be a death sentence. To all who go."

"Fine. We tell the doc what's wrong with her, and he gives us what she needs. We already know she has a fever and is coughing up blood."

"You're serious about this? About traveling to Port Augusta during a hurricane?"

"You go outside every day to face death, all to keep her safe. How is this any different?"

156

"The water isn't some feral animal I can put down with a bullet to the head. You can't fight the waves—you can't keep them from swallowing you up."

August chuckled. "You can't swim."

"Of course I can swim. Can you?"

"Nah, not really." The two of them glanced into the bathroom at Jon and Emma. "What about our masked friend in there? Think he can swim?" he asked, and Grady considered.

"This is crazy. Someone has to stay with Emma. Someone has to keep the house secure. Maybe just one of us should go."

"Two of us, and we draw straws."

After putting Emma back to bed, the Hunters left to develop a plan. They met in the parlor to keep their conversation a secret. Emma would never approve of them braving the dangerous waters on her account.

"So...fever, coughing up blood...anything else?" Grady asked while August snapped pieces of straw.

Jon waved an open palm and outstretched fingers over his neck. *Rash.*

"She's got a rash on her neck," August translated, but Jon tapped his shoulder to keep his attention. He motioned to August's back. "On her back, I mean. Sounds like Scarlet Fever to me."

"That's highly contagious."

August shrugged. "I had it as a kid. You?" he asked while holding out a fistful of straws. Grady nodded and pulled one. "What about you, big guy? Ever had Scarlet Fever before?"

Jon shook his head and took one of the straws.

"He wears a mask at all times around Emma. There's a good chance he hasn't been infected. If that is, in fact, what she has."

"Gentlemen. Let's see 'em."

The three of them opened their palms to reveal their straws. August smacked Grady's back. "Looks like you and I get a little bit of bonding time."

Jon drew the short straw, which meant he stayed behind with Emma. As much as Grady wished to say goodbye since it very well could be his last time seeing her, August convinced him it was best not to alarm her.

They ordered one of the essential workers to guard the door while Jon escorted them to the docks in the carriage. "This is madness," Grady muttered as they rode. The heavy rainfall on the carriage, the way the wind blew so ferociously that it swayed them as they moved, he could only imagine what being on the water might feel like.

August opened the carriage door and leaned his head out into the storm. "Jon! You doin' all right up there?"

"Close the damn door," Grady snapped while leaning over him to slam the door shut. The two sat in silence for a moment, and as Grady pouted, August's eyes burned into him. "This very well could be the last night of our lives; I'd like a bit of peace before we get there."

"You think he'll be all right getting' back?"

"I don't care," Grady snapped. His eyes met with August's hateful gaze, and he sighed—folding behind his tough exterior. "If anyone can make it back unscathed, it's Jon. He can brave the storm and take out any Howlers he might come across all by himself."

"That why you're okay leavin' him with Emma? You didn't really put up a fight there. I kinda expected you to. Doesn't seem like you enjoy leaving them alone with each other."

"I disapprove of Jon babying her, but…when push comes to shove, I know he'd die protecting her. That was never my issue."

"You scared of him?" The carriage rocked, causing Grady to grip the roof for support. Across from him, August smirked.

"I'm not scared of Jon."

"But you know she loves him."

Grady kept silent for a long time—staring at his own reflection in the blackened windows of the carriage. "Yes, I do know that. And the day that Jon gains any sense of self-worth is the day I lose her completely."

"What's that supposed to mean?"

"He doesn't think he deserves her. And frankly, he doesn't. He can't provide for her."

"I don't know if you've noticed, but no man can give Emma anything she doesn't already have."

"It's not just about money. He can't provide the love she needs. You think a man who can't even stand the sight of himself in the mirror can give her the love she deserves? It would be fueled by paranoia and insecurity, and Emma wouldn't know what to do with it. She wouldn't know how to convince him of anything. And how can she? He doesn't even love himself enough to believe he deserves her."

"Do you love yourself?" August asked.

"I do. I don't...love the things that I sometimes do. I have many...many regrets in my life. Things I wished I never did. Things I wish I would have done. Situations I wished I handled differently. But at the end of the day, I do love myself." Grady smirked. "Do I even need to ask?"

"Ask what?"

"You love yourself more than anyone."

A large grin spread across his face—accentuating his perfect white teeth as he twiddled his thumbs. "Yeah, that's probably true. But I can tell you right now, I got love for that girl back there," he said while pointing in the direction of the manor. "Wouldn't be sittin' here right now if I didn't."

The carriage came to a halt, and the door swung open with so much force that it hit the side of the cab. In the doorway, Jon clenched his coat around him.

The three Hunters marched through the storm, the wind blowing fiercely as the downpour soaked their clothes. "Hurry back to the house and tend to Emma. Do whatever you can to make her comfortable and try to keep her fever down!" Grady shouted through the storm.

They reached the wooden staircase leading down the bluffs to the docks. Grady gripped the railing, and it wobbled beneath the force. Beneath him, all he saw was a staircase leading into nothingness. A hand clasped his bicep, and with the storm and the darkness disorienting him, he almost fell backward. "What?"

August smirked and handed him a lantern. "Just making sure you don't blow away. Lightweight."

He yanked his arm from August's massive grip. The lantern's illumination only extended a few inches in front of him. His shaking hand clamped the soggy banister again, and as he took the first step down, his knee buckled. "What am I doing?"

A firm grasp at his coat pulled him back, causing his heart to leap into his throat. "Easy now," August warned. "Wanna hold my hand?"

Vertigo enveloped him. Dizzy, he squeezed his eyes shut and ran his cold, wet hand over his face. "Stop talking!" He shouted, and August only returned a hearty laugh.

He thought of Emma. It's the only thing that kept him going as he descended further—his leg shaking with every step he took. When another violent gust of wind blew through them, August tightened his grip on the back of his coat. It was only then he realized his comrade supported him the entire time.

When they reached the docks, Grady exhaled a breath of relief. The waves crashing onto the walkway reminded him, though, that the worst had yet to come. The waves were monstrous, splashing water all around, soaking the path in front of them. If a particularly large wave emerged, it could potentially take them both out to sea.

Grady held the lantern high to light the way to the Maddox boat—an old sailboat. "There!" He pointed. But the sail was torn—ripped to shreds from the storm, and the mast was snapped in half.

"I don't think that'll get us to the mainland!" August shouted. The waves tossed and turned the boat in its port, and it was only a matter of time before it capsized completely.

Lightning followed by a boom of thunder lit the night sky, and in the distance, the outline of what appeared to be a tug boat came into view. Once more, August's firm grasp on his shoulder startled him. "There! That's our ticket to the mainland."

Grady shoved his hand away. "That's not our boat!"

"No, but it might be his!" He pointed to the dock house buried in the cliffs. Through the window, a faint glow of light pulsed.

Grady banged on the wooden door as hard as possible and waited for a response, but none came. He banged again. "I don't think anyone's here."

"Someone's here. Fire's burning."

Grady banged again, only this time, the door flung open and revealed an old man. "What the hell do you want?"

"That your tug boat?" August asked.

"Yeah! Who's asking?"

"Monsieur, we're the Hunters of Point DuPont!" Grady shouted. "It is of the utmost urgency that you take us to Port Augusta immediately!"

"What?" the old man cried. Before Grady had the chance to speak again, August pushed him forward, forcing their way into the shack and slamming the door shut behind them. "You can't just barge into my house like that!"

"Monsieur, forgive the intrusion. We should speak inside what with the storm—"

"We need your boat," August interrupted.

"What for?"

"There's…a very sick girl on the island in desperate need of medication—medication she can only receive on the mainland. We have a limited amount of time to get to Port Augusta—"

"Have you lost your minds?" The old man bellowed. "There's a hurricane out there; we'd never make it to the port!"

161

"Monsieur, I can't help but notice the conditions in which you're living," Grady began. "The girl I'm speaking of happens to be Emma Maddox. I'm fairly confident that if you shuttle us safely to Port Augusta, Mr. Maddox would be most grateful. He might even consider giving you a reward for risking your neck."

"A reward, huh?"

"A...hefty reward."

The old man considered for a moment, studying Grady and August as he did. "You the Hunters?"

"Yes," Grady said through a polite smile.

"I want two-hundred."

"Done." An easy request as the Hunters made double that amount in a week.

"All right. Gimme some time to get the boat ready. You two just wait here."

The man bundled himself in a thick coat and scarf. He grabbed a lantern and exited the shack, giving the Hunters a moment to get warm and gather their thoughts.

Grady leaned on the table and twisted his body to the papers spread over the surface. "I feel like the wind might just blow him right off the docks," he muttered while sifting through a stack of magazines. His eyes narrowed at the sight of half-naked women on the front. *Pornography.* The realization made him sneer.

"What's he got there?" August asked, and Grady tossed one of the magazines to him. "Man's got good taste." He snatched one of them and plopped into a nearby splintered chair—kicking his feet up on the table while flipping through the pages. "And to think, he's willing to leave all this behind for two-hundred bucks."

Grady stared down his crooked nose at them. "Disgusting."

"What, pornography?" August's eyes met with his disapproving gaze. "We might possibly die tonight, and instead of taking one last look at a naked woman, you just sit there all high and mighty. That's fine."

The two were silent for a moment. He made a valid point, and at the risk of death, Grady set aside his concerns on sexually

162

exploitative literature. His fingers grazed one of the magazines. He turned his back to August and pried open the centerfold—eyes widening at the picture of a young, bare-chested blonde.

August chuckled. "That's what I thought."

Chapter XIII

Jon placed a wet rag on Emma's sweaty forehead. The impact of the cold bath already wore off, and sweat dripped from her brow—soaking her bed sheets. She writhed and groaned, her discomfort reaching an unbearable level.

"Stop, Jon." She pushed the rag away from her forehead. "I'm cold, I don't want it—" she coughed and turned to her side to lean over the bed, gagging from the force. Jon grabbed an empty wash basin for her in case she vomited, but nothing came. Once her coughing fit ceased, she picked her head up. "Why are you being so nice to me?"

He brought his right hand down into his left palm with a sharp motion, as if to slice his own hand. *Stop.*

"Don't tell me what to do!" She triggered another coughing fit and leaned over the edge of the bed. "Where's August?" He didn't respond. She leaned back onto her pillow, panting and grimacing. "My head… it's pounding."

He brought a glass of water forward and lifted her until her lips met with the brim. She took small sips, and when she winced, he replaced the glass on her nightstand. When her teeth chattered, he grabbed the comforter at the foot of her bed and pulled it over her.

Every move he made while tending to her, and even when he sank back into the armchair at her bedside, her eyes burned into him. "Where's Bones? I haven't seen her all evening." He glanced around the room, but the cat was the least of his worries. "You don't have to stay here, Jon."

I want to.

She forced a laugh. "No…you don't. Why, Jon, why have you…stayed for so long? You could have left so long ago…and you're still here."

He had no response. Instead of even contemplating an answer, he waited for her to continue her feverish rambling. Because no matter how many times she asked, his answer stayed the same.

Thunder crashed outside, causing Emma to flinch and grimace in pain as she gripped her head. "There are rats in the house," she muttered. "I can hear their little footsteps scurrying about."

There are no rats, he signed.

"Yes, there are!" she shouted and then coughed, but this time, blood spurted onto her lips. She wiped the wetness from her mouth, and when she saw the smeared blood on her hand, she only groaned. "Am I dying?"

I'll check for rats. He crossed the room and exited. After closing the door behind him, he fell into the wall and ripped the mask from his face. He struggled to take a breath, feeling as though the walls caved in all around him. The strain on their relationship from his rejection followed him around like a demon lurking in the night.

He hadn't had a good night's sleep since that night. And now, he feared he'd lose her forever.

He exhaled a heavy, shaky breath.

After a few moments, he replaced the nylon mask over his head and covered his face with the white kabuki mask. Once covered, he made his way to the first floor. Even though the house remained dim, he knew the halls well enough to navigate the darkness of the corridors.

He was cautious on the first floor—looking for any sign of Bones. The heavy rainfall on the roof made it difficult to hear anything else, but when he reached the doors to the dining room, a distant scratching on wood made him stop. Bones must be in the dining room, he thought. As he entered, though, a large, brown rat scurried away from him toward the kitchen.

The distant scratching continued. The further he walked, the louder it became, and when he entered the kitchen, three rats scurried away from him.

Jon hurried to the pantry and swung the door open. Inside, more rats helped themselves to the food supply, and though the light startled them into a frenzy, Jon realized they still weren't the source of the noise.

He stepped back out of the pantry and looked toward the loading bay. A solitary rat sat in the corner, soaking wet—cleaning itself. Jon set the lantern down, and with all his strength, slid the doors open. An explosion of noise erupted from within, scratching from little claws and squeaking and chirping from the sea of rats before him. He held up his lantern and stared at the invaders in wonderment. Though the loading bay remained sealed shut until delivery—they'd somehow found a way in to hide from the storm. In the center of all of them was Bone's lifeless body—her white fur stained with blood.

ဆာ

August hit the tug boat's deck with so much force that it knocked the wind out of him. The waves cut into the bow—causing the water to shoot up over the boat and splash down on the passengers. The frigid water stung August's skin.

Before he had a chance to grab anything for support, another wave kept him grounded. The water slickened the deck, and

166

August skidded, smashing his back into the winch. He shouted in pain. "Grady!"

Grady slid on the deck next to him, grabbing the winch for assistance. "You okay?" he shouted, but as the boat hit another monstrous wave, he lost his grip and fell to the ground beside him.

August grabbed his shoulder to keep him from sliding further back to the stern. "Hang on!"

Through all the madness of the storm—the rain, the enormous waves crashing into them—laughter emerged. They clung to the winch for support, while on the bridge, the old man whooped and hollered as he steered the boat. "He's absolutely mad!" Grady shouted.

Another massive wave crashed into the bow and knocked them both off-kilter. They collided with the deck again and skidded back to the stern. As August hit the gunwale first, Grady crashed into him, and he fought against the forceful blow and the violent winds. He climbed over his comrade and reached for the hawser—the thick cable used for towing other boats to safety. "Give me your hand!" he yelled to Grady, but the wind and the boat crashing into the waves kept him pressed into the gunwale.

August grimaced. He gripped the winch for support as the boat struck another wave. It was only a matter of time before Grady went overboard, he thought. Holding the winch, he used the other hand to further release the cable so Grady might be able to reach.

"August!" Grady shouted. "This is it!"

"Grab the cable!" When he did, August placed both his feet on the winch for stability and support. He gripped the hawser in both hands and, by sheer brute force, pulled Grady back toward the winch. "Just hang on!"

August's arms trembled from the strain of Grady's weight. He thought at any moment, his strength would give out, and Grady might go skidding back into the stern. But just before he reached muscle failure, Grady grabbed hold of the winch.

"How much further?" August shouted, but Grady only took labored breaths of ocean air—his arms wrapped tightly around the winch. "You good?"

"Here it comes, lads! Hang on to your dicks!"

Though the sea remained black as night, August sensed a towering presence. A large swell formed—preparing to crash down on top of them with a mighty fury.

August's gaze met with Grady's. He knew very well they might not survive. His only option was to interlock his arms and tighten his grip on the winch, just as his comrade did moments before.

୫୬

Jon salvaged the remaining non-perishables from the pantry, but with the storm raging on the island, he knew there wasn't much to be done about the rat infestation. What worried him most was the weakened walls of the house.

If rats could get into the loading bay, Howlers could as well. It was the first time he didn't have a commanding officer to bring his concerns to, and with no way to reach out to Grady and August, Jon did the only thing he could think to do.

He moved Emma to the servants' quarters.

"Why must I…be in here? It's so…claustrophobic—" another coughing fit began, and Jon pulled a wooden chair next to the small bed to be closer to her. He held her hair back with one hand and brought the washbasin to her with the other. "Did you…find the rats?" Jon shook his head. "What about Bones?" His blood ran cold. But once again, he shook his head. "I'm scared, Jon." He hesitated to respond, but he could think of nothing to comfort her with. "Will you draw something? Or…write something. Just…do something."

Jon inhaled sharply through his nose. He left her momentarily to gather his sketchbook and some charcoal pencils from his own quarters. He tore out any old pictures he'd drawn of her—he didn't want to risk her seeing them.

168

Upon returning to her bedside, he contemplated what to draw. He settled on a portrait of her—his most familiar subject. He outlined her face first. His thick, leather gloves made it difficult to detail her in the manner which he preferred. As he switched between pencils, he sensed her gaze upon him.

He drew her from memory. The last thing he wanted was to commemorate her current state, so he recalled his favorite image of her from her eighteenth birthday. Though it was many years ago, she still had so much hope in her eyes back then. And a face full of freckles from spending her days outside.

All her freckles disappeared over the years.

"You seem so peaceful when you draw." He did not acknowledge her. "Do you do it often?" He shook his head. "Do you hate me now, Jon?"

He stopped drawing—his narrowed eyes meeting with her worried gaze. *Never.*

"But you're angry with me."

He sighed, wracking his brain for the proper response. He contemplated being honest about why he walked out on her—his insecurity plaguing him every chance he had to be close to her. But he knew Emma. He knew she'd resent him for even thinking his appearance mattered.

Even though he knew it did.

He pointed to himself, crossed his arms over his chest, and then pointed to her. Despite her distress, she managed to smile. With both of his index fingers, Jon hooked them together, back and forth. And Emma's smile faded.

"As a friend," she whispered. She shut her eyes—her bottom lip trembling as a tear ran down her cheek. "I want you to know something, Jon. No matter what's happened in the past, no matter what's changed… it's always been you." She forced a laugh, but tears streamed down her face. "I've always loved you. Even as children, I always imagined you'd be the man I married—"

Her coughs began again, and when more blood hit her lips, Jon snatched a rag from the bedside and wiped her mouth clean. "All those times with Grady—" he tried to cover her mouth, but she pushed his hand away. Her eyes became heavy—words slurred. "Even when I was with him, I'd pretend it was you instead." Emma closed her eyes, her satisfied smile fading as she drifted away.

Jon's heart plummeted to his stomach and bounded. He grabbed her shoulders and shook her, but she didn't move. He shook her harder, but she remained still. He groaned—whined while shaking her, desperate to wake her, but nothing he did helped.

He pressed his ear onto her chest—her heartbeat weak and thready against him. The rise and fall of her chest, now more infrequent and labored. Jon ripped the covers from her sweaty body. He lifted her into his arms. The heat radiating from her alone made him sweat.

He had to cool her down. The cold bath didn't have a lasting effect, so he only had one option. When he reached the first floor, he set her down at the door to remove the deadbolt.

He cracked the door, but the ferocious winds from outside blew them open—crashing them into the side of the house. Already, the rain sprinkled Emma's face. He carried her into the night, into the middle of the raging storm—the air being cold and crisp enough that even he shivered.

When far enough outside, Jon fell to his knees with Emma cradled in his arms. The heavy rainfall soaked her within a matter of seconds, and steam rose from her skin.

The force of the wind blew Jon's hood back and shifted his mask, but the only thing he focused on was trying to say Emma's name. He rocked her—shook her while mouthing her name, but no sound left his lips.

He ripped his kabuki mask from his face and then the nylon black mask. It had been many years since Jon showed his face to Emma, but his labored breaths forced him to choke on the fabric. He needed fresh air. Now, he choked on the cool, crisp air instead.

The wind grew colder, the rain—harsher. A knot formed in the pit of his stomach and built from within his core only to rise to his throat. For reasons he did not know, his body's defense mechanism kicked in—alerting him of danger. A dark, intimidating presence approached, but only when lightning lit the sky was Jon able to see the surrounding area.

Their figures were unmistakable. The Howlers arrived, and Jon froze. Sudden movements risked a quick attack and brutal death for him and Emma. But staying in the rain, waiting for them to strike was suicide as well.

They stepped closer, and though their fur was blacker than the night, their low growls cut through the raging storm. His eyes adjusted to the darkness, and he made out their figures as they encircled him—ensnared him in their wicked game of cat and mouse.

Jon pulled Emma closer to him and pressed her face against his. He remained as still as possible, but one of the Howlers broke rank and approached. The massive paws hit the puddles of water and mud, the heavy, croaky breath of the animal came closer until Jon felt the warmth on his own face.

The animal jolted, causing him to flinch. Instead of an attack, however, it howled into the night sky. The other Howlers joined the cry, and only when lightning lit the area again did Jon notice the Howler assumed his place with the pack. Their howls weren't a war cry but something else entirely.

Chapter XIV

The tug boat arrived in Port Augusta, much worse for the wear. The two Hunters leaped from the gunwale onto the dock, and despite the storm still raging—splashing water onto the dock all around them—August never felt more relieved.

Through the rain and the gas lamps, a figure approached. "Have you lot lost your minds?" a dockhand yelled while clenching his coat around him.

"We need to get to Maddox house!" Grady shouted, but the dockhand lifted his lamp to August instead.

"Christ, what happened to you?"

He touched his face, wet from the rain, of course. But his fingertips were red—smeared with blood. "Shit, I'm just happy to be alive at this point."

Grady gripped the deckhand's shoulder. "Maddox house. Do you know anyone who can take us there?"

"It's the middle of the night!"

"It's an emergency! Trust me, we wouldn't be here otherwise!"

Maddox house in Port Augusta was unscathed by the storm. Its modern, brick exterior protected all those within and made it seem like the hurricane was nothing but a spring shower.

The short sprint between automobile and house already had them soaked. Before Grady could even bang on the front door, it swung open, and Byron stood before them.

"Come inside quickly."

The three congregated in one of the guest bedrooms. August tended to the wound on his face in the bathroom mirror. "Son of a bitch," he groaned while holding a rag over his face. "Think my nose is broken."

Grady leaned on the fireplace mantle, keeping warm with a towel wrapped around his shoulders. "Where is Arthur?"

"He's in London. He's been gone for a few weeks now. I have no way to contact him, not in time for him to help in any way."

"What about all the doctors?" August called from the bathroom and emerged in the doorway.

"I've sent for Doctor Bernard. He should be here soon. In the meantime, why don't the two of you get some rest? You've had quite an evening."

Grady muttered under his breath while pinching the bridge of his nose. "We can't just sleep while Emma waits for us to return. We need to get back to her as soon as possible."

"I couldn't agree more, Mr. McCoy. But seeing as how…the doctor is not yet here, and the storm continues outside, you don't have many options right now but to wait. Might as well rest for a bit."

August's shifty eyes darted back and forth between the two. "He ain't wrong, Grady. We can't do anything until the doctor gets here. And ain't no way in hell we're makin' it back to the island tonight with that storm bein' how it is."

173

"You dragged me here, convinced me to sail hurricane riddled waters. All to just give up when we've finally made it?"

"We ain't giving up, but let's think about this for a second. We ain't got no medicine, and we won't get any until the good doctor gets here. Even if he does get here tonight, that tug boat we *braved* the storm in isn't going to make the trip back. Not on those waters."

His lips pursed, and he averted his gaze to the rug beneath his soggy boots. "Very well."

August folded his arms across his chest, victorious in his argument. "Now, get out of my room."

"*Your* room?"

Byron smirked. "Mr. McCoy, if you follow me, I can show you to another, equally accommodating one."

The two of them left—closing the door behind them.

Other than the dull pain in his nose disturbing his breathing, everything seemed almost exactly as it was the night before he left for Point DuPont.

August flung himself onto the bed and kicked off his wet boots. He groaned while rolling onto his side. The crackling of the fire soothed him, and even the sound of the rain calmed him to a state of extreme relaxation until his breaths became slower, heavier, and he drifted to sleep.

His dreams, however, only delivered him back into the hungry sea's gullet—the tumultuous waves all but engulfing the small vessel once more. As the water crashed down around him, August clenched the winch that saved him and Grady's life—the cold, wet metal feeling all too real.

As the bow crashed into another ferocious wave, August's knees gave way. He looked to the bridge, but the crazy old man did not steer the ship. Instead, Emma stood atop the vessel.

"Emma!"

She looked down to him, struggling to keep in place on the deck below—fighting to stand through each wave that crashed down on top of him.

"Let go, August!"

"What?" he shouted.

"Let go! Let the water take you!"

To let go and succumb to the sea would surely mean death for him. How could she want that for him? He knew he couldn't hold on for much longer, though, and when the next wave crashed onto the vessel, August released the winch. His body propelled upward—losing all sense of time and space at that moment.

When he hit the water, a million pins and needles stabbed into him, stealing the breath from his lungs, and he gasped for air.

His own gasps tore him from his nightmare. At the edge of his bed, two little green eyes stared up at him. "August, wake up," she cried.

His breath caught in his throat. "Emma." Yes, he knew it was her after seeing the portrait back on Point DuPont. But why was the ghost of Emma's childhood haunting him?

Her little hand grabbed his, only this time, he didn't pull away from her. Instead, he got out of bed. Whatever was happening, Emma wanted him to see something. "Come on, August!" she shouted while running into the hall, and he hurried to follow her.

She led him down the stairs to the main hall. Through the rain and thunder, August detected muffled voices from the lounge.

He slowed his pace and dipped his head to better hear. "August," Emma whispered and then pointed to Arthur Maddox's study—the room where he first met the billionaire mogul.

"There somethin' in there you want me to find?" She only nodded. She ran across the hall into another room, disappearing from sight. "Wait!" But as he tried to catch her, Byron exited the room and crashed right into him.

"Mr. DeWitt? What are you doing down here at this hour?" Before August could even attempt to lie, a painting on the wall behind Byron distracted him.

"Has that always been there?" Byron looked over his shoulder to the panting of Emma as a child.

175

"Yes. It's Arthur's favorite portrait of his daughter, so he likes to display it in the main foyer." His hallucinations of little Emma all started to make sense.

"Everything all right, Mr. DeWitt?"

"Yeah," he grumbled. "Everything's fine. I must've...not have noticed it the first time, guess I just didn't know it was her." He'd lost his mind, he thought. He'd seen a portrait of Emma as a child and hallucinated her—it was the only thing that made sense to him. Not ghostly apparitions of girls who—to his knowledge—were still alive.

"Doctor Bernard should be here by morning. Is there anything I can get you in the meantime?"

Still, the closed door of Arthur Maddox's study beckoned him. Darkness overcame him—a looming sense of dread at the idea of ignoring his hallucination. It lingered even upon returning to his room. But giving in to such notions terrified him, for then he'd have to admit that he'd actually gone mad.

₭₮₱

Doctor Bernard arrived early in the morning. His first order of business was tending to August's nose. The retired fighter groaned when it snapped back into place, the crack of his bones causing Grady to wince.

"See? Told ya it was broken," August said through a stuffy nose while Doctor Bernard bandaged it.

"Does it hurt?" Byron asked.

"It's been broken before," August said through a stuffy nose. "Lotsa times." Still, the feeling of his bones grinding in his face never sat well with him. When finished, August moved to the corner of the room—ducking his head low to hide the tears swelling in his eyes. Arthur Maddox's study caught his attention across the hall from them, distracting him from his discomfort momentarily.

Grady exhaled a heavy breath through his nose—his lips pursed in a scowl. "Has Arthur been made aware of Emma's condition? Surely he'd come back to the island if he knew."

"He's unreachable at this time."

"Regardless, Emma is very sick. She needs medicine."

Doctor Bernard cleaned his spectacles with his coat—his gaze shifting back and forth between August and Grady. "What would you have me do? I am not there to examine her."

"Well, she has a fever, for starters," Grady said.

"She'll need aspirin then."

August scoffed. "Aspirin? That's it?"

"No, but the aspirin will help fight the fever. What else can you tell me?"

"She's coughing up blood."

The room fell silent, and Grady tore his eyes from the outdoors to face the somber men before him. "It's tuberculosis, isn't it?"

"Highly unlikely. She'd have no exposure to the disease while living such a reclusive life. It's more likely that she's coughed so much that the lining of her throat has become irritated, thus presenting blood in her sputum."

August winced. "She's got a rash on her back."

"A rash? Or a hot spot? How long has she been bedridden?" Doctor Bernard asked. "It could potentially be scarlet fever, but...according to my records, Emma had that as a child. She'll need an IV infusion of saline to keep her hydrated, aspirin to keep the fever at bay, and then we make her comfortable."

"That's it. There's nothing that can make it go away?"

Movement from the hall distracted August. Perhaps just a maid. But once more, the double doors leading to Arthur Maddox's study called to him.

"There is...something we can try," Doctor Bernard began. "Though it has really only been experimented with at this time. It's still pending FDA approval, and will be very difficult to get our hands on, though given Arthur Maddox's reputation, not entirely impossible."

"What is it?" Grady asked.

"I'll need to make a phone call. Byron? Have your lines withstood the storm?"

Byron smiled. "Right this way."

The two entered the next room. "Why does everything have to be so god damned difficult?" Grady groaned while sauntering toward the open doorway. "You'd think, given the circumstances, Arthur would have everything Emma could possibly need on standby."

"Who's he calling anyway?" August asked.

Grady leaned against the wall nearby the entrance and lowered his head. After a few moments of muffled voices, he shrugged. "Someone by the name of Flemming."

With Byron and Grady distracted, August knew it might be his only chance to get into Arthur's office. "I'll be right back," he said, leaving Grady to his eavesdropping. He snuck into the hallway and tiptoed across, but the doors were locked. "You gotta be…" Movement at the stairwell caught his eye, though, and upon seeing the young maid from his first visit to the mansion, August had a glimmer of hope. "Hey, remember me?"

She scoffed. "Oui monsieur." She winced. "What happened to your nose?"

August chuckled and touched the bandage, grimacing. "I busted it on the boat. Ain't nothin' I can't handle." She finished her dusting and moved past him to her next assignment, but August grabbed her arm. "Come on, don't be like that. You mad at me?"

"Mad? For what reason? You just disappear, and I never hear from you again?"

He shushed her and pulled her closer to him, and despite her irritation, the edges of her lips turned upward. "Well, had I known you wanted to hear from me again, I woulda written ya. Is that what you want?"

"No," she said smugly.

"Uh-huh. Hey, you got a key to this room?"

Her brow furrowed. "Oui."

"If I beg real nice, you think you'd be obliged to unlock it for me?"

"Why, so you can steal whatever you get your hands on? They'd throw me out on the streets."

"Darlin', I ain't got no reason to be stealin' from Arthur Maddox. The man pays me more money than I know what to do with." Her gaze shifted back and forth between August and the office. "Truth be told, Ms. Maddox asked me…to get something from…inside this room." She bit her lip—still hesitant. "Come on, if Arthur were here, I'd just ask him. But he's not."

She looked down the corridor in both directions, then pushed him aside. "Quickly, though. I can't explain cleaning this room twice today." She unlocked the door and pushed it open.

"Yes, ma'am."

The two of them entered, and the young maid closed the door behind them. She took her feather duster and dragged it along the bookshelves, all while keeping her eyes on August.

He hurried behind Arthur's desk. His hands sifted through everything on the surface, but nothing caught his eye.

"What are you even looking for?"

"Uh…just some…documents…I think."

"You think?" the maid asked, appalled.

He dropped into the chair and searched the drawers, but everything he came across was business-related—nothing of value to Emma. The longer it took, the more frazzled he became, and the young maid noticed. She stopped pretending to clean and watched him while twisting her feather duster between her fingers.

August stood and scanned the room, searching for anything that Emma might want him to find when his eyes landed on a safe embedded in the wall between the bookshelves.

"You have the combination to that?"

"No, of course not." August ran to the safe. It was a standard wall safe with a combination lock. He pressed his ear against the door and started twisting the lock. "What are you doing?"

"Shush!" His own heartbeat pounding in his ears made it difficult to hear anything. He ran back to the desk and rummaged through papers. "Do you know Arthur Maddox's birthday?"

"Uh…16th of December."

"What year?"

She shrugged. "How am I supposed to know?"

"How old is he?"

Her frantic eyes shifted back and forth as if searching the depths of her mind for the answer. "Uh…thirty-eight."

"Thirty-eight? That's not possible. That wouldn't make any sense—"

"No, I…I was the hostess for his birthday last December. He had an exclusive party, and there were thirty-eight candles. I know because I put them on the cake."

But August didn't have time to ponder all the reasons why it didn't make any sense. He ran to the safe. "That means he woulda been born in…1890…" He twisted the lock to 12-16-90. But it remained locked. "Shit."

"We have to go now. I can hear someone coming!"

Her panic made his mind race, impeding his ability to focus on his task. "Just…gimme a second. What about his wife? Arthur ever been married?"

She shook her head. "No, he's a famous bachelor. Never been married."

"What about Emma's mom then?" She shrugged and shook her head, much quicker and sharper in her movements. August wracked his brain. No wife, no anniversary to commemorate. The possibility that the combination was a random series of numbers disheartened him. Emma's birthday was the only thing that came to mind, and they only just celebrated the occasion. "October 26th…"

He twisted the combination to 10-26-04 and pulled the lever downward, and a loud click sent chills down his spine. He opened the safe. Inside, a stash of money and a pistol, but surely that wasn't what he was meant to find.

"Please hurry...someone is coming!"

"Mr. DeWitt?" Byron called from the hall.

August moved the pistol and money aside. He grabbed a large envelope and retrieved the papers within. He found paperwork for legal adoption with Emma's name and custody being granted to Arthur Maddox in 1908. He replaced the paper and shoved the envelope back into the safe.

A series of smaller envelopes hidden at the very corner of the safe caught his eye, though. He snatched and fanned through them. All the envelopes were stiff and weathered at the sides—sealed and then torn open again. They were all handwritten, addressed to a man named Phillip Wiseman from none other than Carlyle Gummar.

"Mr. DeWitt?" A knock came on the door.

The maid cupped her hands over her mouth. "He's coming inside!"

August shoved the envelopes into the back of his trousers and closed the safe. Before the double doors swung open, he looped his arm around the young and frightful maid's waist and pulled her into a kiss.

Byron cleared his throat. "Forgive the intrusion, but is this really the best time given the circumstances?"

August whipped his head to Grady and Byron in the doorway. "It's...a stressful situation." The young maid shoved him away and scampered out of the study, pushing past Grady as she did.

"What a gentleman you are," Grady barked, leaving August feeling rather sheepish. Though he'd much rather be considered a scoundrel than a thief.

Chapter XV

As the day progressed, the storm waned. Bolts of lightning no longer lit the sky, and crashes of thunder were too far to shake the foundation of Maddox House on Point DuPont. The rain continued, but the ferocity paled in comparison to the night before.

Jon stood in the parlor, staring out into the open, soggy field in front of the house. The very field that the Howlers encircled he and Emma, yet for some inexplicable reason, did not attack. But they howled through the night.

A carriage arrived in front of the house. Grady and August returned from Port Augusta with Doctor Bernard, and he hurried to the door to greet them. The three barged inside and marched to the stairwell, leaving Jon to barricade the door again.

"The antibiotics will take some time getting here, but the aspirin and IV fluids should help to stabilize her," Doctor Bernard said while ascending the stairs, and Jon raced to catch them.

Grady led the way to Emma's bedroom. He burst through the door, but her bed remained empty—perfectly made as if no one had been in there for days. He whipped around, and only then, acknowledged Jon's presence.

"Where is she?" he shouted.

Jon pointed to the ceiling.

"She's upstairs?" August asked. Jon nodded and held up four fingers. "Servants quarters." August led the way.

As Grady followed close behind, he nudged Jon in passing. "Why is she up there?"

The four of them entered the room where Jon kept Emma, but she remained asleep—pale and face wet with sweat. Immediately, Grady sat beside her.

"Emma? What's wrong with her?"

"She's unconscious." Doctor Bernard shooed Grady away and sat at her bedside, and after checking her vitals, he confirmed her dire state. "We'll have to start IV infusion immediately. When she wakes, we can give her the aspirin, but not while she's like this."

Jon sighed and ran his hands over his mask. As much as he wanted to stay by Emma's side, his tolerance for the men around him already waned. Too many people at her bedside, and there was no longer room for him, so he excused himself.

Jon wanted peace, but the Hunters had other plans.

"Hey!" August called after him and chased him down the hall. "You okay?"

Jon nodded and then pointed to August. *You?*

"It's been…a crazy night."

Jon pointed to the nose of his mask—questioning August's injury.

Before he could answer, Grady marched into the hallway—his hateful stare on the masked Hunter. "Why was Emma moved to the servants' quarters? Why is she unconscious?"

"All right, easy now," August said while holding Grady back. "Man's had a tough night."

"It's nothing compared to what we've been through." His piercing gaze settled on Jon—who became hardened to that accusatory expression. "What happened? I leave you in charge, and she's unconscious."

Jon signed, aggressive in his movements, and August winced. "He said that she's sick…there wasn't anything he could do. He did what he could to cool her off, but she just never woke up."

183

Grady scoffed and stepped away, but only seconds later doubled back—his face inches away from Jon's mask as if to challenge him. "And why is she up here?"

But Grady did not scare him. He glanced to August, unsure of how to even begin to explain. Instead, he thought it best to show them. *Follow me.*

He led them to the first floor and into the dining room. They followed him to the kitchen. When Jon pulled open the doors to the loading bay, the infestation of rats caused even more concern than the sick lady of the household.

"How could this have gone unnoticed for so long?" Grady muttered as he stared at the sea of rodents in shock and disgust.

"Probably seeking shelter from the storm," August said. "What's this?" he asked while poking a stiff object wrapped in a pillowcase.

Jon sighed. *Bones.*

"Right. We seal off this section of the house until the storm dies down completely. We won't be able to get anyone here to fix it until then. From this moment forward, gentlemen, we're on threat con delta. We'll be working in shifts, but someone always needs to remain on the first floor. In the dining room, preferably. In case a Howler gets inside."

August lifted a lazy hand. "I'll take the first shift."

"Very well. If one does get inside, try to lock it in the dining room and come get me and Jon immediately, understood?"

"Yes, sir."

∞≪

In the dining room, August kicked one of the ornate chairs backward and plopped down, kicking his feet up on the table to relax. He knew he'd more than likely be there for a while, which suited him just fine. Since getting his hands on Carlyle's letters, it's all he thought about.

Jon entered the dining room behind him. He stopped at the head of the table and hesitated—lingering momentarily and then continuing to the dining room's exit.

And then he stopped again. *Need anything?*

"Nah, nothing." Jon pointed to the nose of his mask again. August reached to the bandage on his face and winced at the touch. "I busted it on the boat. Trust me, I've suffered through way worse."

I took Emma outside.

August's gaze lingered as he played back the hand motions in his head, wondering if maybe he misinterpreted them. "You what?"

Outside. Last night.

Unsure of how to respond, he contemplated his options. On one hand, he appreciated Jon opening up to him since their last encounter strained their relationship. On the other hand, he worried he might come off as judgmental if he asked any questions. "Uh…" August laughed in an attempt to ease the rising tension. "Why would you…do that?"

Cool her, he signed.

August nodded. "Okay. Good. Did it work?"

Jon hung his head. *A little.*

"Uh-huh. Why are you telling me this?"

Howlers. Jon refused to look at August for some reason. Shame, perhaps. Or maybe he was just afraid of how August might react.

"Did something happen?"

Jon shook his head. *They left.*

His distress was palpable. Whether it was the fact that the Howlers left them alone or that he endangered Emma's life, something was not sitting well with him. "Jon, listen to me. I don't care what you do, honestly. I know you love and care for Emma, and you're gonna do what you feel you have to do to help her. One thing I am gonna say, though, don't…tell Grady what you just told me."

Jon tipped his head to him. He lingered for a short while, then turned on his heels and left the dining room—closing the door behind him. As curious as the confession seemed, Carlyle's letters burned a hole through his hands.

June 1st, 1928

Phillip,

I know I haven't been as responsive as in the past. Things are going on in this house that I can't even begin to describe. I've mentioned a few oddities in previous letters. The muted, burned man who always wears a mask, the ex-mercenary who (according to Emma) abandoned his wife and family. And the Howlers themselves, unlike any other critter I've ever seen before.

Like a dire wolf, remember from those books you like to read? Least, that's how I pictured them when you read me those novels overseas.

But the strangest thing by far has to be the lady of the house herself, Emma Maddox. I know this sounds crazy, and maybe me having been here for over a year now, I'm starting to lose my mind, but there's something off about her. I always liked her, and even writing to you, the closest person in my life, I feel guilty saying it about her. You'd really like her too.

She gets into these fits, though, these emotional little tirades (like when your mom has too much to drink, haha) only bizarre things happen when it happens to her. I haven't been able to get any concrete evidence because every time she gets all emotional, the ex-merc sedates her.

Things will move, though, only a little bit. The flames dance higher, the wind blows harder. Rain will come out of nowhere.

That's crazy, right?

I'm kind of drunk writing this, too, so maybe I'm just dramatic, but I'm thinking about making her mad just to see what happens before Grady steps in and ruins the fun.

In all seriousness, though, she's a strange bird. They keep telling me she's crazy, but I don't think that's the case. She doesn't seem crazy, just odd. But how could she not be after being locked inside for God knows how long? What concerns me the most is that they keep saying she's dangerous. I don't see how a woman of her upbringing can be considered dangerous.

More to come on that later.

Forever yours,
Carlyle

August would be lying if he pretended to not have similar thoughts about Emma. A very odd woman indeed, but what grabbed August's attention was the conclusion Carlyle started to draw about her nearly a year after his employment.

It was a realization he could not ignore, not after witnessing what happened the night she lost her temper. The night that he provoked her into a vengeful state. "Oh, Emma. What is going on with you?"

June 21st, 1928

Phillip,

I know I've been saying it since my first week here, but there is something very peculiar going on in this house. I'm starting to get scared, which sounds ridiculous, I'm sure. We fought in the war together, and you know better than anyone how I am, how skeptical I can be. But I'm starting to think the Howlers aren't the only thing to be concerned about on the island.

I haven't been sleeping very well lately and have been waking up with headaches. There's something in the walls, some kind of electric current. It's not like normal electricity either. I can hear it when I press my ear against it. There have been people going in and out of the basement for weeks, and Emma hasn't been allowed on the first floor in that time.

They're building something below our feet. I can feel the vibrations. I've tried to talk to Jon, but he acts like he has no idea what's going on around here. All he does is swoon over Emma, the git. If I cared more about the situation, I'd just tell him that she's in love with him too.

Even Emma doesn't seem to know what's happening in the basement. I think my best option is to get closer to Grady and find out from him.

Love,
Carlyle

June 30th, 1928

Phillip,

I can't take this anymore. I'm starting to lose my mind. The treatment of this woman is horrifying, and I'm certain that her doctors have broken every oath they took in medical school. How Arthur Maddox can continue on with his daughter being treated in such a way, I'll never understand.

At first, I tried to ignore it. It was my job to follow orders, but to do this to a young woman is sickening. She's constantly sedated, force-fed when too upset to eat, hydrated through IV when too distraught to drink. I used to justify it by saying, oh, she's rich. She gets whatever she wants, but the men in this house treat her as if she isn't a person but a monster.

We have to help her. If the authorities knew about these things, they'd take her out of here and place her in a hospital, which is maybe what she needs—real doctors who abide by their Hippocratic oath. Perhaps you can speak to one of your friends in social services? What might I need to do to get her the help she needs?

They give her medicine every morning and night, a shot they say that helps her moods. I was a medic in the Army, and though I'm not a doctor, I cannot think of any medication administered that way for moods. Something is wrong.

Carlyle

August 15, 1928

Phillip,

I have not heard back from you since May, and I'm starting to become concerned. I found out what's in the basement! It's a cell for Emma, a prison cell, almost, but without bars. Instead, it's built with some sort of glass and iron casing. I managed to pick the lock one night when everyone was asleep. There's a bed and a bookshelf, everything she might need, but why do they need a cell for her?

For some reason, the electric current I told you about grew stronger down there too. You can hear it the further you get into the basement. The cell is surrounded by circuit breakers, and it smells like copper wire down there. Maybe that's why the Hunters are acting strange; they know that I know they're up to something!

I can't wait around to find out what's going on here. I fear for my safety and Emma's as well. I need to get off this island and far away, and I need to get her help. Did you manage to contact anyone from social services?

Love,
Carlyle

August 20th, 1928

Phillip,

*I can't do this anymore. They know I know something; I
can feel it. Jon has been keeping his distance, and Grady
has been overly friendly. I don't want to cause a scene. I
need to secure my resignation and leave this island
immediately. It's the only way I can help Emma before
they do something that ends up killing her.*

*No need to respond to this letter. I'll be home before you
know it. This is the only way I can save myself and her.
We'll be going hunting today. Once we return, I'll submit
my resignation letter to Grady and hopefully be on the
next ferry to Port Augusta.*

I love you.
Carlyle

Carlyle's last and final letter, never even sent. None of the
letters he wrote in the last few months of his life were ever sent.
August could only speculate that Grady—or Arthur Maddox—
screened all the letters leaving the island. It made sense, given
what they were hiding.

Carlyle discovered the cube, and August became convinced
that his desire to save Emma is what cost him his life. Of course,
it could have just been a coincidence that he died the same day he
wrote that letter to Phillip. But after what Jon said about Carlyle's
death, it seemed unlikely.

For the first time ever, not having any family to write home to
seemed like a blessing.

He folded all the letters and shoved them back into the
envelopes before tossing them into the colossal fireplace. After

that, he built a fire, burning away all the evidence that he ever had them.

Even more suspicious, if Arthur Maddox were truly only thirty-eight years old, that would mean he adopted Emma when he was only eighteen—him having been only fourteen when Emma was born. It was a matter of public record that Arthur Maddox assumed control of his family's estate on his eighteenth birthday. And what eighteen-year-old decides to adopt a child after inheriting one of the largest estates in the world?

Chapter XVI

Just as Grady directed, the Hunters worked in shifts guarding the first level in the event a Howler made it into the loading bay, but it wasn't all that he expected of them. Whoever was not guarding the first floor sat with Emma in case she awoke—and the solitary Hunter caught between those two shifts got to rest.

By the time August made it back to his room, it was nearly midnight—leaving Jon on guard duty and Grady sitting at Emma's bedside. He had her moved back to her own bedroom, knowing she'd be more comfortable and safer now that all the Hunters were back at the house. At her bedside, Doctor Bernard set up an IV to keep her hydrated. After nearly twelve hours of infusion, Emma opened her eyes. "Grady," she murmured.

Her eyes fluttered, and he dove to her bedside, grabbing her hand for comfort. "Darling, you had me worried sick."

"What time is it?" she asked. "Where's Jon?"

She struggled to sit, but Grady pushed her back onto the bed. "It's past midnight. Jon is in the dining room. You still need to rest." He grabbed the bottle of aspirin on the bedside table and poured two pills into his palm. "Take these." He handed her a glass of water, and after taking the medicine, she rested her head on her pillow.

"My throat is killing me."

"You've been very sick. But don't worry, we're going to get you better." He brushed a bit of hair off her forehead, but she whipped her head away. "Emma, don't act like this."

She buried her face into her arm and coughed so hard that her lungs rattled. When Grady reached for her again, she shoved his hand away. "So, because I'm sick, all your past transgressions are forgiven? Spare me your concerns. Your love for me is beneficial to you; that's it."

"Beneficial? You think...loving you benefits me in some way? You think it gives me joy? It's torture," Grady snapped, causing her to flinch. He grabbed her shoulders and lifted her from the bed. He shook her, his fingers digging into her arms. "I've thrown away everything for you."

"I never asked you—"

"You don't have to ask. But you are sorely mistaken if you think me loving you has been beneficial to my life in any sort of way. I fell so hard for you Emma, I loved you...so much. But you just brushed me aside and treated me like trash, after everything I threw away for you." Tears burned his eyes. As his face grew hot, he became unsure whether he felt more angered or heartbroken by her words.

"Grady, let go."

"Nothing I ever do is good enough for you."

"What did you think? That I'd be satisfied being your whore for the rest of my life?"

Finally, he released her and stood. He tried his best to maintain some modicum of composure, but his anger overtook his anguish. Instead of just walking away, defeated and heartbroken, he swung his arm across her vanity, shattering and knocking everything she owned to the ground.

Emma's gasp made him retreat. He refused to look at her, though. Out of shame. "Forgive my outburst. I think…I just need some sleep."

He stepped over the mess. Like a wounded animal scurrying off to lick its wounds, Grady stormed out of her room.

While marching down the hall, a burning rage grew inside of him. He hated her, but his hatred turned to guilt—and great despondency followed. He was torn in two different directions, his heart shattering at her reaction to him, but his ego did its best to turn that heartbreak into anger.

He banged on August's door. When it swung open, Grady grimaced. "I'm sorry to disturb you. I know you've been resting."

"It's okay. What can I do—?"

"Emma's awake."

August nodded. "Oh. Good. Is she—?"

"I need you to sit with her. If you don't mind. I don't want her to be alone, but I can't—" Grady exhaled a shaking breath.

"Whoa…easy, pal." August placed his hand on his shoulder, but Grady pushed him away.

"I've sacrificed everything for her," Grady sobbed. "How…how did I let things get this way? All I've ever done was love her—"

A stinging sensation knocked him back into the opposing wall. His cheek throbbed from the force of August's smack. "Come on, pull yourself together. You know, sometimes you get rejected. And I know it feels fucking terrible, but it's not the end of the world."

Grady leaned his head back. "How do you do it?"

August's eyes narrowed. "Do what?"

"Live your life…entirely for yourself." August only averted his gaze. "What I would give to not…feel for anyone. To live my life the way you do. Without anyone to break me."

August groaned. "You don't have to take this, Grady. I don't for one second see you as the victim in this scenario. I think you've done your fair share of damage to Emma as well. But you can say enough is enough. What's keeping you here? The idea that maybe one day she'll forget all the horrible things you two have done to each other, and you'll live happily ever after?"

Grady sneered. "I don't know."

"You ain't obligated to anybody in this world no matter what people say. Go home, Grady. Or don't. Pack up your shit and go to…fucking Florida, for all I care. Your life isn't over because you fell in love with the wrong person and made some fucked up decisions. But it will be over if you stay here on this island."

"Are you threatening me?"

"No. But this right here, what you're doing? It ain't healthy. And it will kill you, eventually. Maybe not today or tomorrow, but this story doesn't end well for you." He moved past him and disappeared into the dark hallway ahead, leaving Grady with his pain, and even worse, his thoughts.

ഔ൪

August entered Emma's bedroom, and when she picked her head up from her pillow, he smiled. "How was your nap?"

Emma scoffed and folded her arms across her chest. "You have no tact, August. Did Grady send you in here to check on me?"

"What do you think?" His eyes narrowed to the mess of shattered glass and water scattered beneath the vanity. "Yikes." He stepped over it all and settled into the chair beside her bed.

She leaned her head back onto her pillow, but her eyes narrowed to him. "What happened to your nose?"

August chuckled and touched the bandage, wincing as he did. "Busted it."

"On what?"

"The boat."

She stared at him for a moment, trying to piece together the information he shared with her. "What boat?"

"Uh…the boat to Port Augusta." He waited for her to say something, but she only gazed at him. "Grady and I caught a boat to Port Augusta to get you some medicine."

"During the hurricane?"

He nodded. "Yep. So whenever you feel like no one cares about what's going on with you, just know there are at least two men in this household who would take on a hurricane to take care of you."

Her eyes became wide. "Jon didn't…?"

August shook his head. "Nah. But don't let it get to you. He drew the short straw and had to stay behind."

"The short straw," she said pointedly.

"Yeah, but…truth be told, I think he wanted to stay back with you. Not that I don't think he'd take on a hurricane for you—"

"I'm glad you're all right."

"You're gonna be okay too. Your medicine should be here in a few days. It'll be like nothing ever happened. Just…try to take it easy, all right? Don't go gettin' into any heated debates." Emma chuckled, but it escalated into coughing. August handed her the glass of water from her nightstand. "Can I ask you something?"

She took a sip, handed him the glass, and sunk back down into the bed. "I suppose."

"What's your earliest memory on the island? You've lived here…practically your whole life, right?"

"Why do you ask?"

He shrugged. "I dunno. My earliest memory of childhood was…my mama takin' me to the state fair when I was just a little kid. I don't remember exactly how old I was, but I know it was before Jack was born. Me and mama were best friends, we spent all our time together. But she took me to the Georgia State Fair…I don't remember where my dad was, probably workin' that day. My mama bought me a soda pop…a Dr. Pepper, and I thought it was the best thing I'd ever had…to that point." Emma forced a smile. "But I remember they had cage fighters there. I wandered into the tent and just saw these two grown men beatin' the ever-lovin' shit outta each other… 'scuse my language—"

Emma shook her head. "I've heard worse."

"I thought it was…pretty cool, though. I was so close to the cage that when one of the fighters, the losing fighter, got thrown into the chain link, the blood on his face splattered onto me. His opponent thought he had him right then and there. But I remember lookin' into that man's eyes and seeing something incredible."

"What?"

"He hadn't given up. The other fighter dropped his guard because…he thought he had him, ya know? But just when he thought he won, the guy swung on him. Cracked him right in the back of the head. Total knock out."

Emma raised an eyebrow. "This is your first memory? That's horrifying."

August laughed. "Nah, it was amazing. I knew from that day forward I was born to be a fighter. Never wanted to do anything else." His reputation as a shamed fighter overtook his thoughtful moment. His fall from grace, it haunted him. "For a short while, I was known as the best cage fighter in North America. *The Unbeatable August DeWitt,* they called me."

"What happened?"

The memory of Jack's death, the downward spiral as a result, it distracted him from his goal. Now, all he felt was shame. "I took a dive. Another manager paid me to lose to his fighter, and I accepted."

"So, you were no longer unbeatable?"

August's eyes widened, and he chuckled. "No, everyone knew I was still unbeatable. They knew that if I tried, I woulda killed that fighter in the cage. No one bought that I'd lost to this kid from Winnipeg. They knew I'd been paid to do it. That's when everything went to shit." He thought for a moment. "I think if I woulda lost fair and square, I coulda recovered from that. I'd no longer be known as unbeatable, but…people would still wanna see me fight. Thing is, though, when people know you're swayed by money—take a dive there, forfeit the fight here—it ruins everything. I...ruined everything."

"Why'd you do it if you knew you could beat him?"

He hesitated to answer—unsure of whether or not he wanted Emma knowing such terrible things about him. He hung his head, contemplating. He needed catharsis. "A few months before, Jack...he was hit by a car walking home from one of my fights. I usually walked with him, but...not that night. I wanted to stay and enjoy my victory with all the beautiful women and high society. My brother died because...fame and fortune became more important than his well-being."

"August... that's not your fault."

"I appreciate you saying so, Emma. But it is my fault. And after that happened, I just didn't care about anything. I was offered more money to take a dive than I woulda been awarded for winning. I'd fired my own manager in a drunken stupor, so I didn't have anyone lookin' out for me. Hell, I sure as shit couldn't look out for myself after all that."

"Is that why you're here now?"

August nodded. He watched her, deeply appreciative of her at that moment. He wasn't sure if it was because she had no knowledge of the outside world or how deep his shame ran. She maintained a kind smile, and he knew that despite the horrible things he told her, she saw him no different.

"I'm sorry, I was tryin' to find out more about you, and I completely made this about me."

She outstretched her fingers to him. "For what it's worth, I think you're a very decent man. A little rough around the edges, but...with a heart of gold." Her words touched him. He dipped his head to hide the burning of his eyes. Instead of thanking her, he forced a laugh to dislodge the lump forming in his throat. "Would you mind terribly if I went to sleep now? I feel so...tired and drained—"

It was the perfect out. "Yeah, you...you get some rest. I'll be here if you need me," he said in a low, gruff tone.

She turned onto her side and pulled the covers to her chin. With her back now to him, he no longer felt the need to hide the expression on his face—the tears burning his eyes. She accepted him despite all the horrible things he did before knowing her. To her, he was redeemable. It was the first time since the accident that he was able to imagine a world without his shame and grief.

⅋ℴ

Within two days, Emma's medicine from the States arrived. Doctor Bernard stayed by her bedside within the first few doses to assure no adverse effects be present, but within twenty-four hours, Emma's condition improved.

The rain finally stopped, but the landscape of the island remained wet and soggy. A thick layer of fog blanketed the long grass, and the only bit of light breaking through in the early morning painted the scene in light blue and nothing more.

August finally emerged from Emma's room after a long night of monitoring her. He walked into the dining room to find Jon standing at one of the windows, staring out into the thick fog. The days had not been kind to the Hunters, their exhaustion having reached a peak level.

To make himself more comfortable, Jon had removed his jacket, rolled up his sleeves, and removed his kabuki mask, wearing only the thin, black nylon mask to cover his burned face.

The exhaustion in Jon's eyes was unmistakable, but even more discerning, his sincere misery. "Hey," August muttered while nodding his head to the weary Hunter. He sank into one of the chairs and kicked his legs up on the table. "You feelin' all right? Not gettin' sick, are ya?"

Jon shook his head.

The two were quiet for a while. August picked the skin at the base of his fingers, trying to think of anything to say to the brooding Hunter.

Jon turned to him. *I'm a fool.*

"How so?"

Emma. His breath shook as he dropped his hands to his side—his frantic eyes darting across the floor. Finally, he lifted his hands again. *She almost died.*

August nodded slowly. "Yes, she did."

Jon hesitated to sign. *I love her. I want to be with her.*

"You gonna tell her?" he asked, and after a brief moment of hesitation, Jon nodded. August's stomach turned. He shifted in his seat and cleared his throat. "There's, uh... there's just one problem with that, Jon. I...love her too." The masked Hunter faced him—his gaze cold and unwavering. "I just don't think you're good for her. You can't help her." Jon marched to him. With every step, August kept his eyes on the hunting knife at his side, anticipating an attack. When within arm's reach, Jon stopped, and he cocked his head to the side inquisitively. "You wanna keep her locked up here forever. Just like Grady." Jon shook his head. "You know it's true. You're afraid she'll get a taste of the world out there and forget all about you. It's the only reason you haven't taken her out of here sooner."

Safe here.

August stood, slamming his fist on the table as he did. "No, she's dying here, Jon. Can't you see that? Think back on the girl she used to be. Is it anything like how she is now? And you've done nothing to make it better! Why can't you see that if she stays locked up here any longer, she is going to die?" He grabbed Jon's arm and pulled him closer. "If you have any love for her, Jon, you'll keep this confession to yourself. She deserves better. She deserves a man who will stand up for her."

August pushed past him to exit the dining room, but when a loud thud landed next to his head, he jolted. Jon's hunting knife splintered the wood of the door. He looked over his shoulder to the masked Hunter, still standing in his throwing position.

He yanked the knife from the wood. "Nice shot."

I missed.

The retired fighter studied the knife, contemplating. He could kill Jon right then and there, he thought. Not to eliminate competition, but to assure Emma's escape from Point DuPont. When he thought of Emma, though, he resigned himself to practicality, knowing she'd never recover from Jon's death.

August approached him, and when next to the dining table, he stabbed the knife deep into the surface. "You didn't miss. You're not a killer, Jon." He lingered, waiting for the moment where his comrade might drive the knife deep into his chest. But it never happened, and August turned on his heels and marched out of the dining room—certain now that Jon posed no threat to him.

Chapter XVII

Emma awoke later in the evening with no one at her bedside. The fire nearby popped and cracked as the flames danced and devoured the wood. Someone stoked it recently, she thought. The heat made her sweat. She flung the blankets from her body and sat at the edge of her bed—finally having the strength to do so on her own. After taking a deep breath, though, she winced—her chest still tight and rattling from illness.

The wind howled against the house—creaking and shifting its aged foundation. On nights like this, Jon usually sat with her, and she read to him until her eyes became too heavy to keep open. At least, that's how things used to be.

She missed having him at her bedside.

Emma tiptoed down the corridor from her room to the stairwell, taking special care when passing the hall near Grady and August's rooms.

As she ascended the darkened stairs, she tightened her robe—the cold becoming much more prevalent the higher she climbed. The steps she took winded her, and when little black spots invaded her vision, she gripped the railing and took deep, labored breaths. By the time she made it to the fourth floor, her knees shook, and she held the post and lowered herself into a crouch. She stayed that way until the heartbeat in her ears and pulsating vision subsided.

The splintered, wooden floors leading to Jon's room in the servants' quarters creaked with every step she took. With the staff still evacuated to Port Augusta, the fourth floor's isolation unsettled her. Devoid of life and hidden away in the furthest reaches of the house, the idea that Jon preferred ostracization broke her heart. He deserved better. He deserved warmth.

She stopped in front of his bedroom door, and after a few deep breaths, she knocked. "Jon?" No response or movement from within. She knocked again. "Jon?"

She twisted the knob, surprised to find it unlocked. The moon shined through his lone window and illuminated his neatly made bed—the gas lamp on his bedside, cold to the touch.

Jon hadn't been in his room all evening.

Emma sat on the edge of the bed and glanced around the empty, drab room. Despite the isolation, even being in his private dwelling space without him comforted her. His presence lingered, and wrapped around her like a thick, warm blanket—shielding her from the cold and anxiety of the night.

She rested her head on his pillow, his scent wafting up around her and causing her to smile. She wrapped her arms around it, pretending it was him instead. But in doing so, her fingers ran across something small and metal—a silver embellished case about the size of her palm. Inside, an ambrotype of herself from her seventeenth birthday.

She remembered the day she sat for the photograph. Her father insisted. Seeing the photograph, though, broke her heart. Not because her father decided not to keep it, but because Jon kept it under his pillow.

A large pad of sketch paper resided on his desk.

Other than a half-finished portrait of her, the sketchbook remained empty. Floored by his hidden talent—one he did well to hide—the fold of the pad is what intrigued her. She ran her fingers

204

over the jagged, frayed edges in the center. Pages were missing—lots of them. She opened one of his desk drawers where he kept charcoal pencils and a collection of small knives.

The drawer beneath that, she found a stack of sketch paper, and grabbed them to flip through them. In the beginning, drawings and sketches of her in beautiful gowns and ornate jewelry stole her breath away. He drew her in various poses, some close-up and some far away. Yet as beautiful as the pictures were, they sickened her.

Even more impressive than hiding his hidden talent for drawing for so many years—his ability to hide her as his muse. Because by the looks of it, she was his only subject.

She flipped through more pages. As they went on, the portraits became more detailed. And the fewer clothes he bothered to draw for her until he stopped bothering entirely. She threw the papers on the desk and sobbed—snatching her mouth to try and muffle the sound.

Jon betrayed her. As children, they promised never to lie to each other. He told a lie so massive it almost destroyed her. She wiped the tears from her face and looked over her shoulder to his bed again. The painting she did weeks ago hung above his bed.

The bedroom door opened, and Emma whipped around to meet Jon's inquisitive gaze from the doorway. His presence froze her—stopped her beating heart right in her chest. After a few moments, he closed the door behind him and approached her—his boots thudding against the wooden floor with every step.

The cold, metal casing of the ambrotype in her hands brought her back to reality. Jon hurt her, lied to her. And his reasons, whatever they may be, seemed completely irrelevant.

"Where did you get this?" she asked while holding up the ambrotype, and he stopped within inches of her. "Did my father give it to you?"

I took it, he signed.

"Why?" He reached his gloved hand to her. "Don't," she snapped, shoving his hand away from her, and he retreated.

205

He snatched a chair instead and motioned for her to sit.

"I'm not taking orders from you anymore. Not from anyone. This is my house, my life. I'm in charge here." Jon nodded. She held up the ambrotype again. "Why'd you take it?"

Jon's breath shook, and he hung his head. As if ashamed.

He motioned to himself, crossed his arms over his chest, then pointed to her firmly. Reiterating with a shaking finger, *I love you.*

She sobbed again. "You lied to me. You made me think I was…unworthy of your love—" He started to sign, but she turned her back—eliciting a whine from him. "I don't care about the reason. I'm not real to you; I'm…just a fantasy. I'm just…a thought that keeps you company at night—a daydream to pass the hours in the day. You could have had me, all of me, in real life. Instead, you choose…this fantasy version of me that doesn't exist—"

He grabbed her arms—his head whipping back and forth in disagreement. "Get off—" He pulled her into him, tried to embrace her. "Get off of me!" she screamed and smacked him so hard that he staggered into his desk, leaving his mask askew. "Stay away from me, Jon. Stay away forever. You can hide away in here with all your drawings, your paintings, your fantasies…and this." She threw the ambrotype on the ground. "I hope it'll keep you warm at night." She stormed past him, ignoring his attempts to reach for her, and his cries after she slammed the door behind her.

When Emma reached the second floor, her knees gave out. She gripped the railing of the stairs, once more taking labored breaths to calm herself, but the tightness in her chest caused pain with each and every attempt. Only this time, she wasn't sure if the pain came from her illness or her broken heart.

She sobbed. She needed comfort, but the only person she ever sought security from became the reason for her devastation. Her feelings of abandonment, rejection, and debilitating solitude only lasted a moment when her eyes wandered down the hallway to

August's room. The thought of him gave her a sliver of peace. And hope.

She knocked on his door, careful not to alert Grady from across the hall. After a few moments of no answer, she knocked once more but resigned herself to the thought that August might be sleeping. Defeated, she turned away, but the door swung open.

August's brow furrowed. "Emma?"

She hesitated to speak, her words failing her once in front of him. "I was just...I shouldn't have bothered you, I'm sorry—"

He gripped her arm gently. "Hang on now; why are your eyes red?" It's all it took for the tears to start again. When she sobbed, he pulled her into him. "What happened? Bad dream?"

She whimpered into his chest to muffle the sound. "It's Jon."

August inhaled deeply. "Come on." He draped his arm around her shoulder and escorted her into his bedroom, closing the door behind them. A low fire crackled and warmed the room. His blankets were dishevled on the bed. On his table beside the barred windows, *'120 Days of Sodom'* was spread open—face down beside a crystal glass and bottle of gin.

His hand slid across the middle of her back. "Emma...I know things didn't work out with him the way you wanted, but—"

"He lied to me, August."

She sat on the edge of his bed, her knees shaky from the excitement of the evening. She wanted to say more—tell August everything that happened. But her lethargy overpowered her, and she hung her head to cry.

"Emma..." August began while kneeling down in front of her. "Look, Jon had his reasons for...not telling you the truth. I know that doesn't mean much to you, but he never wanted to hurt you."

"You're right. It doesn't mean much." She picked her head up and stared deep into his honey brown eyes. "I want to leave Point DuPont, August. I want to get out of here and live a normal life. If I stay here any longer, I'll only suffer."

August nodded. "Yep."

207

"Will you help me?" she asked.

"Yes," he said without hesitation, and she wrapped her arms around his neck and fell into him. He held her tight, cradling her in his arms while she sobbed quietly. "If you're serious about leaving, we best do it soon before all the servants come back to the island. We got a better chance of going unnoticed without all them people here."

℘℘℘

The recent hurricane left Point DuPont in soggy, wet misery. A thin layer of fog settled around the inner regions of the island, and at the bluffs, the angry waves died down in stature yet continued to claw at the cliffs—waiting for the moment to devour the island whole. Seagulls cawed while soaring through the gray sky, and August shielded his eyes to see them.

Even without the presence of the sun, the sky burned his eyes after being in the darkness of the mansion for days.

He tightened his coat and hurried to the stable to fetch Domino. He told Jon that he needed to check on the villagers—that his conscience would not allow him to rest until he knew they were safe and insisted Jon stay behind to guard the house.

August noted Grady's absence since their run-in in the hall. With the vetern Hunter being preoccupied and Jon scheduled to have the evening to himself, the plan to leave Point DuPont seemed to unfold just as hoped

The ex-fighter rode to the docks—his pistol clenched in hand the entire time. After securing Domino to a makeshift hitching post, contemplated the possibility of a Howler attack.

The field around him remained stilted, and days passed since he last heard their wicked cries from the forests. He ran his hand along Domino's mane, causing his horse companion to snort and bob his head. "Well, what do you want me to do? I don't think the stairs are gonna hold your weight." Domino nudged his arm. The stairwell leading to the docks creaked and shifted in the wind.

While descending the stairs, the sea breeze stung his face, and he wrapped his jacket tighter around himself. The winter months were fast approaching—chilling August to the core. He stepped off the last stair, the dock creaking beneath his boots as he walked. The water came in waves against the dock—shifting boats in their ports and knocking buoys together.

To his right, the dock house glowed.

Without a hurricane dominating the environment, August's knocks resounded, and within seconds, the door swung open. The same crazy old captain stood before him, a wide smile upon his face. "Let me guess. You wanna get to Port Augusta?" he asked, raising his eyebrows.

"No, not Port Augusta. How much would I need to pay you to take a friend and me to Prince Edward Island?"

The old man considered. "This the same friend as last time?"

"No, I'll have a woman with me this time."

"You pay me four-hundred, I'll take you both to Prince Edward Island. Hell, I'll even throw in supper for the both of you."

August cringed. He knew the old man swindled him, that part he didn't mind. He pulled four hundred from his coat and shoved it into the captain's hand. "We'll pass on supper, thanks. Be ready to go by twelve-fifteen. In the morning," he stressed. "You know? When the sun is gone and it's dark outside."

"Thanks for clarifying."

The captain slammed the door in his face, and August flinched back to avoid taking a hit to his already broken nose. He scoffed. "Crazy old coot."

But August's errands were far from over. Even though checking on the villagers was a cover, it was a stop he needed to make. As he rode into town, those passing by tipped their heads to him—a much more warm greeting than he ever received before. He noted the amount of people outside of their homes as well—going on about their business as if the Howlers were just an afterthought.

He slowed Domino and secured him to the hitching post outside of Le Cellier. Two villagers passed with guns slung over their shoulders. They tipped their head to him.

A half-smile spread across his face.

As much as he enjoyed seeing the villagers find a bit of courage to face the Howlers without the Hunters, an ideal world is one without the beasts entirely.

On the porch of Le Cellier, the same middle-aged man who braved the days since the beginning sat in a splintered rocking chair—swigging from a flask he kept clenched in hand.

August stood over him. "Can I join you?" The old man shrugged, and August leaned on the wall beside him. He passed him the flask. "Thanks." After taking a sip, he contorted his face—so jarring and unexpected. "What is that?"

The villager took it again. "Prune juice. Helps the bowels."

He raised an eyebrow. "You mean to tell me you been sittin' out here day in and day out, and you're not drunk off your rocker?"

He lifted the flask to his lips and shrugged again. "Used to drink everyday when I was your age. The only thing it ever did was cause problems."

"You don't realize how dangerous it is just sitting out here? The Howlers could come at any—"

"I'm not scared of the Howlers. They don't want us."

His words boomed like thunder, and August stiffened from the shock. His mouth ran dry, and before speaking he nearly choked on his own tongue. "What do they want?"

He groaned after taking another swig of prune juice. "They want you. The Hunters of Point DuPont."

Terror reverberated his pounding heart. He sank a little lower against the wall as blood drained from his face. As ominous as it seemed, his words didn't make sense. "The Hunters are here *because* of the Howlers—"

"That so? Because I remember them being here *before* the Howlers. They went by a different name back then. The...keepers, I believe." His wrinkled eyes finally met with August's fearful gaze. "That poor girl even still alive?"

"She is. But barely." His breath shook. He contemplated their escape—filtered through all the information the man freely gave him. Another mystery unfolded before him—*the keepers.* Keepers of Emma, no doubt. "Would you be willing to help her?"

ℬↄ◖℞

That evening back at the mansion, Emma sat at the foot of her bed, eyes fixated on the ground while August sat beside her, waiting for her to speak. "So... that's it?"

He hesitated to respond. "Only if you want it to be. I told the captain to be ready by twelve-fifteen. It's the best chance we have of sneaking out of here unnoticed," he whispered—peering to the door intermittently to assure no one listened. When she didn't respond, he brought his hand to her knee. "Emma...we don't have to do this—"

"No, I want to," she whispered. "It's just that...I never thought this day would actually come. And now it's here, and I'm..." she glanced to the door and then lowered her voice. "I'm scared to death. What if it's not at all what I expected. What if...I can't survive?"

August gripped her hands. "I know it's terrifying, but I promise you...the life you could have out there will be much better than any life you have in here. And I'm gonna be with you every step of the way, you hear me?" She nodded, and he shook her leg. "Don't be scared of that. I won't abandon you."

She wrapped her arms around him. "I don't think I'll ever be able to thank you enough."

He rubbed her bony back and gripped the back of her neck to cradle her in his arms. His thumb traced her skin. Life remained

211

inside of her—the desire to live fought to break free despite her oppression. He could still save her, he thought.

She still had fire raging within her.

That night before going on guard duty, August climbed the stairs to the fourth level. The servant's quarters remained dark and ominously quiet since the evacuation. But the door at the end of the hall—even closed—emitted a warm glow from beneath.

August knocked on the door. "Jon? I need to have a word with you. It'll only take a second." Jon rummaged around inside. Within a few moments, he opened the door. "Look, I know you probably hate me now, but I got a favor to ask you. An important one." Jon stepped further into the hall, pulling his door closed behind him. "I know you're supposed to have the night off, but...I need you to come check on me in the dining room at twelve-thirty. Can you do that?"

Jon shrugged, cocking his head inquisitively.

"I, uh...I haven't been feeling well. I don't know how long I'll last tonight." Not the best excuse, and he knew it to be true. He grabbed Jon's shoulder and pulled him closer. "I just need you to come check on me at twelve-thirty, all right?"

Through narrowed eyes, he nodded.

August released him and backed away. As much as he wanted to avoid involving Jon, his conscience would not allow the house to go unguarded without a barricade all night—a barricade that could only be done from inside the house. As soon as Jon realized that August was not at his post, he'd assume the security of the house—it's all August really wanted from him.

At exactly eleven-thirty, he took his post in the dining room and waited for midnight to come. He sat upright with perfect posture, his body tense as his eyes fixated on the oak table before him. The reflection of the flames from the fireplace danced upon the wood, and low jazz played from the gramophone in the corner of the room. In front of him, an untouched glass of bourbon.

He scoffed. One of the downsides to leaving the Maddox employment. No more booze. If they went to the States, America's prohibition laws were much more difficult to get around. He knew from experience. He snatched the glass it took it down in one swig.

When the clock on the mantelpiece struck midnight, August's eyes darted to the kitchen door, knowing a Howler could get through at any moment. Despite his and Emma's grand escape, the idea of a Howler getting inside in the short crossover between him and Jon is what terrified him the most.

His heart pounded when he realized the time was at five minutes past twelve—knowing the window to escape grew smaller with every passing second. But before he even stood to go check on Emma, she appeared in the doorway.

"I'm ready."

ဢဢ

August's arms shook as he took special care lifting the barricade from the door . Every sound made him flinch for fear that Grady or Jon might appear at any moment.

Emma gripped the back of his coat, her head leaning into him while he unlocked the door. She trembled against him.

Once he set the barricade aside, August grabbed Emma's hand and opened the door. For the first time in many years, Emma stepped through the threshold of the outdoors of her own volition.

She stood at the foot of the stairs—her head leaned back with her eyes closed. She took a deep breath. "It's so peaceful out here." Her eyes opened, and she pointed to the sky. "Look, the moon is full."

August draped his arm around her and pulled her close. "We need to be quiet." He pulled the hood of her coat down to cover as much of her face as possible and led the way down the steps,

213

through the open field in front of the house, and then through the gate that surrounded the home.

The iron gate creaked open, and on the other side, the middle-aged man from Le Cellier waited with a horse.

August took one last look at the house. Only then did he notice that above the iron gate, in big iron letters, *The House of Maddox*—illuminated by the moonlight.

He climbed onto the horse behind Emma, and the villager led them to the docks. The entire ride, August kept his hand on his pistol in case of Howlers. He kept his other arm around Emma's waist and leaned his head into her back. After inhaling a deep breath of her, he knew, without a shadow of a doubt, he loved her immensely.

When they made it to the docks, August jumped from the horse and pulled Emma down beside him. "Don't leave just yet," he said to the villager while shoving a wad of cash into his hand. "I don't trust this old coot as far as I can throw him."

He clenched Emma's hand, and assisted her down the wooden stairs. With every gust of wind that blew through them, her grip tightened. "It's cold down here," she said through chattering teeth.

"Can you believe Grady and me came down these things in the middle of a hurricane?"

When they reached the docks, August banged on the old man's door. They waited for a short while, and August banged again, already growing impatient. Finally, the door swung open. "I was beginning to wonder if you were coming."

August groaned. "We're right on time."

The man held up his watch. "It's 12:20."

"Is the boat ready?"

The old man pushed past them. "No, but you can go ahead and wait inside."

August escorted Emma into the dock house. "We don't have much time," he muttered to the captain in passing. "The sooner you get that boat going, the better." The old man saluted and slammed the door as he left. August cursed him under his breath.

214

Behind him, Emma rummaged through the pornography magazines on the table. His heart jumped to his throat, and he rushed to her side. "Crazy old perv," he grumbled while gathering them up and moving them elsewhere.

She sat at the table. "Don't like pornography?"

His cheeks flushed. "No, I…I mean I do, I just—"

"I've read far worse things in my time. Pictures of naked women seem to be rather tame in comparison."

August remembered *120 Days of Sodom*—the naughty book she hid from him the first day they met. He sat across from her. "I forgot you had a dark side."

"A dark side? Or a human side I don't care to hide from others?"

He nodded, thoroughly pleased with her response. His eyes drifted behind her to a bottle of gin. "Would you mind joining me for a drink then?"

"I could use a bit of liquid courage."

The bottle clanked as he poured a shot into a glass for each of them. It would be the last drink he had for a while, he thought while sliding hers across the table. He needed a bit of liquid courage as well. With the captain running behind and twelve-thirty fast approaching, it was only a matter of time before Jon noticed they were gone.

His conscience burdened him more than anything, he thought while sipping his gin. When Emma winced after taking a sip, he smirked. "Not your cup of tea, huh?"

"I'm certainly more of a wine and champagne kind of girl, myself. And you, you like scotch. But bourbon is easier to find." He nodded. "See, I remembered."

The two fell silent, sipping their gin while they waited for the captain to reappear. The buoys in the water clanked together, and a wave rushing into the cliffs broke the silence. As a clock ticked in the background, the tension started to rise.

"You once asked me what…my first memory of Point DuPont was. I've been thinking about it a lot because…well, I've never

215

really thought about it before. Truth be told, I don't remember anything before meeting Jon."

Mention of *his* name unsettled August. But he wanted to be supportive. "How old were you when you met?"

"I was ten. He was eleven. You'd think I'd remember something before then, something from the island, but…I don't. Every memory I have involves him. So, I guess the first memory I have of Point DuPont is meeting Jon." She smiled and looked into her glass of gin as she scooted it back and forth. "I was out playing in the forest. There weren't any Howlers back then, so…even though my father would disapprove, it wasn't as dangerous. I remember I was playing make-believe like I was some…woodland fairy from one of my books. I came across this…little cottage, and I thought, what a great place for a sorceress to live. That's what I want to be. A sorceress!" She lifted her glass with a wide smile, so wide that her cheeks turned red.

August grinned and lifted his glass to his lips. "You seem more like a sorceress than a fairy anyway."

"I wasn't alone, though. I went inside, singing and shouting—trying to scare away anything hiding inside. But it seems I only managed to scare this little boy who was on the floor drawing. And he gave me a good fright as well. He was reticent, never said a word to me, but I didn't mind. He just let me…talk, talk, talk the afternoon away. We were best friends after that, meeting at that little cottage every afternoon to play make-believe."

Her smile faded into melancholy, and it came as no surprise to August. The last thing he needed her to think about was Jon. "Jack was my best friend as a kid. I know how important it is to have someone to confide in at that age."

The clock struck twelve-thirty.

Emma's eyes darkened, as if storm clouds consumed them. Her brow furrowed, and her smile transformed into a scowl. "Something's wrong."

August lowered his glass. "What?"

216

The rise and fall of her chest quickened. With every heavy breath, the veins in her neck bulged. "I...feel like I can't breathe, my heart... it's beating so fast..." She stood, scooting the chair out from beneath her from the abruptness. "Boots swinging in the hall..." she grasped her forehead and grimaced—eyes shut tight.

"Emma, what's wrong?" He reached for her, but she held her hand out to keep him away. "Baby, tell me what's wrong—"

"Jon!" His heart plummeted. "I...I can't do this." Tears streaked down her red face.

"Okay... you're just panicking a little bit."

"No, August, I can't do this, I can't leave him."

It was the one thing he knew would keep Emma on the island if she lost herself in thought, and at that moment, she did. It was a fight August knew he couldn't win.

"You don't want to leave him."

Emma shook her head. "I'm...so sorry, I...I want to leave the island, I want freedom, but I can't live a happy life knowing that he's here...all by himself." He turned away to hide his pain. "Please don't hate me, August. I never meant to...cause so much trouble."

He ran his hand over his face and inhaled a deep breath. "I could never hate you, Emma. All of this was just...to give you a shot at a happy life. And if you tell me that being with Jon will do that, it doesn't matter where you are."

Emma whimpered. She ran to him and wrapped her arms around him, burying her head into his back while she sobbed. "I don't know what came over me. I was so...brave a moment ago."

He clenched her hand to his chest. "We have to hurry. Our taxi will be on his way shortly."

217

Chapter XVII

As soon as Emma and August entered the house, they met with Jon in the foyer. The brooding Hunter stood before them, his eyes darting back and forth between them. And then to the suitcases at Emma's feet. At that moment, for the first time ever, August wished he faced Grady instead. Or even a Howler.

"Jon? What are you doing?" Emma asked.

He snatched her hand—yanked her into him, far away from August. *Upstairs, go*, he signed.

August nodded at her. She moved past them and scurried up the stairs to the second floor. "All right, I know how this looks," August began, but Jon grabbed his coat and slammed him into the wall, eliciting a painful groan from the ex-fighter. "You don't wanna do this, Jon," he said through clenched teeth. "I'll win in a fight every time." Jon snatched the hunting knife from his belt and held it against August's throat. "Guess that changes things a bit." The sharp blade pressed into his bounding pulse. He struggled to swallow through the pressure. "She chose you, Jon. She doesn't want me. She wants you."

Jon's frantic eyes poured over August's pained face. The wait was excruciating—the discomfort from Jon's knife growing more prevalent with every passing second. When Jon finally lowered the blade and released him, August staggered away and massaged his throat.

Jon turned his gaze to the vacant stairwell—his fear and apprehension palpable. He whipped his head back to August. Any shred of courage, any bit of wrath he expressed only seconds before, was now replaced with sympathy. Or perhaps regret. Whichever emotion he felt, August wasn't entirely sure. But after Jon replaced his knife on his belt, he raised his hands and signed, *I'm sorry.*

"Don't even pull that shit with me; if the roles were reversed, you woulda slit my throat."

Jon approached the blackened stairwell.

Despite Emma's rejection—and Jon running off to live happily ever after with the woman he loved—a sense of completion came over August. He competed, he lost. But he lost to the most worthy opponent he ever faced. That loss, to him, was bittersweet.

ഇരൻ

A glow at the end of the hall led the way through the darkened second-floor corridor. With every step Jon took, his heart pounded harder and faster in his chest. His throat became dry. At any moment, he might choke on his own tongue. His palms were sweaty beneath his leather gloves. Still, he continued to the orange glow that painted dancing shadows on the wall across from Emma's room.

She left the door ajar.

He lingered in the doorway momentarily, wracking his brain for anything she might be expecting from him. An apology, perhaps. Or maybe, in a perfect world, just a bit of comfort.

The door creaked when he pushed it open, but the room was empty. He stepped back into the darkness of the corridor; his breath stuck in his throat. She must be in the library, he thought.

Without the servants tending to the house, the library remained dark with only a bit of moonlight breaking through the massive, arched windows. The cold enveloped the room, and Emma was not to be found.

He groaned—disturbed by her absence.

More than anything, he wanted to call out for her. As he marched down the hall, panic raised within him at the thought of her wandering the mansion. It was too dangerous for her to be alone in its current state.

"Jon?"

He came to a halt at the sound of her voice. She stood in the shadows of the stairwell, her slender fingers dragging along the railing as she ascended to the third floor. When she disappeared into the darkness, he chased after her.

He followed her up the stairs, past the third level, and to the servant's quarters, but when he reached the corridor leading to his own bedroom, she was gone. The only indication of where she went was his bedroom door creaking open at the end of the hall.

His room. Where all his drawings of her resided, and all his obsessive thoughts drove him to write love-fueled letters that he never gave.

Fear of rejection dominated him. Even after August's confession, he feared Emma would turn him away if she saw the extent of his burns. Despite this, he followed.

He pushed the door open. From his desk, Emma turned to him—cowering at the sight of him. "Jon," she cooed.

He closed the door and locked it behind him. With every step he took to her, she slunk further back into his desk until his gloved hand lifted her chin to him. He studied her face—looked for any reluctance therein.

"You draw so beautifully." Her fingers grazed the drawings behind her. "I don't want to just be a fantasy anymore."

His thumb traced her trembling bottom lip. He shook his head. For as long as he could remember, he loved Emma more than anything. He pointed to himself, crossed his arms firmly across his chest, then pressed his index finger into her chest—directly over her heart.

She smiled. *I love you*, she signed in return. "I always will, mon amour."

He looped his arm around her waist and pulled her into him. Her body tensed against his. Her shaking fingers slid up his chest, his neck, and to the edges of his mask.

His instinctive reaction was to pull away and grip her wrists to stop her, and she retreated. Her green eyes softened. "It's all right," she whispered and gripped his hand. "May I take off your glove?"

He hesitated to answer. Only when she brought it to the side of her face did he nod. As ashamed as he felt about his burns, he longed to touch her and feel her for real, not through a thick, leather barrier.

She ripped the glove from his hand and brought his palm to the side of her face again. Her warm breath on his skin—her soft lips brushing against him, it weakened him. Once again, he dragged his thumb along her bottom lip and moaned when she wrapped her lips around him.

Her tongue, soft and wet—gentle. A sensation he only ever imagined before. He grabbed the back of her neck and yanked her into him—her face only inches away from his mask.

On the one hand, he was terrified of showing his face. On the other, he so desired to taste her and feel her sweet tongue against his. "I'll close my eyes if you want."

He shook his head. It's not what he wanted. He wanted all of her, every inch of her mind, body, and soul. But it was unfair to ask for that when he hid his true form away.

He stepped back and gripped the edges of his mask. After removing it and setting it on the desk behind Emma, he reached his hand to the back of his head and ripped the final barrier from his face. His black, nylon face covering.

For the first time since the fire, Jon stood before her without his mask—his burned face exposed for her to see. He kept his eyes on the ground with a permanent grimace on his face, waiting for her shrieks of horror or cries of protest.

It never came.

Instead, she stepped toward him and slid her fingers along the sides of his face. "There you are, my love."

Finally, he kissed her for the very first time. As her tongue entered his mouth, a side of him that he always kept hidden away from Emma broke free. He pushed her back into his desk, causing it to shift beneath the weight of her.

He tore the other glove from his hand and gripped both sides of her face. His kiss deepened with fervent urgency like he might never be able to make up for lost time with her.

As sweet as her lips tasted, he wondered what the rest of her might taste like. He broke away from her mouth and kissed her cheek, then her jaw, down to her neck—running his tongue along her flesh. The perfect blend of sweet lotion and salty sweat covered her. But as she gripped his jacket lapels to pull it from his shoulders, he snatched her wrists. Despite revealing his face to her, Jon remained dispassionate about being completely exposed—for the time being, at least.

He spun her around, and she planted her hands firmly on all the drawings of her. He attached his mouth to her bounding pulse in her neck. His hands slid from her waist, up her stomach, and to her breasts.

"Jon," she moaned. "Undress me…make love to me."

Her words ignited desire deep within him. A desire that, up until now tormented his mind.

A master of undressing her, he was. He knew her garments better than any man. His fingers snatched the ribbon at the back of her gown, and he tore them loose. After, he kneeled down and bunched up the hem to pull over her head. After tossing it behind him, he went to work on her undergarments—tearing them from her body and throwing them aside.

He bent her over the desk, admiring her backside just as he'd done so many times before. He got to his knees and parted her legs even further. When he buried his face into her, Emma cried out. His tongue massaged her—devoured her in a way that he only ever fantasized about.

Like enjoying a piece of pomegranate—oh, how he loved fruit. The juices sliding from his mouth down his chin, quenching his thirst. As Emma's knees buckled, Jon lifted her leg onto the desk—a visceral groan escaping him.

As her body shook and writhed against the desk, Jon tightened his grip on her legs. Only when she became rigid—only when she threw her head and moaned in delicious pleasure, did he release her legs. He kissed her backside and ran his hand up along her spine, entangling his fingers in her thick hair as he stood.

With his face buried in the crook of her neck, he smelled her.

"I still want you."

He moaned when she touched him. His fumbling hands unbuckled his belt and hurried to free his erection. When he entered inside of her, she threw her head back and crumpled the drawings beneath her palms.

He dug his fingers into her hips and steadied himself. Just her reaction to him was enough to push him near the edge. As she crashed her hips back into him, he groaned—tensing from the pleasure that flooded his body.

Feeling her for the first time was a transformative moment because for so long, he only ever fantasized—the evidence of which were being destroyed by Emma's frantic hands on his desk.

He pulled her hips back into him again.

As he started to tremble, he contemplated the ways in which he could make this moment last longer. He removed himself and spun her again. With little to no effort, he lifted her onto his desk and spread her legs wide enough to accommodate his body between them, then thrust himself inside of her again.

"Jon!" she moaned—gripping his shoulders and digging her nails into his thick coat.

His long, deep strokes prolonged his climax. Still, her eyes—the sight of her biting her lip and her naked body shifting with every advance he made inside of her—forced him to the precipice once again. He stilled himself.

His breath quivered, and another moan escaped him at the release. A much more satisfying experience than all the nights he pleasured himself to the thought of her. As he loosened his grip on her, Emma slid from the surface of his desk—still holding him for support. She smiled. "I am completely obsessed with you," she whispered against his lips. "It's going to take a lot to curb my appetite for you. You'll be a very tired man."

Jon forced a heavy breath from his nose—his form of laughter. A difficult concept for him to grasp, his frantic eyes scanned her face for any sign of insincerity. He found only her soft, gentle kiss instead.

Chapter XIX

August sat in the parlor with a glass of bourbon, staring deep into the crackling fire. Despite him knowing that Jon deserved Emma's affections more than he did, his heart sank a little deeper in knowing that she'd chosen the brooding Hunter. He wanted to be happy for Jon, but his biggest concern was Emma might rethink her decision to leave the island entirely.

She got the man she loved in the end, but was Jon strong enough to do what she needed? August's tormented mind reckoned the possibilities.

Jon entered the room, breaking August of his thoughts. "Jesus, you're practically naked," he said at the sight of him with no gloves, coat, or kabuki mask—only his black nylon face-covering remained. August chugged the rest of his bourbon. "What's this?" he asked when Jon handed him a folded piece of paper.

August,

I want to thank you for all you've done for me. If it weren't for you, Jon and I would still be acting as if we were only friends and nothing more. I'd still be a victim to Grady's control, and the idea of a free and happy life would seem like an impossible goal. You've given both Jon and me the courage we needed to move forward with our lives and leave this place behind. This island brings nothing but pain for both of us. It's something we both want to forget.

You, on the other hand, I wish to never forget. You've been a very dear friend to me in the short while I've known you, and I know without a shadow of a doubt, this life will be good to you. You will find happiness and fulfillment. I love you, dearly, my brave, white wolf. You'll forever be my savior.

Love,
Emma

August folded the letter. Better than having to face her again. "So y'all are leaving?"

Jon nodded and signed, *Come with us.*

"Nah, that's all right. I appreciate the *'no hard feelings'* between us, but I ain't interested in watching you and Emma ride off into the sunset together. I'll be making my way to Halifax. You two should head elsewhere. Somewhere Arthur Maddox can't get to ya." He placed his glass on the table and stood. "I am happy for ya." Jon tipped his head to him. "And to think, just an hour ago, you were ready to end my life."

Grady entered the room, distracting them both from their thoughtful moment. "Good, you're both here. We need to reinforce the loading bay. Even though the storm's gone, we won't be able to get our workers back to the island for at least another week."

August groaned. The responsibility fell upon him to inform the veteran Hunter of his and Jon's impending departure from Point DuPont. "Jon and I are actually gonna head out. We've had enough of this place, the Howlers. Seems to me the logical thing to do is evacuate the island altogether. There's no reason to keep fighting these things anymore."

Grady laughed. "Very funny. Seriously, we need to barricade the doors. I heard Howlers not too far off—"

He adjusted the veteran Hunter's disheveled shirt. "Grady? We're leavin' the island. We ain't gonna hunt Howlers anymore, ain't gonna try and secure the mansion. It's time Emma get out of here." He clamped Grady's shoulder and lowered his tone. "She deserves better than this."

Grady smacked August's hand away. "Is this a joke?"

Jon pushed past both of them to exit the room.

As Grady reached for him, August snatched his wrist. "They're in love, Grady, just let 'em be."

"Let go of me." He ripped his hand away. His cold blue eyes darted to Jon. "Do you think she'd still love you if she knew what you did, Jon?"

His words kept him from leaving.

"What's he talking about?" August asked.

Jon shook his head.

"Don't act innocent now. You don't suddenly get to choose to be the good guy."

"Just what the hell are you going on about, McCoy?"

Grady sneered. "Why don't you fill him in, Jon? How did Carlyle really die?"

August waited for a confession and hadn't taken a breath since the mention of Carlyle's name. He suspected the Hunters played a part in Carlyle's death, but never that Jon may have been the executioner. "Jon?"

The mute Hunter had no response. His own hateful gaze was fixed entirely on Grady, and as he clenched his fists by his side, August noticed his hunting knife.

He stepped between the Hunters and grabbed Jon's shoulder to usher him out of the parlor. Without knowing who posed the bigger threat, he knew he needed to separate them, at the very least. But Grady snatched the blade from Jon's side.

Jon's instinctive reaction was to shove August out of the way.

Grady plunged the knife deep into his stomach. The masked Hunter tensed—his wide eyes fixed on the knife in his abdomen. As Grady shoved it deeper within him, Jon groaned and fell to his knees. "Oh my—" August darted to Jon and caught him before he fell to the ground. "What did you do?"

"I did what I had to," Grady defended.

"You didn't have to do that!" He grabbed the knife, but Jon gripped his wrist and shook his head. "I don't know what to do, Jon…" August tore the mask from his face, and blood spurted from his lips.

Emma, he signed.

August shook his head. "Nah, you're… you're gonna get her out of here. You can't make a promise to a woman and not keep your word. She'll hold it over your head for the rest of her life." Jon chuckled, but more blood shot from his mouth. He winced and gripped August's wrist, but within seconds, his body went limp. His eyes remained open, fixed on the ceiling. "Hey," August shook him. "Hey, you gotta wake up. Emma's gonna be pissed." His eyes burned from tears blurring his vision.

"Jon?" August's blood went cold. Emma stood in the doorway. "Jon?" she cried.

"Emma—" August began.

"Darling, you shouldn't see this."

Emma collapsed next to Jon's body. Her shaking hand moved to the handle of the blade deep in his stomach. She gasped and covered her mouth, smearing Jon's blood along her face. "Jon?"

228

She grabbed his shoulders to shake him. "Jon," she said again through gritted teeth.

"He's gone, Emma." August gripped her shoulder. "Come on, let's get you cleaned up—" She thrust her hand to him, and an invisible force shot him backward into the wall.

Grady's fumbling hands reached for the sedatives strapped to his belt. Scratches on the large paned, arched windows distracted August. They cracked—spiderwebbing the glass of each and every pane.

Emma wailed—her voice like a banshee.

The windows shattered, sending shards of glass onto all of them. A forceful gust of wind knocked Grady forward, and the sedatives flew from his hands across the wooden floor.

"The sedatives!" Grady shouted as they skidded between August's legs.

As Grady darted to them, Emma raised her hand into the air, stopping him dead in his tracks. His riding boots lifted from the ground. He fought and clawed at his own neck—his face reddening. He couldn't breathe. Emma was strangling him without even having to touch him.

"Emma!" August yelled, but her hateful gaze focused only on Grady. The wind whistled through the shattered windows, and the flames in the fireplace burned so fiercely that it enveloped the wall above. From outside, howls grew closer—fiercer. "Emma, stop! You'll kill us all!"

He grabbed one of the sedatives from the pouch between his legs. He stood—careful not to draw attention to himself, but he didn't have much time. The flames engulfed the wall—the violent wind fueling it more and more.

He approached her slowly, syringe in hand. When within arm's reach, August fell to his knees. He wrapped his arms around her, stuck the needle into her neck, and pressed the plunger.

Only when she fell limp in his arms did Grady hit the ground, gasping for air. "August—" he gasped. "The fire...we have to put out the fire!"

August dropped Emma onto Jon's body and scrambled to reach the massive flames that continued to grow. He and Grady snatched one of the thick, velvet curtains in the window to put out the small, dancing flames on the hardwood. "The fire extinguisher!" Grady yelled and sprinted to the hall.

August stomped on the fabric, putting out as much of the flames as the curtain would allow before it burned. When Grady reemerged, he used the entirety of the fire extinguisher. And only when blackened walls remained did August finally take a breath.

He glanced around the room at the broken glass and the blood, the two bodies in the corner of the room. "What...the fuck just happened?"

Grady gripped his neck and grimaced. He coughed—his breath still labored from Emma's attack. "We have to get her downstairs. We have to get her to the cube. I have a feeling she'll be no more compliant when she regains consciousness."

The cube. My God, August thought.

"What about the Howlers? I can hear 'em outside!"

"They won't get through the bars."

As much as August hated the idea of Emma being a prisoner, seeing what she could do made him reconsider everything. She was dangerous, strong enough to have launched him into a wall without ever touching him. Fear dominated him at that moment, and when Grady kneeled beside Emma, August volunteered to carry her.

Grady led the way to the basement. He unlocked the steel door and held it open for August to enter. Stone steps led the way further downstairs. Burned copper wire dominated his senses— singeing his nose. The further they descended, the warmer he became.

The walls around him buzzed with an electric current so strong, the hairs on his arm stood upright. They emerged from the stairs into a rectangular room with a man in a lab coat at a power grid and a control panel to their right.

They were in an observation room.

"Monsieur, I managed to repair the fuses, but the cube is still only at sixty percent efficiency. The rats, they must've chewed through—"

"It doesn't matter; it's an emergency. Open the doors," Grady demanded, and he flipped a switch—unlocking a steel door in the corner of the room. "Come on, bring her in here."

August hesitated. Before him, a large double-paned window revealing the atrocity within—the cube. "Jesus Christ."

"August, quickly!"

He followed Grady through the steel door and down a hallway made entirely of metal with small windows allowing them to look inward at the cube. At the end of the hall, another steel door clicked, and Grady pushed it open.

The cube was a 12x12 reinforced glass cell with metal edges to further secure the sound structure. Grady moved to the corner of the room—the wall beside them lined with five more power grids. On each corner of the cube, thick, tall pylons stood, meeting at the top with copper wire. A surge of blue electric current jolted into a circular structure that emitted so much electricity, the room glowed bright blue.

Grady flipped a switch on one of the power grids, and the steel door on the cube unlatched and swung open. "Put her inside."

Inside was a twin-sized bed, a painting easel, a bookshelf, and a dresser. A washbasin sat next to the bed, and on the small table in the center of the cube, one solitary chair. It looked as though Emma had everything she'd need, but putting her in a cell disturbed him. "Is it gonna hurt her?"

"I promise; she won't feel a thing."

August lifted Emma further into his arms and carried her into the cube. Inside, the electric current was muted, and it was much cooler than the area outside the cube.

He placed her on the bed and backed away from her.

"Come on out," Grady said, and August obeyed. He flipped the switch again, and the steel door closed and bolted shut.

"How long will she have to stay in there?"

231

"For a long time, I imagine."

The thought chilled August to the bone. He now understood just how dangerous Emma was, but also he knew she was provoked—forced into a vengeful rage when she saw the man she loved with a knife in his stomach. And while nothing she might possibly face in life be so traumatic as that event, he recalled the fire of Point DuPont, now completely convinced she was the cause.

₮℞

The two Hunters walked into the parlor, and August assessed the damage she caused. Or maybe, the damage Grady caused out of sheer jealousy.

The veteran Hunter placed his foot on Jon's chest and pulled the knife from his stomach, and August shook with rage. He grabbed Grady's shoulder and snatched the knife from him, shoving him back and away from Jon. "Don't you fuckin' touch him like that."

"We need to burn him," Grady said. August tossed Jon's knife onto the desk. "Did you hear me?"

But the only thing he really heard was the howls growing louder. "We ain't doin' shit with them things outside." He flung his hands to the side. "Was it even true?"

"Was what true?"

"Jon killing Carlyle? Or were you just blowin' smoke up my ass?"

Grady inhaled sharply through his nose. "It was true. Jon did kill Carlyle."

"I don't believe you."

"You don't have to, but believe this," he began while closing the gap between them. "Carlyle was going to blow the lid on this operation. He was going to leave this island and tell everyone what he saw, exposing all of us."

"So? Maybe you should be exposed."

"You don't understand, August," Grady snapped. "Maybe you disagree with our methods and the things we do. But imagine a world where people know about Emma. Imagine what would happen to her if people knew the things she could do, the powers she had. She'd either be killed, her body being donated to science, or she'd be locked up and experimented on. Do you want those things for her? Could you possibly even begin to understand what…what that would do to her?"

"So…Jon killed him to protect Emma?"

"And I foolishly covered for him. If Emma had known the truth about Jon, all of this could have been avoided." August sneered. "I hope you understand now why I did what I did. Jon somehow became convinced he was strong enough to control her out there in the real world. A very foolish mistake on his part, and I couldn't stand idly by—"

"He could have. You don't know their relationship; he could have saved her."

"Then you still underestimate her."

August clenched his fists by his side. He approached the veteran Hunter, and for the first time ever, Grady cowered before his towering presence. "You underestimated Jon." From outside the window, a large mass of black fur caught August's attention. "What do you propose we do about that? You know as well as I do that they can get inside the loading bay. Only a matter of time until they find it."

Grady dipped his head—his gaze shifting back and forth between the parlor door and the floor beneath his feet. "I don't want to think about it right now." He excused himself from the parlor, leaving August alone with Jon's body and the Howlers patrolling the window outside.

Chapter XX

August brought Jon to the medical bay to prepare him for cremation. When Doctor Bernard asked if he should perform an autopsy, August declined. "I know how he died. He was betrayed."

"Very well."

While the doctor cleaned Jon, August retrieved clean clothes for him from his quarters. Another pair of black slacks, a black vest, but instead of his standard black shirt, August picked a red one from the bottom of his drawer—one he probably hadn't worn for years. Once dressed, August tossed his nylon mask aside. "He won't be needing that."

"It's a shame, really. I quite enjoyed him. A bit misguided, but overall, a good man."

"Misguided how?"

Doctor Bernard sighed while staring down at Jon's face, his eyes having been glued shut. "He always romanticized the idea of Ms. Maddox. It led to his demise, as I suspected it would."

"Emma didn't do this."

"She might not have landed the blow, but she certainly is the reason for…all of this," he said while glancing around the room. "If she never would have come to the island, it would still be a

234

thriving village. Jon would never have been burned. He'd still be alive, more than likely."

"It wasn't her fault."

"Don't mistake me, Mr. DeWitt. I don't hold her completely accountable. If Arthur Maddox never adopted her, she probably would have lived her life without harming a single soul. But as it were, a man like Arthur Maddox has to own anything of value. He has to try to understand everything. Emma became his greatest and most dangerous discovery."

August stood before Doctor Bernard in awe. The entire time, he had someone who'd been privy to every bit of information regarding Emma and Arthur Maddox.

He just never thought to ask.

Doctor Bernard shook his hands dry at the sink. "Those Howlers are going to find a way in eventually. Probably sooner rather than later." The idea of being ripped to shreds brought August back into the severity of the situation. He had to do something. Leaving wasn't an option, not with the monsters lurking outside.

Perhaps the only thing that could save them was the thing they were keeping locked in the basement for their own safety.

Emma.

ഇൈൽ

Even though the basement remained sealed shut through August's stay on the island, the recent events left his superior in a frazzled and distant state of mind. The basement door remained open.

August crept down the stone stairs to the observation area—the electric current in the walls sending a tingling sensation up his arms. Through the observation window at the bottom of the steps, Emma remained asleep in the cube.

"Excuse me?" August whipped around. "Are you permitted to be down here without Monsieur McCoy?"

"Uh yeah. You're Leroux, right? You engineered all of this?"

235

"Oui."

August approached the control panel. "What's all this for?" He dragged his fingers along the warm, vibrating structure. Buttons and switches of different colors and different meanings, a lever on the far left—it all seemed so complicated and complex. All for Emma.

"It's mostly to regulate the temperature in the cube. The reserve power." He removed August's hand from the panel. "The main power source is in there on those power grids."

"What's it for?"

"It's all experimental, really. But it seems that, for some reason, the electromagnetic current keeps Emma docile. The waves have some sort of effect on her, rendering her powerless."

"So, she can't...do anything in there?"

"As far as we know, no. But we're only running on sixty percent power, so I am unsure how well it will hold her when she regains consciousness."

"Looks like we're about to find out." Emma turned onto her back and pushed herself upward. From a speaker on the control panel, she groaned. "Can she hear us?"

Leroux grabbed a microphone and handed it to August. "Press the button to speak."

August brought the microphone to his lips. "Emma?" She searched the room for the source of his voice. "Emma, turn around." She did and stared blankly through the cube at the observation glass. "Can she see us?"

"Oui."

She stood from the bed and approached the glass. When her fingertips met with the surface of the cube, she flinched and stepped back. Her head whipped around to all sides until she found the door, but when she tried to open it, she leaped back, gripping her hand to her chest.

"What's happening to her?"

"The inside of the cube is electric. Only the floor is safe."

"Help!" Emma shouted. "Let me out!"

236

"Emma, listen to me. You have to calm down, or they're never going to let you out of there," August said. "You're considered a danger right now."

"Where am I?"

"You're...in the basement."

"Where's Jon?"

His words became jumbled in his throat. His mind drew a complete blank. The doe-eyed, weary expression she gave him shattered his heart, and he averted his gaze. "He's in the medical bay."

"He's...dead, August?"

August hesitated. "Ye...yes."

Emma's face contorted into sheer horror. She sobbed and rested her head on the glass, but the electric shock sent her back, further away from the glass. So she screamed. "Let me out! Please let me out of here!"

August dropped the microphone. "Open the door," he demanded.

"What? No, I can't!"

He grabbed Leroux by the lab coat and slammed him into the wall. "Open the door now."

August ran into the room housing the cube. He needed to be near her—consoling her through an observation window and microphone seemed so dehumanizing. "Emma," he called to her while pounding on the glass. "Emma, listen to me."

She wailed, never giving him the chance. Even though it seemed the electromagnetic current helped to keep her powers at bay, it didn't stop her from causing destruction on her own. She grabbed the books on the shelf and ripped them onto the ground, tore down her painting easel, and shattered the washbasin at her bedside.

August banged on the cube. "Emma...please just look at me. Talk to me." She ignored and fell to her knees. Only when she grabbed onto a shard of glass from her broken vase did August panic. "Emma, put it down!" He ran to the control panel on the wall and hit the button that unlatched the steel door. When it swung open, he darted through and dropped beside her.

Despite her being the most powerful creature he ever encountered, when he gripped her wrist and told her to drop the glass, she abided.

"I don't want to live anymore, August, not without him." He cradled her, rocked her back and forth for comfort. Sure, perhaps Emma, in her full power, could defeat the Howlers prowling outside the house, but she certainly was not in the emotional state to do so.

August sighed. "It's gonna be okay."

A click behind August's head made him freeze. He knew the sound all too well from his time as a bootlegger, and just like all those times, he lifted his hands in surrender and froze.

"Grady," Emma gasped.

"Get out of the cube, Mr. DeWitt." He did as Grady demanded. "Emma, stand back." He pointed the gun at her. "Leroux, get all the broken glass out, so she doesn't do anything stupid."

The engineer ran into the cube to clean the glass from the floor. The entire time, Grady kept his gun on Emma—much braver than he seemed before. Because now, she was powerless. When Leroux exited the cube, Grady flipped the switch to close the door once more.

Finally, he lowered the gun.

"You didn't have to do that," August said.

"I'm going to pretend this never happened. It's not entirely your fault since…you don't know what all she can do. She's been off her medication since falling ill. Which means she's capable of much more than what you're accustomed to."

"She's broken, Grady."

"And it'll only fuel her!"

August shoved him back. "Let's think about this for a moment. We got a pack of Howlers just waitin' for a chance to get inside,

238

and you're keeping the strongest weapon we have against them locked up? She could stop them!"

"Problems with the Howlers?" Emma mused from inside the cube. She smiled at Grady. "Good."

Her words chilled August.

"She cannot be trusted, August. Letting her out would cause more damage than all the Howlers combined—" August grabbed Grady's arm to keep him from walking any further.

"I wonder why that is. Maybe if you wouldn't have killed Jon, she'd be more willing to help!"

Grady yanked his arm away and scoffed. "You have no idea what's going on here. If Emma could defeat the Howlers, then she would have done it by now. She can't, August. She's powerless against them."

"I find that very hard to believe. Maybe if you didn't keep her so doped up, she could have stopped all of this a very long time ago."

"She's the reason they're here!"

"If that's true, then she can stop them!" Grady dismissed his recommendation, and only then did it hit August. "You're more afraid of a woman with power than a wild animal that would willingly tear you apart. She scares you…all of you. Because you know deep down, you deserve everything she'd do to you."

Before Grady had the opportunity to retaliate, a horrifying scream from above triggered their fast action. Grady darted to the stairs, and August followed behind. They burst through the basement door to see a mass of black fur before them. One of the Howlers made it inside, and in between its sharp fangs, Doctor Bernard's leg barely held on by his tendons.

The Howler dragged the doctor down the hall toward the dining room. He grabbed the rug beneath him, fighting hard to tear away from the beast when finally, his leg was ripped from his body.

"Shoot it, Grady."

Grady pulled the pistol from his side and pointed it at the Howler's head. The beast backed away with Doctor Bernard's leg still in its mouth, but when Grady fired a shot, it yelped and released.

It darted back into the dining room, narrowly missing another shot from the Hunter. Grady ran to the door and closed it, locking the beast inside. "This won't hold it for long. The others won't be far behind." He marched to the stairwell.

"So, what now?"

"Grab whatever weapons you can find. We'll have to kill them one by one as they make it through the door."

But there was only one weapon that could possibly kill all of the Howlers. August backed away from Doctor Bernard's body. He pushed open the steel door and bolted down the stairs to the basement

"Monsieur, I've been given orders not to let you—" Before Leroux finished, August wrapped his arms around his neck—forcing him into a headlock. As much as Leroux tried to break free, the retired fighter's strength and magnitude were too much for him to fight. Within minutes, Leroux's body went limp.

August dropped him and pulled the lever to open the massive door beside them. He ran down the hall and into the room that housed the cube. "Emma?" He pounded on the glass, and she looked over at him. "The Howlers are inside. Doctor Bernard is dead."

"It's a good thing I'm in here."

"No, listen to me; you can stop them. You're powerful; you could…kill them all."

"Stop them? Kill them? Even if I knew how, why would I want to?"

"Innocent people will die."

She laughed. "Innocent? Are these the same innocent people who locked me up in here? Who kept me so heavily medicated that I haven't had a clear thought in nearly a decade? Well, I'm thinking clearly now, August, and I say let them all burn."

"And me? You want me to die too?"

"You could always just…come in here?"

"You and I both know that is a temporary solution. Don't you want to be free? Jon's gone, Emma, and I'm so sorry about what happened to him. Trust me, if I could trade places with him, I would. I would give my life so the two of you could be together. But it just ain't possible, and for that, I'm sorry."

Tears streaked her cheeks. "We were going to run away together. We were…finally going to do it."

August nodded. "Yeah, I know. Don't condemn yourself to death out of guilt. Jon would want you to still escape."

"How terrible of you to use my grief to save your life."

"It's not even about that. We can leave right now, run from the Howlers, and get you off this island. But we're running out of time. I'm not trying to guilt you into anything. Let them all die, for all I care. But I can't get you out of here if I'm dead too."

She closed her eyes and swayed a bit. For a moment, August thought he saw her smile. As she leaned her head back, her eyes opened and darted around the room. "I don't need your help."

He stepped away from the glass when he noticed the electric current above them going haywire. A misfire from one of the blue volts made him dive toward the observation window. Small tufts of fur scattered along the ground as he hit with a massive thud. Rats scurried away. They scratched and squeaked and gathered in one common area—the main power grid.

Emma outstretched her hand to the wall of the cube. "I never liked rats, August. But for some reason, they've always liked me. And since I was a child, seemed to follow me everywhere."

The electricity failed. The lights on the control panel surged, then went black. The blue, electric current above the cube wound down until total blackness consumed the room.

Despite the disorientation from all loss of light, the sound of glass cracking was unmistakable.

The reserve power came on, and the glass that encased the cube exploded from a violent force—sending little shards of glass shooting through the entire room.

August fell back into the observation window—shielding himself from the onslaught of shards. He expected to be ripped to shreds, but instead, a light breeze tickled his skin. He opened his eyes to see all the glass suspended in the air around him—still and posing no threat.

As Emma stepped through the open wall, the glass fell to the ground around him. He stood—skidding on the broken glass as he ran for the exit, down the hall, and up the stairs once more. It was time to leave.

He crashed into Grady after emerging from the basement. With his rifle slung over his shoulder, the veteran Hunter stabilized himself. "What in God's name—"

"I'm gettin' the hell outta here. You might consider doing the same," August said while jogging to the front door.

Grady's rifle cocked—stopping August dead in his tracks. "Do not open that door, August."

"That's the second time today you've pointed a gun at me. It will be the last time," he said while turning to the veteran Hunter.

"Yes, it will be."

August held his hands up. This is it, he thought. Not in the ring, to a Howler, or even Emma. But *Grady*. He closed his eyes and winced. The rifle cracked, causing August to flinch. But he felt no pain. He opened his eyes and only then noticed the dead Howler behind him—blood pooling around its head.

"It seems they've found another way in."

August lifted the barricade. "I'm getting out of here."

"Walking out that door is suicide!"

"Staying in here ain't much better."

"No, it certainly isn't." Grady flinched at the sound of Emma's voice. He whipped around to her, but before he raised his rifle, it flew from his hands and skidded down the hall.

Grady fell to his knees before her. "Emma—"

"You don't look pleased to see me," she said while passing him, keeping her eyes on him until she reached the stairwell. "What's the matter, darling? Afraid you'll finally get what you deserve?"

"Are you going to kill me now?"

Emma stopped on the first step. "No. I think I'll leave you to the wolves." Her green eyes glowed when her gaze met with August's. "You might want to leave now, August."

As she ascended the stairs, Grady grabbed the pistol at his side and pointed it to her. He pulled the hammer, and only then did August realize that Grady intended to kill. "Emma!"

Grady fired. The bullet narrowly missed Emma's head as she ducked, and within seconds, August had Grady on the ground. He grabbed his wrist and smashed it into the hardwood continually until the gun flew from Grady's hand across the floor.

The veteran did his best to hold off the ex-fighter, but his only move was to reach for August's face and dig his nails into his flesh.

August groaned and dropped his elbow onto Grady's nose, weakening him. He punched him again and again until he broke skin and smeared blood over Grady's face and his own fist.

"Stop," Emma commanded. "He doesn't deserve your mercy, August. Leave him be."

August dropped him. He climbed to his feet and stepped over him to reach Emma on the stairs. "Come with me, Emma. Let's get out of here." She looked upward to the second level. "You deserve better than this. We can leave the island now, and you can have a normal life."

"No. Nothing will ever be normal again."

"A happy life then."

Her expression softened. "Without Jon?"

"Look, I know it'll be hard. I know what it's like to lose someone you love. I lost both my parents on the same day. I lost Jack, and... I'll never forgive myself for the things that..." He grimaced. "I'll never forgive myself for what happened to them.

But I have felt happiness since I lost 'em. And...the idea made me feel guilty as sin, but then I met you, and I don't feel guilty for that now."

A tear fell down her face. "August—"

"Let me help you, Emma. Let me take you out of here. You can feel happiness again, even if it seems unlikely right now. Your life's not over."

She considered. Slowly, she slid her fingers into his palm and descened the stairs closer to him—their eyes fixed on each other while stepping over Grady. As they neared the entrance, Emma managed to smile. "You don't know what you're doing..." Grady muttered. "Emma! He's dead because of you!" At his words, Emma stopped. "Do you really want to condemn August to the same fate?"

August's heart plummeted. For a moment, he convinced Emma all would be okay. All it took was one provocation from Grady to convince her otherwise. She released August's hand. "Don't give in to it," August said, but Emma ignored it. "Emma, don't let him do this to you."

"I think it's time for you to leave, August."

The sconces on the wall burst into an oily flame, enveloping the walls in which they stood. "I'm not leaving you—" The front doors behind them burst open. Just like in the parlor, an invisible force knocked August backward far enough to land him in the open field in front of the house.

He groaned from the impact. Before he could reach the doors again, they slammed shut in front of him. He smashed his body into them, but they wouldn't budge. As he tried, smoke seeped from beneath the door.

He fanned the smoke and backed away from the heat growing within.

The flames engulfed the walls around Grady and Emma. "Why provoke me?" she asked as she approached. "You could have just let me leave. You'd still have the Howlers to deal with, but now your chances of survival are slim to none."

He climbed to his knees, groveling before her. "I don't want to live without you, Emma. You can't survive out there. When this is all over, you'll realize just how much I loved you and wanted to keep you safe."

Beside them, a black mass of fur approached. "Never will I look back on these times and think for one second...Grady must have really loved me."

He sobbed. Before he said anything else to her, the Howler attacked—latching its teeth onto the side of Grady's face and taking him to the ground. Unbothered by his cries of terror and pain, Emma focused her attention on the stairwell before her and ascended to the second level.

ᏚᎧᏓ

The sun started to rise. Smoke billowed into the light blue sky from the house, now wildly ablaze. The horses from the stables sprinted through the field with the caretaker running behind, shouting indiscriminately to the burning house.

August marveled at the wildfire and black smoke filling the morning sky. It was only then that he realized the archway in front of the house started to collapse from the heat as well. It no longer read *The House of Maddox*—but *The House of Mad* instead.

August coughed. Despite having moved away from the house, the smoke choked him. The roof caved in, sending him even further away from the burning structure. The walls collapsed inward, and within half an hour, only the foundation of the house remained.

His eyes burned, but through all the flames and smoke, Emma kneeled before Jon. "Emma!" August yelled.

A low growl sent a cold chill up his spine despite the heat from the fire. He looked around as Howlers surrounded him in the open field. They approached him slowly. With each step they took, one by one, they disappeared into thin air until the field was empty once more.

"What the..." He took deep, labored breaths and whipped his head back to the burning structure.

But Emma disappeared into the flames.

Chapter XXI

December 5ᵗʰ, 1928
Halifax, Nova Scotia

In a dingy motel on the coast of the ocean, August DeWitt drank himself into a stupor—just like he'd done almost every night since leaving Point DuPont. He fled the island and caught the next ferry to Halifax, avoiding any sort of contact with his previous employer. Not only did he want to avoid interrogation—he had no idea how to explain what happened that morning—but he also feared persecution. He knew that if Arthur Maddox knew he survived the fire, he'd have him killed.

Just like Carlyle.

He managed to find a bootlegger in the area—an easy enough task for someone who used to be part of the game. And without any concern for his own safety or freedom, he grew bold in his search for liquor. It was the only comfort he found.

He planned on heading back to the States for safe passage but then remembered Arthur Maddox's hands reached every country—any city he went to, he could be found. Even though he had quite a bit of money saved, he lived a modest existence, using most of his money to pay off bootleggers for more booze.

He mourned the loss of Emma, but more than that, the loss of his sanity. Every night he replayed the events that happened that morning—the things he saw didn't make any sense. The Howlers disappearing into thin air, Emma's ability to manipulate the elements around her, it all sounded like a terrible dream.

The news never reported anything about the fire on the island. However, he suspected Arthur Maddox covered everything to avoid questions from the authorities. Point DuPont was privately owned—no one cared to check on the inhabitants.

In an attempt to sort through everything in his mind, August started writing. He tried to recount all events—to document the sequence from memory, but his drunkenness made him question his own mind, and it wasn't uncommon for him to toss his writings into the fire, only to start the next morning anew.

The winter in Nova Scotia was a brutal one. Despite August having bought himself new clothes to brave the inhospitable season, he found himself in a perpetual state of cold. A similar depression to when he lost Jack and losing that bit of warmth in his life left him feeling frigid and alone in the world.

Just like he did every night before, he trudged through the snow wearing a thick coat and winter boots. He bought a bottle of bourbon from his main supplier down the street and then trudged back to his dingy motel—ready to drink himself into a stupor again.

August sat at the shoddy table in his motel room, the bottle of bourbon beside him as he hunched over a sheet of paper with a pencil in hand. He tried writing about the cube, but every time he read the words back to himself, it all sounded too ridiculous—like he ripped it all from *Mary Shelley's Frankenstein*. He crumpled the piece of paper and tossed it onto the ground.

A knock on the door echoed throughout the room and ripped him from his thoughtful state—putting him on alert. He stared at the door for a long while, wondering if he just imagined the sound entirely. But another knock sent him to his nightstand, where he kept a revolver. Could be the authorities, he thought. Maybe they followed him in a sting.

He pointed the gun at the door. "Who's there?"

"August?" It was a woman's voice. He lowered the gun. For a long while, he remained frozen, once again questioning his own sanity. "August, it's me. It's Emma."

The revolver hit the floor. "Emma's dead!"

"I'm not dead, darling. Please, open the door, and I'll show you."

He remained skeptical. It's just what an impersonator would want him to think. No doubt Arthur Maddox had the means to find someone to impersonate Emma perfectly. "If you're Emma, then prove it!"

"You don't recognize my voice?"

He hesitated to respond. "I'm...a little drunk."

"Oh, August," her muffled voice groaned. "Your brother was killed in a car accident, walking home from one of your fights."

"That's a matter of public record!"

The woman sighed. "Your earliest memory was of a cage fight in Georgia. Your mother took you—" August ran to the door and unlocked it, swinging it open so fast that Emma flinched before him. "Hello, darling."

There she stood, a weak smile on her face. She looked very different—her hair much shorter and her clothes looking as if they'd been purchased from a high-fashion catalog. She looked the part of a gilded era aristocrat. Her eyes, though, were unmistakable.

August grabbed her and pulled her into him, holding her tightly—afraid that if he loosened his grip on her, she'd disappear completely. Like the Howlers. "Emma," he murmured.

"It's all right. I'm right here." She forced him into bed, and within minutes, everything went black.

August awoke the next morning in a haze. The sun blast through his window, blinding him—the brightness of which creating a shooting pain up the side of his head. He groaned and turned to rip the curtains shut.

"You're like a vampire."

August flinched at the sound of her voice. At the table across his room, Emma sat with her fancy jacket now draped across the back of her chair. Despite his severe headache, August managed to smirk. For a moment, he thought he dreamt the whole thing.

"Sorry, I'm a terrible host."

"Yes, you are." Emma found a memento from the fire—Jon's white kabuki mask. She held it in her hands, running her thumb along the edges. "Where did you find this?"

"The house. In a pile of dirt and ash. I was looking for you, but...I found that instead. Felt wrong leavin' it behind."

"Can I have this?"

August nodded. "Yeah...of course."

"Thank you." She set the mask on the table and wiped her tears. As she approached August's bedside and sat beside him, he tensed—knowing he more than likely reeked of booze and sweat. "Why are you doing this to yourself?"

"Is that a serious question?"

Emma sighed and touched his hand. A warm sensation moved from her fingertips all the way up his arm—similar to the electric current he felt in the basement of Maddox house. "You're killing yourself," she said solemnly.

"I thought you were dead."

"That's no reason to—"

"It's not the reason," he grumbled and then grabbed the bottle of bourbon at his bedside. "Not the only reason—"

Emma snatched the bottle from him and replaced it on the bedside table. "If you have any desire to continue your services to me, you'll stop drinking. Immediately."

250

"Services?" August squinted his eyes to refocus her. "Jesus Christ, Emma, after all the shit we went through to get you off that island, you mean to tell me nothin's changed?"

"Everything's changed."

"What? Your hair, your clothes? Where you been, Em? What happened to you that day? You expect me to believe that what we went through was for nothing, but then you turn up on my doorstep with a fancy new hairstyle and fresh new duds talkin' about employment. Did Arthur send you?"

"No," she spat, appalled. "My father has no idea that I'm alive. He thinks I burned in that fire along with Grady and Jon. And you."

"He thinks I'm dead?"

"He has no reason to think otherwise. You left everything behind. You snuck onto a fishing boat as a stowaway to avoid being identified and have been keeping a low profile ever since."

"Yeah, and how do you know all this if you've been '*dead*' for the last few months?"

"I have my sources."

"Uh-huh." August reached for the bottle again, but it skidded away from him. His eyebrow raised when his gaze met hers. "I think you and I have a lot to talk about, Emma."

"Yes, we do. But first, you need to get cleaned up and eat a proper meal." She crossed the room to sling her coat around her shoulders.

"You're leaving?"

"I'll be back once you've washed up. And you'll be needing something to eat besides canned beans and liver."

"It's high in protein."

"Ah yes, protein." She smiled warmly at him. "I'll be back in an hour. Please be presentable. I don't wish to baby you."

After she left, he drew a hot bath to wash away the smell of booze and sweat and clean the dirt and grime from his body. After climbing out of the bathtub, he stood in front of the dirty, cracked mirror above the sink.

He grew out his beard—covering his youthful, fresh face. He grew out his hair, too. It's a miracle Emma even recognized him, he thought. He squeezed his stomach. A high-protein diet with little to no exercise and a steady intake of bourbon robbed him of the athletic physique he once boasted so proudly.

"Don't be too hard on yourself, kid. You wanted to be dead up until about ten hours ago." He grabbed the razor from the sink's edge—wondering where to begin.

෪ඏ

August wiped the remnants of shaving cream from his face with a damp towel. The sight of Emma holding a brown paper bag stopped him in the doorway of the bathroom, and she smiled at the sight of him. "There you are." She set the bag aside and slid her fingers along his smooth face. "Just as handsome as I remember."

"I think I got carried away," he said while running his hands over the sides of his shaved head. "I ain't a fighter anymore, I shoulda done something more…inconspicuous."

"You'll always be a fighter, August." She stepped aside and pulled a chair out for him. "Sit down; I brought you food."

Emma sat across from him as he devoured his meal—the first real one he had in months. As he ate, Emma told him her side of the story.

"I stayed on the island longer than I should have, mourning Jon's death. For nearly two weeks, I stayed in the forest at this…little cottage he and I used to play in as children. I buried him nearby and just… didn't have the strength to leave him."

"You got him out of the fire."

"Of course. Jon's afraid of fire. I didn't have the heart to let him burn." There was a moment of silence for the fallen Hunter and Emma's true love. "It was only after a few weeks that I convinced myself it wasn't the life he wanted me to live."

"So, you left."

"I caught a ferry to Prince Edward Island. I knew stopping in Port Augusta was too dangerous; I couldn't risk being recognized."

Emma went on to explain that she had every intention of disappearing forever. Thanks to an anonymous friend, all of Jon's estate was legally transferred to her—him having listed her as his beneficiary many years ago when he first became a Hunter. His fortune amassed to over one-hundred thousand dollars—enough to give Emma a happy life far away from Point DuPont.

"But after a while, things started happening outside of my control, or...perhaps not outside of it completely. But I'll get angry, and then things will catch on fire. And when I'm sad, it'll start to rain."

"What about the Howlers?"

"Subconscious manifestations, I fear. A defense mechanism, so to speak. Just like the white wolf many years ago." Emma stood and moved to the window, looking out into snowy terrain and choppy, rough waves of the Atlantic Ocean. "I don't understand what's happening to me or why, but it's something I need to learn to control, August. Not only for my sake but...for my child's as well."

The blood drained from his face. When Emma turned to him again, she cradled a small bump that her clothes did well to hide. "Emma?"

"I'm going to be a mother, August." Through tears, she smiled. "I'm really hoping for a boy. And maybe, he'll look just like his father."

Jon.

August grimaced and hung his head. The idea of Emma carrying Jon's son ripped his heart to shreds, only because their fallen friend would never get to meet his child. And then, there was the fear of the alternative. He groaned. "No offense, Emma, but...how do you know it's Jon's?"

He hesitated to meet her gaze—afraid his words might cause her undue pain and stress. But she wasn't angry. Instead, her eyes

253

became wide, and she bit her lip. "Because I can feel him growing inside of me."

It's all he needed to hear. So long as she was convinced, so wa he. "That why you're here?"

"I'm here because…I want what's rightfully mine. And I nee your help."

He raised an eyebrow. "Rightfully yours?"

"The money Jon left for me will give our child and me a happy life, but it won't be enough for the research that needs to be don on my condition. For my baby's sake, I need to learn more abou what I am."

"So…you want your dad to fund it? How is that any differen than the arrangement he had before?"

"No, I need to be in control this time. But the only way tha can happen is if he gives me all his money."

August chuckled. "You really think he'd do that? Just han over all his money?"

"He won't have to," she said while approaching him, the loo in her eyes cold and full of hate. He'd seen that look before, an he knew what came next. "I am his rightful heir. If anything wer to happen to him, his entire estate becomes mine."

"You want to kill Arthur Maddox."

Emma hesitated. "I want what I deserve—"

"Count me in," August said, without hesitation, and a wid smile spread across her face. Truth be told, if Emma opened wit *'I want to kill my father,'* August would have agreed withou question. One, because he loved her. And two, after all he'd see the past few months, he truly believed that Arthur Maddox wa evil.

Chapter XXII

December 10ᵗʰ, 1928
Port Augusta, Nova Scotia

The sun disappeared behind the horizon, leaving the air surrounding the port cold and icy. As the temperature plummeted, inhabitants of the port retreated to their homes for the evening. August walked slowly, the wood creaking beneath his boots, sounding as though it might crack beneath him at any moment.

On the main road nearby the docks, the mixture of water and snow created a thick sludge along the gutters. A car waited for him, the heat from the machine being thrust from the exhaust, melting the ice and snow below. August stepped into the vehicle, and though not much warmer inside, he was relieved to be out of the thick sludge that seeped into his boots—freezing his toes.

Maddox house came into view, and suddenly August's cold feet became a distant thought. For the first time since becoming a Hunter on Point DuPont, August was to meet with Arthur Maddox face to face. At Emma's encouragement, he'd written in advance.

Dear Arthur,

I'm sure you've been left in mystery as to what happened that day on Point DuPont. It is my utmost regret that I left you tortured, wondering what may have happened to Emma. Truth be told, I still don't know how to explain it myself. I ran away, afraid of what might happen. I've spent many sleepless nights wondering if what I did was fair to you. Leaving a man wondering about the safety of his own child.

I've been harboring a lot of guilt for leaving without an explanation. Hell, I'm sure you figured I was dead as well. I know now that I'll never be able to move on from the island until I speak with you. You have a right to know what happened. You have a right to know everything. Please accept my offer to meet with you and tell you everything. I fear I won't know peace until then.

Best Regards,
August DeWitt

Mr. DeWitt,

I was thrilled to know of your safety. Please, whenever you can, come to Port Augusta. We'll share a glass of *scotch, and you can finally tell me what has become of my sweet angel. I look forward to your visit.*

Arthur Maddox

August emerged from the vehicle and once again marveled at the grand structure of Maddox House. He tightened his coat as a gust of wind chilled him to the bone. After climbing the steps, he hesitated to knock. The idea that Arthur Maddox might shoot him dead on sight stayed at the forefront of his mind.

"Please, come inside," a young maid welcomed and stepped aside. The foyer was dark and lifeless, but in the parlor to his left, a fire burned and low-playing jazz emitted from a gramophone. At the same time, servants hung a *'Happy Birthday'* banner.

"Mr. DeWitt!"

August's heart launched into his throat. Upon seeing the billionaire mogul, his courage abandoned him. Arthur Maddox— a powerful man looking no worse for the wear despite his daughter's disappearance. Same as he did the first time they met many months ago. He approached August with a warm smile and a glass of scotch in his hand.

"Y'all having a party?"

"Just a little birthday soiree before I leave. I'm headed to the states early in the morning, so you can imagine how thrilled I was to hear from you when I did. Excellent timing." He patted August's back. "Not to worry, though. My guests won't be arriving for at least another hour, so we have plenty of time to talk."

He extended his hand toward his study, allowing August to take the lead. A fire burned in the fireplace, warming August's frozen toes the closer he stood. On Arthur's desk, a solitary lamp lit the papers scattered along the surface. "Work never ends, huh?"

"Not when everyone's asking for your money," Arthur joked and extended his hand to the armchair in front of his desk. "Please, sit down. Make yourself comfortable. Now, I promised you scotch, but it seems I've drank all our supply. How's bourbon?"

"None for me. I'm trying to quit."

"Good for you. Nasty habit." He took a sip of his scotch, the same twinkle in his eye as when they first met. To an outsider, Arthur Maddox seemed harmless. But August knew better. After sitting behind his desk, Arthur sifted through papers. "Now, you say you have information about what happened to my daughter."

"You never told me that Emma was adopted."

Arthur lowered his glass, his eyes looking upward through a furrowed brow. "Should I have?"

"It was just…kinda surprising. Here I thought I'd be protecting a little girl. Got to the island and realized I was sorely mistaken."

"Little girl or not, the job was always the same."

August chuckled. "Nah. No little girl can do the things your daughter was capable of. She was a force to be reckoned with."

"You speak of her in the past tense. Have you come all this way to tell me my daughter is dead?"

August shook his head. "I don't know."

"And what about Jonathan Moreau and Grady McCoy? Do you know what happened to them?"

"Jon's dead."

Arthur nodded slowly. He grabbed a pen from inside his desk and began writing on a sheet of paper. "Terrible tragedy. I always liked Jon. He's been living under my roof since he turned eighteen. And Grady McCoy? His wife hasn't received any payment from him since the incident. They risk losing their home."

"I didn't see it with my own eyes, but…I suspect Grady burned in the fire."

"I see. Well, without a body, the McCoy family isn't entitled to Grady's life insurance. Terrible news," he said and then continued writing.

"What about Jon's money?" August asked, worried that Arthur Maddox might know more than he led on initially.

"From my understanding, it's all been donated to charity," he said in a cold, uncaring tone of voice. "Do you know what started the fire?"

"I suspect it was the same thing that started the fire in 1921," August muttered, grabbing Arthur's full attention. "It'd make sense, right?"

"I'm...not sure. We still don't know what started the fire back then." Arthur studied him skeptically and set his pen aside. "Mr. DeWitt. You said you had information about what happened to Emma. Do you know what happened to her?"

"Not entirely, no. I saw her in the fire. The Howlers surrounded me, and...I thought that would be the end of me. But one by one, they just started to disappear into nothing. When I looked back to the fire, Emma was gone. I don't know if she burned. I don't know if she escaped."

"So, you don't know...anything," Arthur accused. "Was this all just a ploy to waste my time? Or perhaps you thought you could get more money out of me?"

"The Howlers disappeared into thin air. And you accuse me of wasting your time?"

"Where is my daughter?"

"I don't know."

"Where is she?" he shouted.

"I said, I don't know—"

Arthur snatched a revolver from his desk and pointed it at August, silencing the ex-Hunter. He stood, now towering over him. "The Unbeatable August DeWitt cowering before me. The way I see it, Mr. DeWitt, you were only of value to me if you had information on the whereabouts of my daughter. And since you have no such information, you're now more of a liability than anything. Or maybe you do know, and you're just trying to protect her." August raised his hands in surrender. "I'll ask one more time."

"Oh, for goodness sake, there's no need," Emma said from the doorway.

"Oh, thank Christ," August gasped.

"Emma!" Arthur exclaimed while tucking his revolver behind his back, a wide smile on his face. "My darling girl, I've been worried sick about you."

"Yes, the party across the hall certainly paints the picture of a father riddled with grief." Emma moved beside August, who stood and took a step behind her.

"I'd rather not have those vultures assume the worst. That my one and only daughter, the heiress to my estate, be dead when it might not be true."

"So, you've been mourning in private?"

"The wealthy do not wear their emotions on their sleeve. Something you'll do well to remember. We're easily controlled and manipulated if we allow the world to see what we're thinking and what we're feeling."

"What are you feeling?" Emma asked.

Arthur hesitated. "What?"

"Right now," she said while stepping closer to his desk, sending Arthur a few steps back. It was then August noticed that her own father was afraid of her. "What are you feeling?"

"Disappointment," Arthur said. "Regret. Dread."

"Dread," Emma whispered.

"Dread…over what might happen to this world if I let you leave."

"What else are you feeling?" she asked, and he wiped his forehead. All color vanished from his face.

"Anxious…my heart is…pounding…" Arthur fell into his desk, and his knees buckled. He lifted his pistol to Emma, but she took it from him and set it aside. "Emma?" Arthur groaned.

"Can't find the words to describe what you're feeling? It's called death, father. Embrace it."

Arthur grabbed the hem of Emma's skirt, but within seconds, he released the fabric and hit the ground, motionless. The lifeless body of the man who caused every bit of horror and atrocity in Emma's life lied before them, pale and vacant. To watch a man of such grandeur fall to his knees, having crumbled beneath the powers of the woman he tormented her whole life, astonished August.

Emma peered over her shoulder to him, then pouted. "Oh, don't look at me like that, August. He had it coming."

"I just hope that I never piss you off."

She smiled. When by his side again, she kissed his cheek. "Don't be afraid of me. I'd never hurt you."

He believed her. He believed that even though she may have felt a small bit of enjoyment for exacting her revenge, she maintained a good heart. And perhaps it was his duty to assure she maintained her compassion. Because anyone with that much power could easily fall prey to the intoxication.

The office door opened, and Byron entered.

August stepped in front of Emma and braced himself, ready for a fight. "Byron, how are you?" Emma asked in a calm and soothing voice.

"I'm doing well, Ms. Maddox. And yourself?"

August hesitated to speak. "Is he...a friendly?"

"Yes, darling," she said while patting his chest.

"Mr. DeWitt. Happy to see you're alive and well." In his hands, Byron clenched a thick, manila envelope. "Ms. Maddox, all the legal documents are in here." He crossed the room and handed her the envelope. "You are now in full control of the Maddox estate. I've also included your passport."

"Thank you, Byron. You've been most helpful."

"Wait, you're the guy who's been helping Emma?"

Byron smiled. "I've been an advocate for Miss Emma since she was a little girl and have been waiting for this day for a long time.

When she told me she located you, I drew up all the necessary paperwork to assure a smooth transition of the Maddox funds to her name."

Emma tipped her head to him. "A most egregious process, I'm sure."

Byron's eyes fell on Arthur Maddox, and he cleared his throat. "Right. You two would be wise to catch the next ferry out of Port Augusta. A heart attack is easy enough to diagnose, but we wouldn't want anyone suspecting foul play," he said. "The car awaits."

Byron paid off the servants, and the driver taking Emma and August to the port. Once on a ferry, they sailed to Halifax. Emma stood on the deck, admiring the Atlantic in the moonlight, her coat fastened tightly around her. Her breath visible in front of her lips and her pale skin in the bright moonlight consumed August while he lurked in the shadows.

He never thought he'd see her again after leaving Point DuPont, and now she stood before him, a faint smile on her face, breath in her lungs. And more beauty and vibrancy than he'd ever seen inside of her.

As the ferry docked in the port, he approached her. "Looks like we're here," he muttered.

"You're here." She pulled a small envelope from inside her coat and handed it to him. Inside, more money than he'd seen in a long time. "I appreciate your continued service to me. Without you, I don't think I would have had the strength to face my father."

"Emma, what the hell is this?"

"Payment for all you've done. You no longer need to stay by my side, though, August. I've returned you to Halifax. I'm hoping you'll find some reason to move forward, but if not, at least the money will help."

"I don't want your money."

She sighed. "What do you want?"

"To be with you."

She hesitated to speak. "August, I…" she shook her head. "Jon is still so—"

"I don't mean like that." He grabbed her arms and pulled her closer. "I'd be lying if I said that I didn't love you. But… I'm not expecting anything from you. You know I'm nothing like Grady; I'd never hold anything like that over your head."

She sighed and nodded. "I know, darling."

"I just wanna be near you. I wanna help you figure this thing out, and…on days you're not feeling well, I wanna take care of you. Days you're pissed off and hating the world, I wanna be there to distract you." She laughed, but August saw the tears burning her eyes. "And I want to be there for…this little guy too." His hand moved over her belly. "You don't owe me anything, Emma. But I owe you everything. Don't send me away."

"After all you've seen, you still choose to remain by my side?"

"Always. And hey, if you're goin' to the States, you'll need an American to show you the ropes, you know. Teach you all about American society." She laughed and leaned her head into his chest. "I ain't ever gonna leave you. You and me, we're family now." She sobbed, and he swayed her back and forth to soothe her. "Come on, don't start crying. This is the beginning of a new life for you." She picked her head up, and he wiped the tears from her cheeks. "So, where we headed?"

She smiled and looked outward to the smooth, calm ocean before them—illuminated by the brightness of the moon. "Anywhere we wish."

Made in the USA
Coppell, TX
13 February 2021

50309277R00155